TEMP TALES

TEMP TALES

A Survival Guide

Tom
Thanks & Enjoy ~
Judy M Crouse

Judy M. Crouse

To order additional copies of this book, contact:
Xlibris Corporation
1-888-795-4274
www.Xlibris.com
Orders@Xlibris.com
67157

TABLE OF CONTENTS

DEDICATION

Dedicated to my husband, Jeff, for his loving encouragement and support, and to Liza Loo, my childhood friend for cheering me on.

PREFACE

Your can't stop the waves, but you can learn to sail

I have been working on and off as a temporary employee for nearly thirty years. I never thought I would look back one day and realize how much time I wasted making employment agencies prosperous. I don't have a retirement package and I've never had medical benefits. Few of my holidays were paid. It's almost impossible to rack up twelve hundred uninterrupted hours working as a temp to acquire one week's vacation. I always had the oldest car in the parking lot.

I have always been a good employee, always punctual and I refused to call in sick. I never ruffled feathers and created waves. Rather than deal with distasteful situations, I would quit. When I did stand up for myself, I usually retreated in defeat. The catch was I could always get a temp job and so my professional life turned into a vicious circle of temp jobs and lousy full time positions. The great jobs I took on were never going to become full time. If it turned out to be a good job, the person I was subbing for was *always* going to return. They were good jobs after all.

I received such extensive on the job training that I mastered Windows 3.1, 95 and 98, NT, Office Professional 2000, Microsoft Office2007, Microsoft Dynamics, Peachtree, QuickBooks, Microsoft Money, Lotus123, Quattro Pro, Profit 21, Continuum, scanning software and AS400 systems and on and on.

I worked a variety of clerical positions as an administrative assistant, an accounting clerk, a credit clerk, an invoicing clerk, a DOT audit clerk, a customer service representative, data entry clerk, auto and homeowners Insurance P & C Licensed Agent, a retail and warehouse accounting clerk and a traffic and shipping clerk. I've also worked in a bindery, a food processing plant, a plastics manufacturing plant, a restaurant, a cocktail lounge, a group home, a sheltered workshop, and a greenhouse. There was not one job I was sent to that I did not give it the old college try.

If I had known the pitfalls of not applying myself in high school and thereby not attending college, I would have studied harder. Unfortunately, I never had much direction from family or a mentor when I was a teenager. My parents had not attended college. They worked hard and strove to live the American Dream after WWII. My father served in the military during the war and was able to obtain his high school diploma though the G.I. Bill. My mother did not complete high school but was a licensed practical nurse. If I had aspired to go to college, I would have had to pay for it myself. It was easier and less complicated at the time to obtain a job and get married.

So, I worked at jobs I hated. I would grow so sick of working temp that I would take any position offered to me. When I would go on temp to permanent jobs, I was usually offered the position. Some I accepted and others I declined. I often accepted jobs because nothing else was on the horizon, not because I actually wanted to work at that particular company.

I had worked at so many temp jobs, when I did go on interviews for positions I really wanted, the interviewer was put off because I had worked at so many different places.

I've always been anal retentive. I still have my taxes for the past twenty five years and every bill for the past ten years. One bored afternoon, I decided to write down all the places I had worked since graduating from high school. I used old W2 forms, day planners, and bills to reconstruct my life.

I was shocked to see that I had held one hundred and two different jobs or assignments throughout my illustrious career. That does sound dreadful. But of that total number, there are only sixty-six companies. I was such a great temp that a company often requested I return for more torture. Of the sixty-six companies I've worked at, twenty-three are no longer in business. Like temps, they come and they go.

My husband would tell me, " . . . you're like Joe Btfsplk from the Little Abner comic strip. Nearly everywhere you work goes out of business." Well I guess you *could* think that but I prefer to think it was just lousy timing. After all, I have to look on the bright side.

One evening after a horribly distressing temping day, I was relating to my husband the days events (I don't recall what the circumstances were now), and Jeff told me, "You should write a book." As you can see, I did.

This is more than a survival guide; it's also a cautionary tale. The stories you'll read are if nothing else, interesting and though the names have been changed to protect the guilty, they know who they are. The "clues" are planted among the tales. Was it Mrs. Raven in the break room with a knife, was it Bert in the mailroom with a letter opener, or was in Mildred in the Cafeteria with a candlestick? To the many fellow workers and employers whose moral compass has always directed their success, I tip my hat.

I hope by reading my tales you'll be able to avoid some of the pitfalls of working as a temp. I have tried to add the humorous times, after all, life isn't all doom and gloom. Too often, the tale is just one of another sordid day at the office.

CHAPTER 1

If you can maintain your cool when all about you are losing it you will be the perfect temp

I awoke to a dark and stormy morning. Oops, wrong story line. My coffee is getting cold. As I slide my cup into the microwave, the phone rings. I run to grab it before the second ring. It's the temporary agency's representative. I'm worried, she is too excited. This is one person I must not alienate. In short, she is my pimp. I am NOT her equal. She is the happiest person this side of paradise. The reason being, she has a job.

"Hi Judy," Miss Bubbly gushes, "I have this absolutely wonderful position, at an absolutely wonderful company. And you're going to be a "perfect fit." Love that term. She even has the gall to say, "It might go full time." Now this is a total lie, as I find out during the course of this job. So, I listen and say, "Yes, when do I report?" I am sooooo excited too.

I make sure Miss Bubbly gives me all the information . . . parking, dress code and the contact person. She will not have any or at least not all of this on the first phone call to me. She will probably have to ring me back once, if not twice. I must remember that she is just so busy!

I have decided, no matter what any one thinks, I am a very brave person. I get to go to the first day of middle school every time I start a new job! Remember that day; I have that old sinking feeling. "Will I fit in, will they like me, am I dressed right, and where is the bathroom?"

All those horrible misgivings I thought were left behind years ago. They are front and center this morning.

"I have to get this terrible attitude out of the way this morning." I pry myself out of the car. I take a deep breath, walk towards the building, struggling with my coffee mug and tote bag. This should not be so hard. Here I go, another temp job, big sigh.

Something happened in America about 20 years ago, it was the emergence of the Temporary Staffing Agency. Someone in a corporation decided that instead of hiring people out right, they could turn millions of people into indentured servants. The company would save all this time, no interviewing, no making decisions, and in turn hire people who would really grovel. "Temporary employment has stripped the American worker of independence, pride and the ability to earn a decent wage." Ugh.

O.K, I am in the reception area meeting Miss Wonderful, my guide to hell. She proceeds to trot me to the department I will be working in. I just try to keep up with her, she is so busy too.

Miss Wonderful introduces me to the department head or The Boss and vanishes down the hallway. Usually the boss is a woman. It is unlikely I will have any more contact with her. The Boss is very capable, or she would not *BE THE BOSS*. She is probably badly over worked and her department understaffed. Even though she is always the best dressed, there is always sadness surrounding her.

If you get in truly tight with your co-workers, you will find they have no respect for her. They all agree that she is both ineffectual and an idiot. Perhaps climbing that ladder has taken all the fun out of her?

You find yourself feeling sorry for her. Don't get sucked in with that thinking. She will turn on you in a millisecond if you screw up. Don't be caught up in her false friendliness. After all, it is all about the "Act".

I must explain the "Act." This is the behavior everyone, including you, displays on the first day of an assignment. You are friendly, smiling, and will accomplish any task given to you in record time. In turn, they are smiling, helpful and patient. This is only going to last, at the utmost, one week, and your first week. After that, everyone is back to their back stabbing, sniping remarks, and foul deeds.

The boss, in turn, trots me to the person responsible for my training, and she too disappears. This over worked person doesn't "feel" it is their job to train me. So, imagine what I'm going to learn today. Better figure it out for my self. What I am being given to do is not what I was told I would be doing by my cheerful temp agency Pimp. This is called the "bait and switch." Onward, after all I need to get though this and make some money.

I have been told that the dress code at the company I am going to is "Business Casual." I am wearing my very sharp black silk cashmere blend suit with a crisp white blouse and great black shoes. My bulging ebony tote is of the best top grain cow hide. My idea of Business Casual and what I see at this place are two different things. I am dressed better than nearly everyone. The only exception being the manager, she looks sharp in her knock off designer suit from Kohl's. All the other women are attired in double knit pants, beautifully coordinated with a big sloppy top. Now I stick out like a sore thumb. I am not management and

I am not support staff. I am myself, an all around original lost in the corporate world which demands that I conform to their standards. The cubicle I will be sitting in is interesting though. Here we have pictures of the absent person's ugly kids, husband, her pet guinea pig, and so on. The guinea pig is the cutest one in the photos. Maybe I should have temped for the guinea pig. Their cage was probably nicer. Well when no one is looking, I can turn the pictures over? I must be careful and not move anything! Or if I do, I have to be sure to make a mental picture of this "bed room" style decor. Love the little bears.

There is a very good possibility she (I am going to use she, as I have never been a temp for a man) will return while I am still here. This is especially true if the person being replaced is out due to any type of surgery. Her return to work will be a big surprise for all, including the company's human resource department.

If she was out to have a baby, you're trapped in her cubical with no way out until the day she comes in with her bundle of joy to visit. Oh, the dear baby isn't nearly as cute as that guinea pig! Oh well, she does have a sweet beating little heart. Everyone will hold the baby and the baby will cry and cry. Nothing much will get done in the department for hours.

In regards to the IT department and company preparedness for a temp, you can forget about any of that happening. Even though the IT department has known for at least a week that a temp was arriving, nothing is set up. So now, the manager, IT Tech and of course the cube neighbor all will get into the act. No one knows any of this person's passwords, not for the computer or the phone. Voice mail is going to be a real problem. If they are short a computer, guess what, you will get to stare at a lap top for weeks.

Now, it's "let's meet everyone time." This is fun, as if I'll remember all of the names of this bunch of lard butts. Note here to self: make a map of the area. Nothing complicated, just some rectangles, and jot down associated names of the people around me. Say the one who is the department sex pot, Barbie, equals the B.T.P, Blonde with tummy piercing, the huge woman next to her, Vicky, equals V.C.K, "Vicious Cake Killer". You get the idea. Smile so sweetly and be the good little temp. During these introductions, I get to walk around the area for a while killing time and getting paid for it.

First and Primary Rule, "No one sees what "they" do, but everyone sees what YOU do." The people in this office will consider you no more important than wallpaper. They will speak of you in the third person, so get used to hearing, her, she, and the temp. You have become a pronoun.

Hope you don't smoke. If you do, it is very possible you will meet one other smoker during this assignment. She will be a sullen witch. If it is a man, you will be too "below" him to have a conversation with while you are freezing your buns off. The non-smokers will let you know, "smokers get to take breaks as I sit here and slave away." I think, "How stupid are you? Get up and waddle to the snack machine, chill out for 15 minutes. Maybe you'll feel better and even be nicer with a wonderful sugar rush." Of course I don't say any of this, I am a sweet temp. Oh well, back to "Area 51."

It is break time for the non smokers. If you're an eater and not a smoker there's a good chance you may make a friend or two. Boy will they eat. Warning: don't go there unless you are content with adding to your girth. There are bags and bags of salty, fatty snacks *everywhere*. If you're watching your weight, good luck. This is what these people live for. Yet, they drink diet coke; I have never been able to figure that one out.

When it is lunch, your coworkers may invite you to join them the first day. They want to appear friendly to you. Don't think this is going to continue. Since I usually pack well balanced stuff for lunch, that usually ends the lunch invites. It is too intimidating for them.

The first lunch conversation usually goes like this, " . . . is that all you're having?" Not a good sign, as your coworker stuffs a double burger, large fries, and a chocolate bar in her face at the speed of light, washing it all down with a diet coke. Then someone at the table will eventually remark, "I bet you love temping, you get to meet new people all the time and never have to be involved in office politics." I stare in wonderment as to how anyone in their right mind would think this. "Yeah, I love it.", I say with a beautiful toothy smile. Thanks goodness lunch torture is nearly over.

After lunch, I am back training with the disgruntled employee. Take notes the best you can, she is going to "fly" though the system with the how to's. It could be days before you get any hands on experience. She is not going to make this easy for you.

As she will tell you over and over, "I **never** got training. I had to pick this up the best I could." Yep, she's a genius. Hopefully she will not run to the manager saying you're not picking it up fast enough.

You're going to very bored and very sleepy during these training periods. For this, they have the coffee station, if you remember from the morning tour where it is. Be sure and get coffee in the afternoon, that way you don't have to make any more. They just throw it out anyway. It's good enough for you.

Temps have developed their own language over the years and I will share a few of them with you. First you may suffer from "Office Butt." This is an occupational condition that results from always using the lumpiest, most uncomfortable chair in the office. This is a common complaint of the veteran temp. Next, we have the "Filebots." These are the unsightly drones who prefer to file in a back room but who surface twice a day to deliver the mail. Filebots and temps are equal in social status and share an unspoken bond of respect. Finally there are the "Bacterianators", temps with a severe cold or flu who show up for work because they don't get sick pay. Bacterianators are identifiable by brilliant swollen noses and extremely low productivity.

Believe it or not, the day is finally coming to a conclusion. I am out the door. At least I know what tomorrow is going to be like.

If you have found yourself reflected in the people you have met here so far, then so be it. If you don't see yourself, good for you. Don't worry; I have not forgotten the kind, appreciative, helpful, decent people. I will get to them later.

I have been subjected to degradations that a full time employee would never be expected to endure. Many of the people I have had to work for have been rude, unkind, and mean. I have had managers make suggestive remarks, and a human resources vice president even stroked his private parts with a pencil as he gave me morning instructions. I wonder how often he needed to do that a day? Or was he just trying to tell me his *is* a pencil? I would cringe when he beeped me on my intercom phone. The foulest language you can dream up has been spoken around me and to me, not to mention I've had to duck flying manuals.

Now, I need to take you back to the day I walked into the Placement Agency. The hierarchy in a privately owned company is the following: There is the owner, various placement personnel, the receptionist, and the bookkeeper/accountant.

First impressions are lasting impressions. Your first impression does not matter. The lowly receptionist is the only one you're really going to talk to on a regular basis, so be very nice to her. The Placement Person, i.e. the Pimp, will always be on another call. You will at least be put into your Pimp's voice mail.

Let's get back to the PIMP! After tons of paper work which covers everyone's butt except yours, it is time for testing. I have lots of practical experience, but I don't test well. If I can convince the Pimp of this, I usually get an assignment. The Pimp is always a great dresser, fabulous hair; she is younger than you and pretty. These attributes are part of her job description.

The basic thing the Pimp is concerned about is keeping and increasing her client base. If things don't go well on an assignment, this could mean the Pimp would lose an account. So, do not cause this. If you do, you will never work for them again. No matter what the reason, it will be your fault. You can circumvent this by keeping lines of communication open with the Pimp. It is best to let her know if something is amiss.

For the most part, you will be able to do the job. Usually the company is happy with the outcome, and there is always the possibility you may even be hired. Pimps don't get the list of the good jobs to fill and the low jobs you will get are full of bologna. Indeed, you have never been given reason to think you'll actually get hired full time, therefore don't bother wishing and hoping.

When you work as a temp, you not only represent yourself, you also represent the agency. As long as your work is of the highest quality that you can give and you live up to your own high standards, they will be impressed.

Next we have the Bookkeeper/Accounting Person at the Pimp House. This person, usually a woman, is very nice. All she is concerned about is whether or not your hours are correct and that you called in on time. It is unlikely you will have much contact with her.

Now we come to the wicked witch of the East Coast, THE OWNER, or Head Pimp. You may or may not meet this person. It will depend mostly if she is passing though a hallway or not. In some smaller Pimp Houses, you could work directly with her along with your personal Pimp.

The Head Pimp is usually very stylish, good looking and smart.

She might be a college graduate; maybe not. She will handle all the prime accounts and best placements. She will only place her "favorites" in these positions. If she takes you under her wing, don't be mesmerized into thinking you're a friend. She is a business person who got to where she is by using and manipulating people and situations to her advantage. She did not get to where she is by being nice. Don't forget to send these lovely people a thank you note! Be sure your note conveys how appreciative you were of the time they spent with you and don't forget to grovel. They love a brilliant groveler.

Class is now dismissed! You have successfully completed Temping 101. As I progress through my narrative, I will have more details and personalities to hang out on the clothes line, so stay tuned. They have lots of *dirty laundry*.

CHAPTER 2

In the beginning someone created Temp Agencies

In the beginning, I had a great job. Really, once I did. The first involvement I had with an employment agency was after I graduated from high school. It was August of 1967, The Summer of Love. I would discover that there wasn't going to be much love that summer. What I did find was an employment agency in Baltimore, The Olsen Employment Agency.

My first assignment, only for a week, was at Coopers Company in Glen Arm, Maryland. Coopers was situated in a scenic area of Baltimore County. As I drove my little VW down the picturesque winding road, I felt so grown up.

I don't remember much about this place; after all it was 40 years ago. About all I recall was that the people were old fogies and the building was dark and dank. I did the basic temp file job with another lady. I think I was replacing someone who was out for vacation. After all, it was summer. Little did I know than I would spend most of my professional life catching up to everyone else. Over the years, I slowly drifted farther and farther from a real career.

Somehow I ended up at a Chemical Company in Cockeysville, Md. This job was short and sweet. I just walked in and filled out an application, they hired me on the spot. After a few days, I figured out why.

I would be working in the area that manufactured sulfur drugs. I would walk out to production every few hours and pull the time in process sheets. This information was then transposed by me onto graph paper in loose leaf notebooks. This information was used to track production and shipments. No problem, I could do this. But could I work for the boss of this department?

This was the very first time I was exposed to a disgusting bigot. My parents raised me to accept all people regardless of color; there was no color, only people. This was a code my Mom and Dad firmly believed in. When I was confronted with a boss who ranted and used the N word making derogatory remarks about the people of color who worked in production, I was outraged.

Even if I could have worked with this guy, I could not deal with the sulfur drug dust that settled on my desk during the day. It was so bad I could write "please dust me" in it every morning. All I could think of was that I was breathing this stuff in all day, and that couldn't be good. Enough of this, I called in the following Monday and quit, they did not seem surprised.

As the chemical company was a total wash out, I went back to Olson and they found work for me at the Department of Welfare on 33rd Street in Baltimore City. I was a file clerk, very excited at working in the big city.

The woman I worked for was a drunk. She kept a bottle of vodka in the bottom drawer of her desk. She would slide out the bottom drawer very slowly so it would not make any noise and pour a shot or two into her coffee cup. By lunch she was pretty mellow. She had very little contact with any of the "floor" employees.

There were four of us filing and pulling card requests from Case Workers. These cards were about 5" by 10". The cards were a tool used by the case workers to update a welfare recipient's status. Looking back, it is pretty amazing how everything at the time was hand written. They used the "Soundex Filing System". This type of filing converts a surname to the corresponding soundex code (4 characters). There was this huge banner on the wall and all you did was figure out what the 4 characters were. Once done, you did a burnout in your little wheeled chair, zipping up and down the rows all day. These filing bins were in 6 foot sections. Once you got the hang of it, you could really put some work away. File room employees were always either leaving or getting promoted. Even though this was a state job, they used temporary employees.

I made friends and was enjoying being a working woman of the world. One of the gals I worked with moonlighted as a stripper at the Gaiety Bar on Baltimore Street. I was totally in awe of her.

Then Martin Luther King was assassinated. On April the 6th, 1968, Maryland Governor Spiro Agnew called up the National Guard to quell the riots and restore peace to the city. From Friday, April 5th to Tuesday, April 9th, there was rioting and looting. I was at work on Friday when the building I worked in was torched. As the outdoor unit burned on top of the roof, we were all taken into the basement. There were at least 100 people working that day, and we were informed that we could not leave the basement area. The National Guard Units were arriving with four school buses to evacuate us out of Baltimore. This was pretty scary stuff.

Those of us that drove into Baltimore had no other way out, and I would have to leave my car behind. I was parked on a side street off Green Mount Avenue. My little 1963 Green VW was doomed! It was my first car. Sadly I thought, "I will never see you again."

As the buses and troops arrived, we were divided in four groups. The Guard Troops barked orders and herded us into lines according to what direction our homes were: East, West, North, or South of Green Mount Avenue. I got on the bus going towards my home and hoped that when the bus got to a Baltimore County final destination, I could find some one to pick me up.

As we were driven out of the city, we were told to keep our heads down. Of course, we were all peeking out the windows, the city was in flames. I was astounded by the noise and the smoke. I could not believe my city by the bay was totally out of control like this. It was terrifying.

My bus went as far north as the Hutzlers Department Store in Towson, Md. This worked out pretty well, as my mother worked in Cockeysville and could pick me up later that evening. I would have a few hours to kill, where to go and what to do?

The sky was bright, sunny and cloudless, one of those "not a care in the world days." I could not help thinking how wrong that seemed. It would have been a perfect spring day, except the streets were eerily empty. I don't remember being scared, just feeling kind of lost. As I strolled around the streets in Towson, I spied the library, great! I could hide out and feel safe.

The next few days we lived under a Marshall Law Decree issued by the Governor. No one was getting in or out of Baltimore. On Sunday the curfew was lifted and my dad took me into Baltimore to see if my car had survived the rioting. I could not believe it. When we turned up the street, there it was. Not a scratch. I jumped in, buzzed up the road and back to the safety of the county. That was pretty much the end of that job. My Dad told me in no uncertain terms I was not going back there to work. My misfortune could not have been worse, back to searching for another job. I answered ads in the newspaper but without much luck. A neighbor, Gloria, told me Eastinghouse was looking for file clerks. Gloria worked as a secretary there and could get me in. Naturally I took her up on that.

Working at Eastinghouse was my first introduction to the manufacturing work place. I was a clerk in an engineering department. Gloria was my friend there and we did lunch with the other girls. She and I rode together in a car pool. Gloria was a very humble and kind girl. She had gold 1968 Dodge Hemi. She used a beautiful crystal key chain, and was *the* style setter of the office. I always thought she had that car to make up for her physical appearance. Gloria had harelip surgery, and it wasn't successful.

I was very naive at that time in my life and had no idea how people carried on at work. There were love triangles, company romances and inter department squabbles in every area of the company. During the Christmas holidays, the shop area had a big party and everyone was invited. This was an on site party in the shop area. I had heard there was booze of every type, and tons of food at this celebration. Gloria and I decided to walk to the shop to check it out.

To our surprise, one of the women who worked on the line was dancing on the work area table, attired only in a skimpy red baby doll pajamas set. Now these people knew how to celebrate. We quickly returned to our office.

My naivety played out in another unsavory situation with an engineer I worked for. I had no idea how to deal with the men in the department. I was used to handling boys at school. I was totally out of my league on this. This man, Engineer Mac, exposed himself to me, right there in the office. Looking back, I suppose he might have thought I was being bold and flirtatious. I trotted around in spike high heels with short as hell mini skirts, typical late 60's fashions.

Maybe he thought I was coming on to him, but in my mind that had never happened. Mac was at least 15 years older than I, married and not very good looking. There was no way I would have been interested in him.

I stupidly went to my manager and reported what had transpired with this creepy engineer. After Mac was demoted to the shop area, I was laid off. The lesson learned here was that men rule, take what is dished out, keep your mouth shut, and enjoy the ride.

Wandering the streets of Towson looking for another job, I noticed a help wanted sign in the window of an insurance company. As luck would have it, I got the job.

The company was GEICO, you know, the talking lizard? I started out as a file clerk. This was the best company I ever worked for. I was hired as a file clerk. In the course of 6 ½ years, I was promoted into one job after another. My friend Jamie used to call me, "The Star of GEICO." I was eventually promoted to the position of Claims Adjuster. This was a job that required compassion and excellent customer service ability. Talking with accident victims all day requires tremendous patience. At the time, my idea of success was having an office chair with arms and a briefcase. Finally I had a chair with arms, but I never did get an illustrious brief case. At one point in my tenure, I supervised the claims information call center. I was never very good at supervision. I just never had the heart for it. I like being nice, and that's something you can't always have when you supervise others.

GEICO had continuing education programs that were held at the home office in Chevy Chase, Md. These trips were great! Everyone in the claims department was required to attend. I got to go with a gal named Ruth. Ruth was my buddy at the office. We usually did lunch with the other young people in the office. It was just like high school, but in a grown up scenario.

So, Ruth and I are going to D.C for a week long training seminar and we will be staying at the Holiday Inn, just like the "big wigs" in our office. Neither one of us had ever had been on a "business trip". We were so excited, and we would have our own expense report vouchers!

We left on a Sunday night going to the most adult thing we had ever done, absolutely giddy with excitement. Up to that point, the most grown up thing we had done was to get married. Ruth and I had both walked down the aisle the previous summer. As we pulled up to the hotel in Washington D.C, Ruth said "I feel all grown up now." I did too. We were now officially professional women of the seventies.

The seminar week was great for "country girls" like us. We got all dressed up each day to go our classes. Every night we were riding in cabs going to the finest Washington D.C. restaurants. The night lights of D.C. were so exciting; my brain just sponged up every accent and face I saw. There were employees from many GEICO branch offices taking this seminar; we savored this great adventure together.

One day after class Ruth and I and about 10 others from class got on an elevator to leave for the day. All of a sudden, *wham*! The elevator got caught between two floors. Up and down up and down, it just would not stop on the ground floor. When the doors would open, it was about 2 feet short of the floor. Well, at one point everyone except Ruth and I climbed up and got off. I don't remember now why we would have stayed on but we did. Up and down, up and down it went. Finally it stopped, the doors opened all the way and we got off. We didn't realize it at the time but we were five floors down in a subterranean parking garage.

As we walked up the ramps in the dark parking garage, our high heels were ringing and echoing off the concrete walls. At one point Ruth asked me, "Are we in the Twilight Zone?" With all the courage I could muster, I said, "no, don't say that." We were scared little girls! All of a sudden we saw a sliver of shimmering daylight, and *ran* up that last ramp into the sunlight. To this day I hate taking elevators. I take them, but I hate it.

The people I worked with were intelligent, fair, and friendly. I like to think we were a family. I miss my manager Bill; he was encouraging and could always get the best out of me. I miss the other women I worked with too, Billy and Sioux. No kidding, that is how she spelled her name. When I answered her phone, I had to correct people and tell them that it was not SUEX, it was Sioux. We would go window shopping at Hutzlers Department Store on our lunch hours. We enjoyed strolling to the Jewish deli where we devoured magnificent corned beef sandwiches. I miss those two crazy auto appraisers, Jamie and John. Jamie used to take statements from clients after hours and always used my desk. I often found empty beer cans in my lower desk drawer. I had to figure out how to get them into the trash. John had a wicked sense of humor. They used to call me, "The Snow-Pak Kid". Once, when shaking up a bottle of correction fluid, the top flew off and Snow-Pak went everywhere. I did not realize how lucky I was to have had great coworkers who were also friends until years later.

GEICO ran into financial problems in the 1970's. No Gecko to the rescue in those days. There seemed to be a problem with "Reserve Funds." Geico had been struck with two big hurricane catastrophic losses back to back. As an employee, I was not privy to the actual facts. When the Federal Auditors' walked in, we figured out things were not going to end well. The company was forced to re-organize if they wanted to continue writing insurance. The solution by the Federal Government was for the company to close all branch offices and re-organize at their central location in Chevy Chase, MD.

This was very sad for all of us. There were about 40 employees at the Towson Branch Office. Some took the opportunity to relocate to the Chevy Chase office, and others did not. I lived in Baltimore County, committing to D.C. just wasn't an option. At this time in the U.S., the gas embargo was going on. President Richard Nixon announced a voluntary "share the gas shortage" plan on May 10, 1973. Commuters faced gas shortages. I decided no more odd or even days for me. I chose to take my severance package and become a stay at home farmer.

My first husband and I had a farmette in Baltimore County. He was a land surveyor and worked for the county government. He made good money and did not want me to work. My working had always been an issue of dissension. I began raising dairy goats. This was something I was very good at. I have always had a natural bond with animals.

We had a working dairy and I showed my goats up and down the East coast. We were winners in the show ring and I enjoyed traveling to State Fairs. I had developed as a person, gotten to know many wonderful people and had made friends.

As time progressed, I grew up and grew apart from my verbally abusive husband. My friends helped me see that I could make it on my own, and were always there for me. They gave me the courage to believe in myself, and encouraged me to get out of a life that was going nowhere fast. As in most situations like this, divorce was not far off. I will always cherish the time I spent raising my goats. They were wonderful companions. When I think back on my life, I don't have many regrets, but losing my dear goats was one.

I left my first husband on Mothers Day, 1980. That was a good day. I went back to live at my parents home and began looking for a job. After being out of the job market for so long, it wasn't going to be easy to rejoin. I had no choice but to contact a temp agency.

I desperately wanted out of my parents' house. I needed to get enough money together for an apartment. It is tough to go back home after 15 years of living on your own.

My parents lived in a thirteen room Victorian home which had originally been built as the summer home for the Blacks of the Black and Decker Company in the early 1900's. Looking at the house now, it is very beautiful, with huge old oak trees, lush green lawns, and twinkling stain glass windows. As a child, I did not see it that way.

To me the house was dark and gloomy. A house that had given me scary dreams and convinced me there were oogie bogie men living in the closets. It had a melancholy atmosphere even on the brightest summer day. It was furnished with massive Victorian furniture. My mother chose dark maroon velvet chairs; the end tables had old statues and banquet lamps on them. There were Rayo lamps shoved in every corner. Hanging on the walls were paintings of the Spanish Inquisition. The drapes were deep blue velvet with gold fringe.

My Father refinished antique metal items for antique dealers and private customers. The smell of the chemicals would drift up from the basement resulting in the house having an arid smell. It was a cross between an antique shop and a funeral home. Even the birds did not come there during the day. They would mysteriously return after dark and sing outside my window late at night. Edgar Allan Poe's poem, *The Raven,* could have been written in the parlor. Even though I had come back on Christmas holidays and family gatherings, I had forgotten how oppressive this place could seem to me.

There I was back in my old room lying across the bed staring at the twenty foot ceiling looming ominously above me. I could not help thinking to myself, now I have come back to square one. "No", I would say myself, think positively. This is square *two*. Stay focused, get a job, and get out of here. If you can get up the courage to leave a mean husband, you can do this too. I looked out the window; it was dark out. I would shutter to think "I hope the wicked witch from the Wizard of Oz doesn't hover outside this window anymore."

The days are long in my mother's house just like when I was a child. I couldn't wait for evening, where I could escape to my room and read. Now I was even a prisoner of that room. I didn't want to go downstairs. My mother was always hovering over me touching my hair, I hated that. She would constantly pick at my choice of clothing and how I styled my hair. "Your hair looked better its natural color." I never thought mousy brown looked a whole lot better than blond. Anyway, I felt sexier with blond hair. All girls look better when they go blond, you know? My father still worked second shift so he did not have to be around the house during the day. Nothing had changed between them; they still sniped at each other and bickered over the most trivial matters.

Things began to turn my way when I got a part time job working for a local veterinarian. Doctor Kerchmer was the same veterinarian we used when we had the goat farm. He gave me enough hours so that I could begin to sock away some bucks in my apartment "fund". My plans were beginning to fall into place.

I was now dating a guy from Anytown, PA. I would travel from Maryland to visit him. I had known John before I had left my husband. We had mutual friends but now our friendship went to the next level. I would go to Anytown to see him and on occasion stayed over night. After all, I was 28 years old.

This did not go over very well with my parents . . ."This is my house, my rules, in by eleven", The Parent Sermon. I had forgotten that part about living at home. I had moved on to being a capable woman, certainly old enough to make these kinds of decisions. I like to think I am a good house guest. I always clean up after myself and volunteer around the house. I am quiet, I read a lot. As a child I would read my books by flash light. You can image how shocked I was to overhear the following exchange between my parents. As I was descending the long winding stair case one afternoon, I heard my father speaking loudly to my mom. "This is my house. I don't want any of them back here." My mom snapped back, "They are my kids, and I want them here. This is my house too!" My father left the house and got into his car, He pulled out of the driveway kicking up gravel in the process. I was frozen on the staircase landing. I slipped back up the stairs into my room and plopped down in a chair. Boy, I thought, nice to be wanted. Feel the love. Now I knew I had to move onward with my plans and make things happen quickly. Two weeks later I went to work at Cottage West Apartments. John was a tenant there and told me they needed a rental agent.

Within eight weeks, I had enough money to get a small efficiently apartment in Anytown, Pa. My mother was having her normal; "I lost control" hissy fit. "Why the rush?" she would say to me. "You can stay here forever." I muttered something back and pretended to be very busy. She stomped around for the next few days with her best "Mother Martyred Face". I never mentioned the "stairway' conversation I had overheard. I felt it was something best left unspoken.

The following week a girl I worked with at the veterinarian's office helped me pack up my furniture. I was on my way to my new life. It was the Fourth of July weekend and I knew in my heart it was a better day.

CHAPTER 3

A Bartender is just a pharmacist with restricted inventory

I wanted to stay in Baltimore but it's a big city to live in with no friends and a mean ex-husband close by. Susie, who I had met at The Open Way Tavern in Anytown, suggested I move north. She thought that I might be happier making my new beginning in a smaller, safer town. Anytown had gobs of clothing outlets and the rents were cheap. I would be able to live cheap and look good. That made sense to me. Anytown is very picturesque on the surface, but beneath you will find a very cliquish, unfriendly population, terrified of strangers and change. I was also dating John and he lived there. It is not a good move to work where your boy friend lives.

The apartments were nice, surrounded by big trees and rolling green lawns. The tenants were average middle class families, with a few singles thrown in. I was the day rental agent. This consisted of showing empty apartments, collecting rents, and scheduling maintenance. There was only one other office employee. Mr. Crisp was the supervising agent and my boss. Mr. Crisp was a fine old gentleman, a dear to know. The complex was owned by a company in Baltimore, MD. The owner came up once a month to go over the books and generally check up on us.

This was a rather boring position except for the crazy busy time, the first of the month. The only thing that was unsettling was the manner in which they handled the money. It surprised me how many people paid their rent in cash. By the end of the day, I would have thousands of dollars in cash. Instead of making a daily bank deposit, I placed the receipts and cash under a piece of carpet in the supply closet. Mr. Crisp would at some point in time take it to the bank. I really never knew where the money went. The owner would arrive from Baltimore once a month and it would be my job to take his big shiny Cadillac to the gas station and get it filled up. I liked driving his car.

Three months later John and I broke up. I wanted a serious commitment from him. I was not into a casual affair. I have never been the jealous type but I was not happy competing with his stable of girlfriends. I discovered something in his closet that was disturbing. One afternoon John called me at work asking me to go to his place and let myself in with a pass key. He asked me to retrieve a paper from a suit jacket. He needed a number written on it. All he wanted me to do was get the number and call him back.

I went to his apartment and let myself in. I rummaged through the closet searching for his suit jacket with the papers. As I pushed his suits around, I spied this wooden board mounted on the wall behind the clothing rack. I could not believe what I was seeing. It was an old fashion horse racing game. The game board was about 3 feet by 3 feet with five or six metal horses mounted on wires. Each horse had a woman's name taped on it. To my amazement, I found out I was in second place. I suppose children used to play this game by throwing dice and moving the horses down the wire to the finish line. He had invented a new game to please himself. I was hurt and humiliated. "What kind of man does this?" Right then and there I was done with John. I did call him with the number he wanted. After that I made myself unavailable. He didn't seem terribly surprised or upset. There was always another filly.

Now a new problem developed. Suddenly John came into the office all the time. He had to pay his rent or he needed all kinds of minor maintenance done in his apartment. He was making it very difficult for me to work there. Perhaps he was trying to keep an eye on me. John's visits were becoming such a nuisance and a distraction that I could not do my job properly. I knew it would never end so I made the decision to find another job. However, working at Cottage West had made it possible for me to live on my own in my first apartment. I knew I would have to go forward and try to make the best of it.

I started checking out employment agencies. My thinking was that I could get another job with no lost time. I was happy because I was able to give two weeks notice and begin working temp without skipping a beat.

My first assignment was with the Peanut Temp Service. This company was a little nut in a large can. The woman running this temp factory was **THE Peanut** queen, with lots of little peanut princesses working for her. I got short assignments from this company. I could not be picky at this point. At least, it was work.

In pretty quick secession, I was sent to Leotards & Lace, a Chevy Auto Dealer and a retail store called Postmen's. The assignments were all quickies. The longest was the auto dealer which was about four weeks. Leotards & Lace was a good company to work for if you could get hired. They used a lot of temps. I was an "Order Re-Checker." This pretty much speaks for itself. I would make sure the phoned in order matched the packing slip. This was only going to last through their seasonal ordering time. I was surprised to learn that their clients were dance studios from all over the world. I found it interesting that they sold to so many European troupes and schools.

The D'namra R. Smith Dealership was a decent assignment. It was the first place I had worked where you could wear jeans. I always had to dress up. There was a reason for the jeans, the place was very dirty. I worked upstairs in the title and correspondence department. The other women I worked with were only friendly enough not to jeopardize me leaving the job. If I left they would have to train another temp. Apparently the last one just up and left in the middle of the day. They were getting a lot of cars in so the extra help would be needed for about four weeks. I was glad when it was over; parking was a real challenge as they had cars parked everywhere and in every direction.

Postmen's was a crappy company to be sent to on an assignment. The people there were very unfriendly. I entered the little tag skew numbers from items sold. I had never worked with a computer, and I screwed up their inventory. This really wasn't my fault, as I wasn't given much training. Sometimes you get the bear, sometimes . . . Looking back on this, I totally blame Peanut Agency for sending me on an assignment I was not prepared to do. I had told Little Peanut Princess when she called me about the assignment that I did not have computer experience, but she said, "You can pull it off." Guess not.

I found employment though another agency, Walnut Personnel Placements. This company was a somewhat bigger nut in the can. The owners were husband and wife, very professional without being chilly. They were nice people, who did a great deal of community service. I had a good feeling about this agency. Things did eventually go south with them but not before I made them a lot of money. I worked for them off and on for years.

The first assignment they sent me on was to a Biller Skating Company. I would be the assistant to the bookkeeper, Sandy, who had worked there for ten years. I had no accounting background at all, but Sandy taught me all I needed to know. Back then, bookkeeping was done by hand, double entry; there was no Excel to do it for you.

Sandy was one of the sweetest ladies I have ever met; she had the patience of Job. We were a good team. After the standard three month waiting time, I was hired. Happy Days were here again.

Mr. Biller, the owner of this company was involved with many other rinks located up and down the east coast. He was a very capable man; but a man of dubious integrity. I never felt comfortable around him. He perceived himself to be god's gift to women. Even though he had a beautiful wife, he was always on the prowl.

He employed his family members and they knew every trick to live off of the business. However, in my mind, what they were doing with the receipts and petty cash reports was nothing short of stealing. But then, what do I know? When I would point out inconsistencies in the receipts, he would get defensive and tell me not to concern myself as he would address the problem. At the time

I did not realize that small business people all legally steal from themselves. So the "problem" was never addressed.

During this time, I was single and dating lots of losers. My girlfriends were always fixing me up with someone. These dates never worked out. Living alone can be very depressing. I usually went out dancing on Friday and Saturday nights. I loved to dance and it kept me thin. But I could hardly afford this high flying lifestyle. I met a gal at the Open Way Tavern and we had become friends. She was the bartender there at the time. Susie was now working at El Jefe's and suggested I get an evening job. It would take up some time but I would have some extra money. She could get me "In" as a cocktail waitress. Susie was one of those people who naturally twinkle. She was great looking and was an excellent professional bartender. She always had a following. It was great to be friends with her. She could read people and was able to steer away from trouble. We had tons of fun, there were no bad times. To this day, she is the one person I can depend on to tell me the truth, no matter how hard it hurts.

I continued working at Biller Skating during the day and hung out as a Cocktail waitress Friday and Saturday nights. I loved the atmosphere there. They had live bands so the place was usually packed on the weekends. The floor waitress wore skimpy Leotards & Lace outfits and killer high heels. I was not a very good waitress, and my feet hurt by the end of the night, but I looked drop dead gorgeous!

It was fun, like going out to party and getting paid for it. I never experienced a bad situation with a customer. It is often said that tables of women don't tip. I did not find that to be true, they always left me something. I got orders mixed up and never could get a customer the right "lite" brand beer the first time around. Bartenders really don't like it when you return drinks. Mary, the head bartender, often gave me the look. She was a tough cookie. As bad as I was, I made money hand over fist. As long as your boobs are hanging out and you're wearing sexy shoes, men will tip. Imagine what I would have made if I had been good at it! After three months, I had saved enough for a little nest egg and I quit.

I was still working at Biller Skating during the day but things were getting weird. At this time Mr. Biller decided to purchase a computer. In 1981 computers were not small. The hard drive was the size of a small freezer. Sandy and I did not use it much. Mr. Biller and his son used it as a play toy. Mr. Biller's son i.e. "He thinks he's a brainyack" crashed it and there was hell to pay that day.

At that time the owner was also getting involved with a bar and motel business. This would prove to be a disaster. Mr. Biller had no experience in the bar/restaurant business and relied on a very knowledgeable woman, Ms. Loon, to direct his investments. They opened two bars and renovated the money pit motel. This motel was horribly run down. The prior owner hadn't done maintenance in years. The bars were successful for a time, but Mr. Biller's wife hit him with a pretty nasty divorce. Ms. Loon had a better contract with Mr. Biller than Mr. Biller had with his wife or any one else for that matter. It all got very ugly.

Susan and I continued along like nothing was amiss, but we knew money was evaporating. I realized one week, that there was not enough in the accounts to cover payroll. I walked over to the Motel and cashed my check out of the receipts drawer. Following my lead, so did everyone else. When Mr. Biller got the drawers from the bar, motel and roller rink, he was surprised to discover that the only thing in them were paychecks. He was furious. It doesn't get any better than that. He stopped speaking to us. He would go in his office, shut the door, and just sit there. We were all waiting to hear the single gun shot. It was not much longer after all that when I got my pink slip. Mr. Biller eventually gave Susan a layoff too, and his daughter became the bookkeeper. His children continued to work for him until the near demise of the company. I had been there for two and a half years, not a bad run.

I now placed a phone call to the Walnut Temp Agency.

CHAPTER 4

The wind in your face and a paycheck in your pocket

I was laid off from Biller Skate Company but The Walnut Agency was happy to have me back in the fold. Mrs. Walnut informed me that since it was summer they were slow. She assured me that business would be picking up and I would be working in no time. I was living with a guy I had met while working at the Skate Company. Consequently I was not experiencing the panic of being out of work. Given that I was collecting unemployment, there was no urgency for a temp to permanent position.

Life was fun; the guy I lived with was a biker. The first time I met him was with a group of gals at the Day Tripper Inn. Sue, Kathie, Kim, and I were following a band called The Pep Boys. They were performing at the Day Tripper Inn, and I had come into their circle of fun when I started going to the New Wheel Tavern in the city. The New Wheel was a little on the rough side, but they always had live music on the weekends.

Kim was the real shinning star in our group. She was a very beautiful girl, with raven black hair and crystal blue eyes. She was tall and lanky. When Kim batted those crystal blues, the men melted. Kim was never into picking up guys, if she came with a group she left with the group. I loved going out with Kim, she was a people magnet.

When I arrived at the Day Tripper Inn, I joined up with Laree, Joel, Carol, and Steve. I knew this was going to be a fun night. As soon as the band began, we were dancing and having a blast.

Smithy stood out from the rest of the guys playing pool. He had sun bleached blond hair, indigo blue eyes, a golden tan and was wearing bib overalls without a shirt. He hadn't been at the beach. Smithy worked on a farm. He was a diesel mechanic, welder and the fix anything guy. The sparks were flying, the booze was flowing, and the band played on, loud and strong. Before long we were dancing and getting acquainted. He invited me to go for a motorcycle ride. I have found Harley Davidson motorcycles are very seductive. I was hooked. We dated for a couple of months. Smithy's friends soon became mine. Most of our friends had Harley's and those that didn't wanted one. I was meeting people who loved to have a good time. We went to biker parties and tubing parties at the river.

Smithy and I decided to give living together a go, we moved into a little house across from a junkyard out in the countryside of Anytown. Smithy rented from his friend Tom, who had at one time owned the lovely junk yard across the road. It wasn't as bad as it sounds. The house was a cottage and Tom had taken good care of it. The house was surrounded with big old trees and a small yard. The house was heated with a wood stove. I never liked wood stoves; they always seemed too dangerous and messy.

By the end of the summer, it was time to get back to work. Walnut Agency called with a short assignment at Agway. This was only a week, filling in for someone on vacation. I would be a file clerk. The one thing that sticks out in my mind about this assignment was the stunning African violets. The ladies had them on the top of the file cabinets. They were the size of full grown heads of cabbage. To this day I have never seen violets that large or with as many gorgeous blooms. Agway was a pleasant experience, too bad it was over so abruptly.

Walnut Agency soon called and had a temp to permanent job available at CCC. Was I interested? You bet I was. I would be working as a receptionist for an insurance company called Rock Solid Insurance. They were opening "satellite" offices within the CCC family. There would be three office locations in Anytown, Hangover, and Gettysburger. When I heard the words "start up" and "satellite", bells should have gone off. This was a great opportunity for me and I accepted the assignment readily.

Rock Solid insurance was another example of what can be good in employment. Once again I was working with smart professional people. My manager Bill was a dream, the agents were kind, friendly, and helpful. Since we were all hired on the same day, a comradeship developed between us all.

We were required to be licensed in the state of Pennsylvania to sell and service insurance policies. Rock Solid paid for our training and the testing. I passed my test and was an official P and C Insurance Agent. I did not go out on calls. Being licensed gave me the advantage of writing policies and helping customers who are known as "walk ins". Usually I was alone at the office as Bill, Rick, and Brad would be out on the road doing the salesman thing.

For the next three years all was good. There were some changes in personnel. Our manager took a transfer back to Philadelphia. His replacement, Rick, previously worked at a Pennsylvania prison as an instructor at the school. It might seem strange that a prison instructor would end up in the insurance industry, but then people working in law enforcement had often drifted into insurance jobs. Rick was an okay guy but a bit rough around the edges. His suits never seemed to fit right, maybe that's why he seemed so gruff?

I was also working with two wonderful women, Pauline and Dee. Dee was a sweetheart; she was raising a beautiful little girl on her own. Pauline had a very happy outgoing bubbly personality, so the sales job was a perfect fit for her.

I had left Smithy, our parting of the ways was mutual, and as it turned out in the future we would end up living together again. We were always good friends rather than star crossed lovers. I had a dear little apartment on Duke Street within walking distance to the office.

One morning Rick called us to a meeting. The sales agents and I "knew" something was in the wind. No one in CCC would make eye contact with us any longer. They would shy way from us in the break room and bathrooms. At this meeting, the "start up" word resurfaced. Rick informed us that the management of CCC in Anytown had decided their insurance department should be making the money, not splitting the policy premiums with Rock Solid. Rick also said the arrangement with CCC was always referred to as "experimental" so this was not a huge surprise. Again, I was not privy to the details. I believed there were other issues. The satellite offices in Hangover and Gettysburger were also closed. As the saying goes, without bad luck I wouldn't have any luck at all.

Rick took Pauline, Dee and I out to lunch at the Greek restaurant across the street on the last day of work. We stood in the sunshine outside the restaurant and hugged and said our goodbyes. I had a wonderful experience working at Rock Solid. I would miss Pauline and Dee. Little did I know I would have the pleasure of Dee's company in the future but in a very different situation.

It was now the summer of 1984 I and was collecting unemployment again, living on my own but scared. I had no one to cover my back financially. I decided to bypass the temp agencies and find a position on my own. I got the local newspaper and began answering ads.

I received a phone call from a company called Edward S. Old and they wanted to interview me. I should have known this was not a reputable company when the man on the phone requested I meet him and the office manager at the Sportsman's Restaurant on Market St, not far from the Agency. Being desperate, I went to the interview anyway. Of course the reason for this secret meeting was they were going to fire the person I was replacing. I aced the interview and began working there the following Monday morning.

I was dating a younger man, Ricky the Rock Star, who was the lead singer in a metal band. Ricky was a rock star, at least to himself. He looked the part with his long black curls and tight jeans. Ricky was separated from his wife and lived at an old hotel near the Edward S. Old Agency. Ricky was looking for a soft spot to land. I was not interested in living with anyone again. It was a fun casual relationship and I planned on keeping it that way.

I had never worked for an insurance agency. It was a big change from working for an insurance company. Insurance agencies write insurance coverage for many different companies. There are different requirements and guidelines for each company. Agents have the ability to circumvent underwriting guidelines and insure people with questionable driving records. On the other hand, insurance companies have hard and fast underwriting guidelines that are NOT flexible.

The office was in a converted house that was a small and dingy. As I recall, there was the owner, a salesman and two women working in the front office. I am at a loss as to the name of the young blond woman I worked with there. She was pretty and very capable. The office manger, Belinda, was not as nice and certainly not pretty. She was tall, skinny, with acne scars on her face. Belinda was very defensive and took an instant dislike to me. I never could figure out how I offended her. I got very bad vibes from her. Funny, but I *never* forgot *her* name.

I did not have a problem working with Belinda; for the most part I just ignored her. She was always behind in her work. I volunteered to help her out but she never wanted me to assist her. I wasn't very happy working there. I sensed she deeply disliked and resented my presence.

One thing I never got used to was the difference in *company* insurance philosophy and insurance *agency* philosophy. There is a concept called "agent exception". Agent exception gives the owner of an agency the ability to make exceptions and insure bad risk drivers.

These people are usually the Agents' friends and golf buddies. I was not comfortable working for a company that did not play by the rules. I had enough claims knowledge to realize the folly in "agent exception". Edward S. Old at some point in time went out of business. I could not help but wonder if this could have been part of the reason. This was the first time I took photos of my work area and my co-workers. I would continue to take photos everywhere I worked after this. When I thumb through an album page, I remember the people and places I have been. I even have a photo of old mean Belinda.

One afternoon I decided that I would start looking for another job. I did not deserve the treatment I received from Belinda. She would come to my desk and slam files down that she had audited, and bark instructions for me to follow. When I would leave for lunch, she would make snide remarks, referring to where I went and what I did on my lunch hour. She seemed to have found out I was meeting up with Ricky at lunch. Ricky lived two blocks from the Edward S. Old Company. We would have romantic interludes during lunch; I don't know how she discovered this. Why this was such a thorn in her side I did not know. After all it was my lunch hour.

I had only worked at Edward S. Old for three months. I did not think it was going to get any better. I had seen an advertisement in the newspaper for a Property and Casualty agent at a company called Bowen Insurance. I applied for the position, went on the interview, and was hired. I was to start at Bowen in just two weeks. This would enable me to give a two week notice at the Edward S. Old Company.

Belinda was such a nasty witch in the days following my interview I decided to leave with no notice. When I would ask her advice on a policy question, she would give me short rude instructions. If I offered to help out, she would say, "I don't need **your** help" giving me the *your dismissed hand wave*. On my last Friday, Belinda was being her usual nasty self and I just got up out of my seat, put on my jacket, walked to her desk and handed her my notice of resignation. As she stood there reading my letter of resignation, I could see her expression go from puzzlement to disbelief. "You're just walking out on me." Her voice was normally rather deep, but it was shrill now. "Yes," I replied, "please mail my check." I walked out the door and into the brilliant afternoon sun light. My apartment was about ten blocks from the office, I enjoyed every scenic moment of my stroll home that afternoon. As I was walking, I realized I had left my old white office sweater over the back of my chair. Oh well, no big loss. Bowen Insurance would turn out to be a huge disaster. I had unknowingly stepped out of the frying pan and into the fire.

Bowen Insurance handles commercial as well as private accounts. The office manger, Mary, fell all over herself telling me at the interview, "We have all the gold plated accounts in Anytown." And they did. Mary was a very, very large woman of Dutch German descent. She was *atypical* of the women living in Anytown. I would soon find her to be judgmental and jealous of the other women in the office.

I was hired under a standard ninety day probationary period. I was training directly with Mary and she was a very knowledgeable person. I worked hard at learning the job. The job was very difficult. The computer system was new to me. There was a big learning curve; I was basically starting from scratch. I would go in every Saturday (without pay) just to get some quiet time and improve on my skills. I knew I was in over my head, but I kept plugging away anyhow. I was into my third week of employment when I noticed Mary had developed an attitude towards me. Since we had gotten on so well at the initial interview, I was mystified as to what was going on.

The other employees at Bowen were all so aloof and unfriendly towards me. I was never able to make any friends; the receptionist was the only person that even spoke to me. She was a very lovely girl, and might I add, she was Bowens' token African American. Anytown County has a reputation for being a tightly closed redneck community. This reputation was well deserved.

Since I left Baltimore and moved to Anytown, I had to deal with overweight women who had an instant attitude towards any woman with a normal waistline. In many instances I have barely known these women. I can only assume it is because I am not one hundred pounds overweight. It surely must be frightening to those women!

I am a reasonably good looking woman. I am not a beauty queen but I have never had a problem turning heads when I entered a room. I dress well and take care of myself. I like to have manicures and pamper myself. I have never judged anyone by their appearance. I would never decide to instantly dislike someone because they were over weight. When I lived in Baltimore I had large girlfriends, no problems.

One payday afternoon, Ricky came into the office to borrow money. We were standing in the reception area talking, and I was trying to get him out of there. I could tell the people employed at Bowen were appalled that someone of Rickey's *type* had the nerve to enter their castle. Suddenly everyone was strolling past us to get a look at the new employee's *Rock Star* boyfriend. I was so embarrassed.

The following morning Mary spoke to me in a very sharp manner. I had enough of this. I politely asked her, "what is wrong, what have I done to cause you to speak to me in that tone? If I have offended you in any way, I apologize." Mary did not respond to me, she just walked away. Later that day she came to my desk and told me to join her in the conference room. "Oh my," I thought, "this is not good." I walked the *longest mile* to that conference room. Mary was sitting at the head of the long shining wooden table. "Judy, take a seat." She barked. "I need to explain something to you." I sat down, trying not to let her see my wringing hands. "Judy," Mary continued, "Each year we have a group picture taken of all the employees. This photo is used in our company magazine and in our advertising. We have decided that you would be out of place in the picture." In other words, you just don't fit our corporate picture. She added, "oh, and you are not grasping the work for this position quickly enough either."

Well you could have scraped me off the floor. I did not know how to respond. I just sat there frozen. Mary went on to tell me I needed to leave immediately. Before I could say anything, she left the room. I got up and went back to my desk. The walk back seemed even *longer.*

I retrieved my handbag and mug. Standing as tall as I could, I departed the office. The receptionist stopped me on my way out to say how sorry she was. Apparently everyone but me knew what was going on. What could I say except, "Thanks for being so nice." I had only worked at Bowen for five weeks. How could they possibly expect me to learn what was involved in just five weeks? I had been told I would have ninety days. What happened to that? When I got out onto the street it was hot and humid. Everything had blown up in my face. I had burned the bridge at Edward Old. I could not go back there. That walk home was very long for me. Darn if I didn't leave another white office sweater over the back of my chair.

I was devastated emotionally with the treatment I received at Bowen Insurance. I filed for unemployment and Bowen actually had the nerve to fight my claim. I won that round; at least I had a little income for a while. The summer of 1984 was almost over. Ricky and I were over too. When things go badly in your professional life the rest of your life goes south too. Nothing was fun anymore. I felt I was a failure and couldn't do anything right. Since I wasn't doing so well finding employment on my own, I called Mrs. Walnut of the Walnut Temp Service, once again.

CHAPTER 5

The more I learn the less I comprehend.

Mrs. Walnut was very compassionate and understanding during the terrible weeks following the situation at Bowen. Her agency was very busy and they offered to find me work immediately. The only problem was that none of the job orders they had were temp to permanent. This made no difference to me; I would worry about a real job later. Right about then, I needed the money. I went to Serpentine Cadillac to work in their leasing department. It was September of 1988 and the new cars were being delivered. I would be typing the new leasing agreements for customers trading in older model vehicles. This was right up my alley; I had all the skills needed for this assignment.

I would be helping a woman who had carpel tunnel surgery who could not type. She would still be there but working in another department. This was great, if I had questions, she was there. I don't remember her name, but she was super to work with. The office I was assigned to work in was beautiful, as was the entire dealership. The building was circular, with a huge crystal chandelier in the show room. Parked under the chandelier were brand new sparkling Cadillac's. It made me wish I could buy one. This placement was only to last six weeks. I learned that the great places to work are never the jobs that go full time. The employees at Serpentine Cadillac were a fun bunch to work with, everyone was helpful. I was sorry to see this assignment end.

Next, Walnut Personnel sent me to Tri-Glory Electric to help out in the filing department for one week. I never liked one week assignments. It seemed that by the time I knew what I was doing it was time to move on. The employees at Tri-Glory seemed stressed out. No one smiled much or seemed very friendly. I just went in each day and did my job. There was a terribly sad situation that happened while I was working there. One of the men who worked the counter did not come into work or call off that day. It was discovered that he had committed suicide. This affected everyone there, he was well liked. Needless to say a pall fell over that job for the next two days. This had occurred on the Wednesday of my one week assignment. Boy was I glad I would not be going back there any more.

The end of the year was approaching and I was unhappy living alone in Anytown. Since I lived downtown in a high crime rate neighborhood, none of my friends would come to visit me. They were all afraid of the people who lived around me. I never felt afraid living downtown. My neighbors were friendly and pleasant. They always greeted me as I traveled to and from my apartment. All my friends lived in East Anytown and I always had to be the one to go visit them.

About this time Smithy and I hooked up again. He was renting an adorable summer house in East Anytown and wanted me to move back. I decided that rather than live alone and be blue I would give it a try again. Maybe I was ready to settle down.

My next assignment was very strange. It was a temp to permanent position at Venezuela Products located in Anytown County. This company manufactured the steel bases for blow mold machines. I would be working in the reception area. I would be the administrate assistant to the newly hired plant manager. I would also track steel inventory and production.

Apparently Mr. Bailey, my boss, was hired to "straighten" out the shop and manufacturing areas. I was not informed what these problems were, and I did not ask. I figured I was better off *not* knowing the whole situation. The reception area where I worked was glassed off from the doors so it was private and quiet. The only visitors that came in were steel delivery drivers and salesmen. I really liked Mr. Bailey who was an older man with a twinkle in his eye. He always had a smile for me and we worked well together. The office manager, Barbara, was very pleasant and upbeat. She did a lot of my training. Mr. Bailey and I were learning the procedures of The Venezuela Company together. Mr. Bailey had given me a *special project* to complete, but instructed me not to tell anyone, including Barbara about it. He gave me time sheets from the second and third shift shop personnel. I would track the parts and the times that had been entered on the time in progress reports per shift. Mr. Bailey told me that if I noticed anything unusual to let him know. I discovered that the part numbers completed on the day shifts were in conflict with the part numbers fabricated on the night shifts. Apparently first shift personnel were re-working parts that did not exist. Consequently, overtime was being charged and paid to employees for work that was not being done. Mr. Bailey did not seem one bit surprised by this. He asked me to get all the documentation together. He wanted to go over everything to make sure the data was accurate.

Another situation was playing out at the same time. When steel was delivered, the drivers would come in and I would sign for the deliveries. One day when I was preparing to sign a bill of lading, the driver informed me the delivery would require immediate payment with a cashiers check. I buzzed Barbara and told her of this. Barbara came right down to the reception area with the check. I knew enough about accounting by then and realized this meant cash flow problems.

Mr. Bailey presented our findings at a meeting with management. There was a big blow up at the meeting with the second shift manager. I had never seen Mr. Bailey so upset. He had been hired to make the company more efficient and to eliminate waste. When he tried to do this all, he got was a lot of static. The big bosses did not want to hear what he had to say, since it wasn't what they *wanted* to hear. The outcome of all this was that the second shift manager was fired on Friday. He refused to leave his office. The situation got out of hand, people were yelling and doors were slamming. Since the manager would not get out of his chair, Mr. Bailey had two men from the shop pick him up in the chair and then carried it out into the parking lot. He sat in that chair all day. It was a hot, humid summer day. I could not believe he was still there at quitting time. He was also blocking anyone from leaving the parking lot. When the company called the police, he left. The show was over. The outcome of this did not play out pleasantly. Mr. Bailey left Venezuela Products; he was totally disgusted with the manner in which they did business. He had far too much experience and ability to waste his time working there. He needed the support of upper management and he wasn't getting it.

I just sat there wondering what was next for me. This position was to go permanent in another week. I did not have to wonder for long. Barbara came in and told me that due to my being Mr. Baileys' *girl,* I would not be hired. She assured me this was not her decision and she was not happy about it. There was nothing she could do. Barbara told me they were going to eliminate my position entirely for the time being. At least I could work out the week. She told me not to be upset and that she would call Walnut Personnel and explain what had occurred. That was easy for her to say, she still had her job. Well at least for now her job was secure. I was so disappointed at not getting this position; I had been there for three months and now was back on the street once again. As I pulled into my driveway, I realized I had once again left a white office sweater over the back of my chair. Oh well. Maybe I should have stopped wearing white office sweaters!

After getting in touch with Walnut Personnel, I was distressed to hear that they did not have anything for me. This would mean I would have to call around to other Agencies. The only job I could find at the time was with Peanut Temp Service.

Peanut Temp Service placed a lot of temps into light industrial jobs and I did not like working for them. The Little Peanut Pimp spoke condescendingly to me, making sure I knew how lucky I was that she had taken the time to place me. I had built a relationship with Walnut Personnel and they had better paying positions. I would take what I could get; after all, it was just a money game.

Until now, I had never worked on the line in a factory, that was about to change. The only position Peanut Temp Service had was at a snack food company. I was to report to Anytown Snacks in the city for second shift. While working on the line, I discovered I was a girly girl. The women working there were tough and mean. They took great delight in bullying the temps. I was absolutely scared to death to work there after the first week. I was sure one of these tough girls would beat me up.

I called Peanut Temp Service and related my fears to them, they were not surprised. Little Peanut said they had a lot of problems keeping temps at that location. Since I had a week's experience, would I go to the Anytown Snack Faculty in the County? Miss Peanut said it was a totally different atmosphere, but it was still second shift. I said, "Sure I'll try it!"

I ended up really liking this job. I worked on the line packing boxes with little bags of popcorn, corn chips, or whatever was being made that night. Second shift was easy for me to get used to. I could party after work for a few hours, do my house work, and get enough sleep. The people at this Anytown Snack facility were fun and friendly. They invited me to go out after work for drinks at the local watering hole. They also included me in silly pranks they played on each other.

One night Shellie, a permanent employee, got into an empty box as it was going down the conveyor belt. At the end of the belt she sprang out and scared Mr. Macho Bobby, who was standing at the end of the belt (he was putting the boxes on pallets) almost to death. He grabbed himself and screamed like a little girl. Mr. Macho wasn't so macho now. We laughed and laughed. The building was hot and steamy, they only had standing fans, and the heat became oppressive at times. However, the plant was very clean and everyone worked their best to produce a good product. By the end of my shift, I smelled like a cheese curl. One Friday night a couple of us girls went to the Day Tripper Inn after work. We sat at the bar enjoying our beers when someone behind us said, "I smell cheese." We shrunk in our seats. Before you knew it everyone around us was ordering cheese plates and snacking. When I would get home early in the early morning hours, my dogs would greet me with bounding joy. Maybe all they really wanted was to lick the cheese off my shoes and my jeans.

I had begun the job in May which is the beginning of the Snack Food Industries busy season. I worked all summer and it was very hectic the week before every holiday weekend. By September things were slowing down and the assignment came to an end. I did not have a lot of money that summer but I had a lot of fun.

Peanut Temp Service placed me in one more assignment that summer. It was at the YWCA but only for a week. This was another vacation replacement position. I would be working the front desk with another young woman. The

YWCA was a pleasant organization to be a part of for me. The desk was very busy. There were children running and laughing all around us. I did my best to help out and keep up with the constant stream of people. I finished up the week feeling very good about my performance. The YWCA people told Peanut Temp Service what a great job I did and they would request me again when needed. I was such a good little temp. I hoped that this would be the last time I had to deal with the Peanut Princesses. I did not like the agency. In the future would only call them as a last resort.

Smithy had a friend who needed part time seasonal help in his greenhouse and asked me if I was interested. I jumped at this opportunity. I am an avid gardener, and knew this would be a great job for me. I took the position at the greenhouse during the winter of 1985. I started work early in the morning. I would water the plants and then clean the potting tables and plant seedlings. I loved it. It could be snowing outside but I was warm and snug enjoying the dazzling beauty of the plants and flowers inside. It was so calm and peaceful. This was another job I wish could have become full time. The holiday season had come to an end and they no longer needed extra help. I will forever remember walking into the greenhouse at Christmas when it was filled with white and red poinsettias, their splendor was breathtaking.

CHAPTER 6

She's like a Cadbury Easter egg, sweet on the outside, yucky on the inside.

It was January 1986, the Greenhouse job was over, and I was pounding the pavement once again. My old friend Susie was married now and had an adorable little girl. Susie was now working at the Highway House. I often stopped in to hang out and have a beer or two and catch up on current events with her. The Highway House is an up scale bar/restaurant. The woman who owned The Highway House, Liza Loon, had been in business with Mr. Biller from Biller Skate Company. When the bars that Mr. Biller and Ms. Loon owned closed, Ms. Loon took her end of the deal and opened her own establishment.

The Highway House was a beautifully decorated swanky bar, but casual enough to have that neighborhood tavern atmosphere. It is one of those places you go to for a birthday celebration, a business lunch, and a romantic rendezvous. I was sitting at the bar one night when Ms. Loon sat down next to me. "Hey Judy, can you make a salad?" she asked. I looked at her a bit puzzled. "Of course I can, why?" "Well," she sighed, "My salad and pastry chef just walked out." The restaurant was a very busy and Ms. Loon was in a predicament. Mrs. Loon made me an offer I couldn't turn down. "I know you are a good worker from the time we worked together at Biller Skate Company. If you need a job you can start right now."

I was a taken back a bit by the suddenness of all this. I answered, "I don't know if I can do something like that, I have never worked in a restaurant.' Ms. Loon assured me, "if you can make a salad at home you can do it here. We will train you. If you're interested come with me and we will get started." Right there and then I became a Salad and Pastry Chef. I worked with two great cooks, Alfred the lead chef and his sidekick Terry. There was a young guy, Anthony, who worked with the cooks as a runner. Anthony was eighteen and had just come out of the closet. Anthony was so silly and we loved him. So began another adventure in employment 101.

The Highway House is a very busy restaurant to this day. It is *the* place to go for that special meal out in the East end. I eventually got the hang of everything, and believe me it was more involved than making a salad at home. I liked working in the kitchen where everyone was truly a *real* team player. The cooks were fun but serious about making scrumptious meals. The waitresses and bartenders I had already known so I did not have to go though the getting to know you routine. We were all about the same age, single, and hung out at the Day Tripper Inn. We enjoyed some ruckus good times together. If it became really busy on Saturday nights, the waitresses would let me know, so I would get the lead out and fly around busing tables to help out.

I found it soothing to walk away from a busy, hot, hectic kitchen into a sparkling dining room with beautifully dressed patrons enjoying the wonderful food. The dining room was a tranquil island. The flames from the table candles reflected off gleaming silverware and sparking wine glasses. I could hear the soft drone of conversation spattered with laughter. I enjoyed thinking that I was a part of someone's special evening.

One Saturday night it was ungodly busy, we had prepared over two hundred dinners, and it was only eight-thirty p. m. All of a sudden, whoosh! The hood on the stove caught fire. The flames were shooting down onto the grill and licking up the sides of the hood. Alfred ran and grabbed the fire extinguisher. Anthony was standing on the inside of the cooking area, against the wall, and was in a full panic mode. As Alfred was franticly spraying to put out the flames, Anthony was yelling, "I'm twapped, I'm twapped!" in his shrill little man voice. Alfred blew up at him, "I'll twap your ass, now shut up!" Poor Anthony, none of us had ever spoken to him like that before. Alfred put the fire out but now there was white sticky foam dripping from everything. It was on the monkey dishes, plates, pans, silverware, counter tops, nothing was missed. Alfred said to me "go out, **calmly**, and tell the hostess we have stove problems and can't sauté anything for forty five minutes. Then get back in here, we have to clean this mess up as fast as we can."

Without skipping a beat, I walked from the chaos of the kitchen into the twinkling lights of the dining room, when this little mischievous voice in my head wanted to scream, **"FIRE! FIRE!"** Of course I did not. As I am walking towards the hostess station, I could not help but notice all the diners eating and laughing. I thought to myself, 'if they only knew.' I told the hostess what Alfred told me to say with no mention of the fire we had just put out and then I high tailed it back to the kitchen as he had said. Some news is best keep secret.

I was helping the dishwasher clean the foam up as fast as we could. Alfred and Anthony were getting dinners out as quickly as they could when Ms. Loon entered the kitchen. She yelled, "What the hell is going on in here?" She immediately saw what was going on, and spied the soot covered vent. Alfred just turned and stared at her with that 'go away . . . we got it covered' look. Nothing more was said. Ms. Loon backed up and walked out of the kitchen. She knew Alfred would have everything back to normal as quickly as possible because Alfred was truly a pro! During the eight months I worked at the Highway House, this had to be most dramatic thing to have occurred. Alfred taught me how to sauté, make casino mix, prepare a perfect grilled cheese sandwich and whip up chocolate meringues to die for.

Some of the employees at the Highway House thought Ms. Loon was a callous, difficult person to work for. In her defense, I must say she was always fair. She had worked hard to get to where she was. She never asked anyone of us to do something she would not do herself. My job at the Highway House was part time, and I needed more hours to make more money. In as much as I loved working there, I had to find something else. Ms. Loon totally understood, and we remained friends afterwards.

So after some job searching, I answered an ad for a Property and Casualty Agent at State Ranch. Since my license had not yet expired I hoped that working for State Ranch would be like working at GEICO. I interviewed and was hired immediately. Well, it wasn't like working for GEICO at all. The State Ranch office was small, just the writing agent and myself. The required duties were the same as at Rock Solid or the Edward S. Old Company. I had no problem with the job requirements. I aced the position in two weeks. State Ranch had a great computer program that was user friendly; this certainly helped me grasp their system for reporting claims.

The agent I was working for was a ball of fire. Maria was of Spanish decent and had grown up in Arizona. She was *transplanted* to Pennsylvania, and like me, she also had a hard time with the area's attitudes. Maria was a gorgeous woman. Her career spanned a gamut that ran from law enforcement to the armed services. To look at Maria you would have never guessed what a tough cookie she really could be.

State Ranch was a very innovative company to work for. They firmly believed in the concept of the *Paperless Office*. I personally thought this was a joke, since the computer age, if anything, has killed more trees then the fires in California. Everywhere I had ever worked, all we did was print, print, and print again. No one ever trusted their computer systems. But Maria was adamant that this could be accomplished. She strove to make it a reality in her office.

Maria was married to an ex-police officer. There was a lot of drama in her life as you would expect, and she always brought it to the office. Her husband, George, was always stopping in to pilfer the petty cash drawer. They would play hugs and kisses in her office. It was rather embarrassing having to listen to what was transpiring in the office behind me. At least they were not yelling at each other or slamming doors. When it came to money for office expenses

Maria was so tight she squeaked when she walked. Half of the time I had to purchase my own office supplies.

One day a nicely dressed woman walked in to get an auto insurance quote. She was recently separated from her husband and had two small children. She told me she was having a tough time and her finances were in shambles. After I had given her a quote, she assured me as soon as she received a support check she would purchase our insurance. I was confident that she would be back. I told her we would hold the paperwork until she was ready to proceed. A few days later as Maria and I were working, the prospective lady customer returned. Maria was in her office and could overhear us talking. This lovely woman told me she was going on a job interview and would I make a few copies of her resume. "Sure," I tell her, "no problem." I made her a few copies and then she dashed off. After she left the office, Maria stormed out of her office and started yelling at me. "What are you doing? That is my paper; you're giving away my paper!" Honestly, I had only used six sheets of paper. "Maria, she is a prospective customer, if we help her, perhaps she will come back, and we can write her auto policy." I responded. "Well, O.K." she says, "but that is my paper!" She stomped back into her office. I was flabbergasted and thought, 'What a tight wad!'

The entire situation with Maria was totally ridiculous. Between her lover boy husband, the drama surrounding his children, and Maria's stubborn unyielding ego, I had enough. It was time to start looking for another job; it had only been three months this time out. I kept chasing my dream job. I knew if I just kept looking I would find another company like GEICO to work for. I put a call into the Walnut Agency. As always they would try to find me work, after I gave Maria my two week resignation. Walnut did not have an office position to offer me at that time. They did have a forty hour a week job at a printing company working in the bindery department. The position did not require any experience and they would train the right person. I was not so keen on this, as it was going to be factory work again. Factories are usually hot and require a lot of standing. Mrs. Walnut assured me that this would not be true in a printing company. The building was climate controlled and most of the work was done sitting down. So I thought " . . . why not. Let's give it a go." This was a chance to learn something different and expand my horizons.

Off I went to Btines Printing very early the next morning. No more dressing up, back to blue jeans and sneakers again. I went to the office and the receptionist buzzed the bindery supervisor. I was nervous about this assignment. The supervisor who came to take me to the area seemed nice. He was a big man but walked so quickly I could hardly keep up. He marched me to a table where six young women were collating a manuscript of some type. He introduced me and disappeared. Those women reminded me of ravenous hyenas. Memories of Anytown Snacks came flooding back to me. There was one friendly face at the work table, Robin. Robin was from a temp service too, so we had an instant bond. Robin was gregarious and adventurous. It was great to have company at break time and lunch. Robin was a terrific gal; she had short black hair, beautiful blue eyes, and porcelain skin to die for. Robin never acted like a diva, she was very unassuming, but she was a tough girl. Those so called bad girls at Btines did not mess with Robin.

I was fitting in at Btines and learning to use all types of bindery equipment. For a time I ran a stitching machine. A stitcher is the machine that puts those two little staples in the fold of a brochure. I also learned to operate a paper driller. I would spend days drilling three holes in ream after ream, skid after skid of printed manuals. The working conditions were good. The building was climate controlled and I could sit for most of the jobs.

The jobs were repetitious and it was hard to stay focused. I would get so sleepy that I would almost doze off. I was concerned I would end up hurting myself. That was when I knew it was getting close to break time. I always looked to Robin for direction at Btines. She had been there longer and knew the lay of the land. When she would catch my eye, we would give a high five to each other and go out for a smoke. At the end of the day, Robin and I would occasionally go to a local watering hole with some of the Btines employees (Btines was not far from Anytown Snacks.) I would run into people I had worked with previously from Anytown Snacks. Everyone was glad to see me again. I was having fun and had a buddy to pal around with to share the good times. Robin and I worked together at Btines until September when the Carnival came to town. One Friday Robin called of from work. As usual, I stopped at the local bar where we usually went to for a beer before going home.

I walked into the bar and there sat Robin. I was delighted to see her; it had been a long day without her company. She waved me over to join her and her new friends. She was sitting with some young guys, and they were playing a game of eight ball. Robin was in a great mood; everyone was laughing and having a bang up good time. Friday was the opening day of the State Fair in Anytown and she had gone to the fair for the day. Robin proceeded to tell me she was running away with the Carnival. Robin was my age, divorced, no children and living at home with her mother. Since we did not make good money working for temp services, she could not afford her own place. Robin was sick of living at home and having to answer to her mother at the age of thirty-five. She introduced me to her new male friend, he seemed nice. He had tattoos and long hair. He ran a Carney game and Robin was going to work at his booth. I was envious of Robin's sense of adventure, how she could just pull up stakes and take off with someone she hardly knew? I was happy for her. She was so excited; I could not bring myself to express my fears to her. She was a big girl and could take care of herself. Robin was not afraid of anything or any one for that matter.

Robin ran away with the carnival and I was stuck at Btines without a buddy. Btines was never going to be a permanent placement job. The assignment was long term temp. I had learned a lot at this job, and later it would serve me well, but I wanted to get back into office work. I had never been proficient at the jobs I did at Btines. Most of the jobs required working at a speedy pace. I am after all, a plodder, and could never work as quickly as was required. I did not make "bonus" money like everyone else. After six months it was time to *move on.*

Years later I ran into Robin at Builders Square. We saw each other at the same moment and did the female squeal greeting. She was doing great, she never married but had a ten year old son, and they lived in Florida. Robin was in town to visit her family. She looked like the same *Old Robin*; it was wonderful to see her again. We exchanged phone numbers and promised to keep in touch. Today I wonder where did that phone number end up.

I had called Walnut Agency and told them I was not doing a very good job at Btines and wished to be reassigned to something else. This they did not understand, as Btines just loved me. They had gotten very good feedback about me. I again told Miss Pimp I wanted off the job. I was not happy there anymore. This went over like a lead balloon. The pimps at the agency will tell you, "if you are not happy at an assignment let us know, don't just walk off. We will find something else for you; after all, everything is not for everybody." That is just fine until you call and request to be removed from a company. When you do this, everyone had an attitude and you're the loser. Walnut agency's pimp was a bit miffed at my request, and told me they did not have anything that was a fit with my skills at that time. Imagine that! It seemed like revenge to me.

I continued to work at Btines and check the want ads in the newspaper. One day I ran across an ad for an accounting assistant at McCoy's Corporate Headquarters in East Anytown. The position was an assistant to the Accounts Payable Manager's Assistant. It would only be thirty-five hours a week but it *might* go full time with benefits. I thought it was worth the gamble. The driving distance was half of what it was to get to Btines.

I applied for the position and was hired. I immediately called Mrs. Walnut and gave her my two week notice. She was very understanding, as always, and told me if I needed them again, just call. It was always nice to deal with Mrs. Walnut. The Walnut pimps were such little snots but I did not want to alienate The Walnut Agency.

I really enjoyed the time I worked at McCoy's Corporate Center. I was in the Accounts Payable Department. I worked in a huge room with thirty other people. I was at the front of the room; my desk was next to Janet's. Janet was the Accounts Payable Managers Assistant. The Manager, Mr. Falkner sat in an office directly in front of us.

There were no such things as cubicles in those days. Behind Janet and I were seven rows of desks with five desks across. The department handled the accounts for everything that McCoy's purchased for their stores inventories. These women handled monstrous accounts that were assigned to them by alphabetical split. Everyone in the department had a phone, and the din was unbelievable. However, these ladies were conscientious and helped each other out. I had a hard time concentrating on my work; it was so noisy for an office environment. Janet told me not to worry, I would get used to it. She was right; I learned how to tune it out. Mr. Falkner was a very approachable boss, but he kept his door shut, maybe he couldn't tune out. He would also disappear into the executive lounge for hours.

I did all types of projects that Janet did not have time to do. I had a lot of various duties and I was never bored. Janet was a dear to work with. She knew how to train and always had time for me. This was the first time I worked with an AS400 computer operating system. I was able to learn so much there. The hours flew by.

I remember at Christmas McCoy's had a party for the employees. I was invited. I did not know that the ladies in my department had a Pollyanna. Apparently Janet was to have told me but forgot. Janet was so busy, I was sure this was the truth, but it really did not bother me. Janet, not wanting my feelings to be hurt, had gotten me a gift. I was so touched by her graciousness.

McCoy's was owned by a company called Rapid America based out of New York City. Our office did not have the authority to pay for whatever we wished. Each Wednesday Janet and I would prepare accounts receipts report that showed which vendors were up for payment that week. We would then give it to Mr. Falkner. He would eliminate vendors he thought could wait for their payments and return the revision to me. Janet would then submit the report to Rapid America for approval. Usually Rapid America would eliminate even more vendors. The end result was that McCoy's was always sixty to ninety days late on many of their accounts. Hence, the reason the phones never stopped ringing.

As the months flew by, Mr. Falkner was spending more and more time in the executive lounge. I answered his extension when Janet was on another line. The vendors were becoming more and more insistent on payments and cutting off deliveries. I sensed that things were not going well once again. We often had vendors come to the office to pick up payments. I will never forget the day that the owner of Coats and Clarke arrived. The Owner of Coats and Clark had flown to Anytown from California. McCoy's purchased all the items for their stores that were classified as notions from them. This included buttons, thread, bindings, lace, all the things needed for sewing.

Mr. Falkner told me to go down to the lobby and escort our visitors to his office. When I got to the lobby, a slick black stretch limo was pulling up to the doors. Three men stepped out of the limo. I opened the door and greeted them sweetly. The owner of Coats and Clark was a younger man of about thirty-five. I cannot remember his name. He looked like Antonio Bandera. He was dressed in a Ralph Lauren cashmere blend suit with a white silk shirt and black tie; his shoes appeared to be very expensive too. You don't see men dressed like that in Anytown, at least not at ten-thirty in the morning.

I guessed the two men with him were bodyguards; at least that is what they looked like. They were big men and not dressed nearly as well, with very serious looks on their faces. One of the men carried the owner's brief case. I took our visitors to Mr. Falkers office, and they seemed to have a gay old time. The door was shut so we could only see through the glass. When the meeting was concluded, Mr. Falkner escorted them out of the building. Everyone seemed happy with whatever had transpired in his office.

Needless to say by the end of the following year, McCoy's had closed their doors. For good or bad, depending upon which side of the coin you are on. Once again, darned if I didn't leave another white office sweater over the back of my chair.

It was time to call the Walnut Agency, once again.

I concluded the year of 1989 working for the Walnut Agency on two short assignments. I was sent to Maple Squash for one week as the front desk receptionist. This was a hard position for me to pull off. It required being quick on the draw and the ability to handle phone calls, visitors and in keeping track of who was in and who was out of the office. There was no such thing as voice mail back then. I had to use those little pink pads to write messages down. But since it was only for a week, I accepted the assignment.

The lobby of Maple Squash was breathtaking. On the far wall was an eight foot waterfall, there were huge living trees placed though out the lobby. The chairs and couches were strategically placed so visitors would be looking out the full-length glass windows into a beautiful wooded vista.

The major problem with running a switch board of that size was getting accustomed to who the people were in the office. In one week I was not going to figure this out. So I was given a list of names and extensions. This sounds simple, and it would have been better if the names would have been in alphabetical order by LAST name. But no, the listing was in alphabetical order by FIRST name. Who does this? It was insane. With the help of the human resources lady, I was able to quickly type up a list of employees by last names, like most other places I had worked.

When I had my training on Monday, the young woman from Human Resources was adamant that I must keep an eye on the parking lot. I could see the first two parking spaces from my seat at the switchboard. She said "the owner has a black Mercedes, if you see ANY other vehicle parked in that space, Call me immediately!" I am the type of person that does not know a BMW from an Audi from a Mercedes. The next day the human resources gal came running towards the switchboard, "there is a BMW parked in the owner's space! He is very upset and had to park five spaces away from the door! You are supposed to be watching the parking lot!" She was nearly hysterical. "I'm sorry," I told her in my most pitiful puppy temp voice, "but I am having a hard enough time keeping these calls straight." She turned and vanished. I found this to be ridiculous. He had to walk an extra twenty feet, boo-hoo. He probably needed the exercise. I was glad when the assignment was over at Maple Squash, the people who worked there did not even acknowledge me. They were too busy running around like chickens with their heads cut off.

Next, the Walnut Agency sent me to The Out of Date Plates Company. The building was located downtown so I would be able to walk to my favorite shops on my lunch hour. I missed being downtown, I am a city girl at heart. This is where my prior bindery experience would come into play. This company made all of their own forms. I worked with a darling older man; the people at this company were wonderful. I was able to run all the equipment without much training or supervision. It was a pleasant way to spend the day, and get paid for it too. After two months, the woman in charge offered me the position full time. This was a surprise to me since I had been told by the Agency that it was just a temp job. I declined their offer. This was not something I wanted to do for the rest of my life. The gentleman I worked with came into the room where I was working and was rather upset. He asked me "who has offended you, or has someone been unkind to you? If so, please tell me. We want you to stay." I told him, " . . . no, no, that's not it; I just want to work as an assistant and use a computer. That is what I love to do." I was taken aback that he was so concerned for my feelings. I was not used to such nice treatment. Looking back I should have stayed there, but hind sight is always 20/20. I was immediately removed from the job since I turned the offer down. The Walnut Agency agreed to call me when something came in that was more suited to my needs.

I began looking for a *real* job again. Temping is a source of a means to an ends. I was not satisfied with the assignments I was being given and I was smart enough to realize what it would lead to nowhere in the end. My dear friend Nancy suggested that I look into working at her company, Shadowfax. I was seriously considering her suggestion.

CHAPTER 7

Was today really necessary?

I met Nancy when I was living with Smithy. She was a part of the biker society of East Anytown. Nancy was living with Jeff. He was a sardonic but brilliant man. Jeff had very little use for stupid people. I enjoyed Jeff's caustic sense of humor. He thought the biker mentality was intellectually dull. He loved Nancy and had to put up with the rest of us. Nancy was ten years older than I and became my mentor and dearest friend. She had raised four children on her own. When I met Nancy, her children were in their twenties. They had flown the nest and were off on their own life's adventures. Nancy was the person I went to for heart to heart talks. She always had a kind word for me or stern advice. She had a lively spirit and was in tune with the world around her. Nancy had a great love of birds and nature. Nancy and Jeff would spend long afternoons watching the hawks down at the river.

We were gathered at the Day Tripper Inn one Saturday night to see the Pep Boys Band. Nancy and I were talking and the subject came up that I had been laid off. Nancy suggested I try something different. She worked for a company called Shadowfax. This was a company that owned and operated group homes for people with mental retardation. There was an opening in the home she worked in. If I was interested, she could put in a good word for me. I did not think I had the skills required for a job of this nature. I had never had children or been exposed to people with handicaps or disabilities. Nancy said that did not matter. "You have a big heart, and you like people. Caring is what the job is all about. Stop in and shadow with me at the home and see what you think." I told her I would think about it.

Out of curiosity, I called Nancy later in the week and told her I would like to see what it was all really all about. She made arrangements with the management of Shadowfax for me to spend the morning and evening at the home and meet the residents. I did not know what to expect, I thought I would be scared of the people in the home. When I got to the home, Nancy introduced me to three young girls about nine or ten years old. They looked like any other little girls. The only exception was that they were suffering from severe mental retardation.

I shadowed at the home that morning and again in the evening. The girls went to school during the day.

I don't think I would have ever gotten into this line of work without knowing Nancy. I decided to try it out. I applied and was hired. I would be working with my friend Nancy who was the group home program manager. There were other women working in this home, Missy and Kate. Missy was a joyful buxom blond with the sweetest disposition, she loved heavy metal music. She cherished the children. Kate was going to college to be a social worker. Kate had a lot of intellectual input and loved the kids too. We all loved these kids and the kids in all the other homes too. The feeling for these children came naturally, they were not helpless, but they were dependent on us to keep them safe from themselves and from the outside world. We had so much fun with the residents of all the homes owned by Shadowfax. We would go to the swimming pool and shopping at the mall. Their favorite spot was McDonald's, what kid doesn't love McDonald's? We worked on teaching the residents living skills and helped with homework. We did everything with our children any normal family would do. As the residents can not be left alone at any time, we had to sleep over. At the time, Shadowfax had not changed the shift from sleep over to wake overnight. We would get the residents ready for bed, have snacks, and retire for the night.

There was an urban legend surrounding the home I worked in. Missy told me one evening after the girls had gone to bed that the previous home owner's wife had left him. In his distressed state, he had committed suicide in the garage using the car's carbon monoxide. Missy continued the story by saying that this man was a ghost in the home. She told me that on the full moon you would hear him walking on the roof.

The house was a very nice split level rancher with an attached garage. When I took the trash to the garage, I got the creepy crawlies. Our staff bedroom was situated in the finished basement directly next to the garage entrance.

One night after the girls were tucked in, I got ready for bed and went down to our sleeping quarters. I could not sleep, the only book I could find was one someone had left on the end table. It was of all things, *Rosemary's Baby*. I decided that it was better than just laying there tossing and turning. At one point, I looked at the clock and it was eleven forty-five. I had been reading for two hours. As I continued reading, I started getting an uneasy feeling. I glanced at the clock. It was eleven fifty. I read a little more and glanced at the clock on the end table and it is was eleven fifty-five. I was really getting spooked by now. I just knew something was going to happen at midnight. I was staring at the clock, as the hands moved to midnight; I was waiting and waiting. All of a sudden the furnace kicked in, *Roarrrr!* I screamed, threw the book up in the air, and flew up the stairs and into the kitchen. I was scared out of my wits.

When I got to the kitchen I realized how silly I was and that there w.
boogie man behind me, but I was rattled. I peeked out the kitchen windo
was snowing softly and the flakes were lightly floating to the ground. The street
lights had eerie snowy *full moon* halos that shown brightly in the stillness of the
night. Still, a shiver went down my back.

I decided to call Nancy at home. She picked up the phone sounding very
sleepy. "Hi Nancy, it's me Judy," I said. "What is wrong?" Nancy replied in
instant supervisor's mode. "Oh, nothing, nothing, I'm just lonely and I thought
I would call." "Well," Nancy said to me, "it's a little late for chit chat, *what's
wrong?*" Being a mother, Nancy could tell something was the matter. I related
what had happened and told her about the ghost story I had been told. Nancy
disgustingly replied, "That Missy I am going to skin her alive. Yes the story is
true, but you know that there's no such thing as a ghost. Put the Steven King
book away, go back to bed. I will see you in the morning." She hung up the
phone abruptly. That was the last time I read a chilling book at work. I usually
brought along something of lighter fair, just in case I had another sleepless
night.

All jobs have drawbacks and working in a group home is no exception.
At the time I worked seven days on and seven days off. This sounds great in
the beginning. After two years I began to suffer from burn out. I found myself
becoming a bit moody and unhappy. The first five days of the week were fine,
but the last two were agony. I was tired of everything and everybody. I was no
good at my job because I was becoming short tempered and stressed out. The
job was very demanding emotionally and I had less and less to give back. I loved
my seven days off. On my last two of those days off, all I would think of was
going back to work. I could not enjoy my precious days off either.

Shadowfax paid its employees extremely well. I knew I would not make
as much money anywhere else I might work. Money is not everything. There
is absolutely no way anyone could work in a group home just to make a good
wage. You have to have it in your heart. The job is all heart. I left Shadowfax
and returned to the world of corporations. I did not realize how much I was
going to miss the girls.

Before I move on, I would like to mention here the great admiration I have
for the all the employees and the owners of Shadowfax. Julie and Dave began
Shadowfax with a vision to do the best for people whom society would like to
forget exist. Their motto was *"Where People Count."* Their goal was to get these
kids out of institutions where they were ignored and neglected. They created
a company that cared for and kept them safe. Julie and Dave bought these less
fortunate people into all our neighborhoods and we are all better for it. The
ladies I worked with Missy, Kate, Nancy, Barbie, and "Lean Mean Emma", I
thank them for their unending patience, and kind words of encouragement.

My experiences at Shadowfax gave me a new awareness and appreciation of the *special* people in the world we live in.

During the time I worked at Shadowfax, Smithy and I moved into a farmhouse in southern Anytown County. The farmer Smithy worked for purchased another large farm. Smithy was offered a very nice house on the property as part of his salary. They needed a diesel mechanic at the new farm. This farm was the largest acreage farm in the county. The house was very nice, except Smithy had to bring his cook stove along. I brought a microwave and it was my first choice for fixing a meal.

I had accumulated some vacation time during my employment at Shadowfax and used it all to chill out. As my savings were dwindling away, I called Mrs. Walnut. She was happy to hear from me, but sorry to hear my job at Shadowfax had not worked out. The agency had work and sent me to a company called Washington Inventory. The pay rate was nothing to shout about, but it did not appear to be a very difficult job. Washington Inventory was a company that did inventories for other companies. They had devised a simple and efficient manner of doing inventories while a company was open and operating. By using a professional inventory service, the company did not have to shut down for a day and pull employees off their normal jobs just for the purpose of inventory.

Upon arriving at Washington Inventories Offices, I met up with about twenty other temps from various other agencies. We were herded into a conference room (mooooo!) for a three hour orientation and training session. We were given electronic hand held counters. The personnel at Washington Inventory did a great job training us. I felt confident I would do first-rate work for this company right of the bat.

That afternoon the temps were split up into four groups of five people each to form teams. Each team had two job supervisors with them. Washington Inventory provided the transportation to the job sites. They also provide us with transportation at lunch time and paid for our lunches. Typically they would drive us to a McDonald's or a Wendy's. "*I' am lovin 'it.*"

My team was sent to a small pharmacy the first afternoon. Each person was placed in an aisle of the store with the hand held counter. I would enter the UPC of the item I was counting, count the items on the shelves, enter that number and go on to the next item. The supervisors floated around the store helping us out if we were not sure of what we were doing or if we were making an error. At the end of the day, the supervisors would take the counters, total the information we had collected, and hit the *send* key on the counter. At orientation, we were instructed to NEVER hit the send key. That was the supervisor's job. Wow, what a job. At the end of the first day, we were all at ease with what the position involved and enjoyed the van ride back. We were the esprit de corps of Washington Inventory! On Tuesday my team was taken to a somewhat larger store, it was a large national chain pharmacy. That was a bit more challenging. It was especially tricky maneuvering around customers and their shopping carts. For the most part it went well. By Wednesday we were in the big time. We pulled up to a MAJOR grocery store. I thought, "This is going to be a long day," and it was. Thursday and Friday were much of the same. I believe we lost some temps along the way. These were tiring days, standing in one place for a long time, moving at a snail's pace up the mile long aisles. By Thursday afternoon my calves were throbbing, my feet were screaming and my back was killing me. Knowing that Friday was the last day of the week, I persevered. I would have the weekend to mend. This assignment went on the same, day after day for one month. Those temps who had hung in there and gotten the job completed we were given a modest but much appreciated bonus. They took us to Pizza Hut instead of Mickey D's for lunch on our last Friday of the assignment. After that experience, I did not accept any more assignments from the agency for an inventory counter.

My next assignment was a bit longer and much less painful. I was sent to the Boon Tune Department Sore. The offices I would be working in were on the second floor of the department store. This would be for three months. I would be entering the payments from customers in the customer service department. I was covering for someone out on surgery leave. This was a gem of an assignment. I was working on a computer again in an AS400 system. It was different then what I had been used to but I picked it up rather quickly. The older ladies I worked with provided me with excellent training. They were pleasant and always made sure I was *sincerely* included in any department parties. There was a baby explosion going on at the time. It seemed like there was a baby shower every other week. Jennifer was one of the girls I met while at the Boon Tune. We would go to lunch and breaks together. We both were smokers. Each morning around ten thirty, we would go out in the front of the store and sit on one of the concrete benches and relax. The benches were situated directly in front of the department store's plate glass windows.

While we where smoking, we would watch the elderly ladies arriving to shop. Being the perfect drivers that we were, we would joke about their driving abilities. We marveled at how they backed up a million times to get into a parking space you could have fit a Sherman tank into. Jennifer even remarked, as we watched a blue haired woman struggle to get a Lincoln Continental into a space, "hope she doesn't hit the gas instead of the break, if she does we're goners." We laughed all the way back to our department. About twenty minutes later, the fire alarm went off and the employees calmly but quickly exited the building out the back doors. Once out in the parking lot we snuck around the corner of the building to see what was going on. There was the Lincoln Continental inside the store! The car had gone up the side walk, crashed into the plate glass windows and continued into the perfume counter coming to rest in the shoe department. As we watched in amazement, the EMT's were bringing out an elderly lady on a gurney; she was smiling and clutching her Boon Tune Bag. The car had taken out the bench we were sitting on not twenty minutes before.

I made lots of friends there and actually stayed in touch with Jennifer for some years. As with Robin, I have lost track of her. It was a sad the day for me when the person I was replacing returned and the assignment came to an end.

Next, I was sent to the Coon & Noslack Accounting Firm. It was tax time and I would be assembling tax returns putting them in envelopes and mailing them to their clients. The assignment was only for the final week of April. By day two, I was glad that it was only for one week.

These people were so hoity toity. They walked around with their noses so dreadfully high in the sky that icicles dangled from their nose tips. The owners (I *think* they were married) were CPA's and dressed in incredibly expensive suits. This seemed a bit over the top, as there were only three people working in this office. Another young female junior accountant worked upstairs. Most of my contact was with the junior accountant. She kept me supplied with tax returns to copy and mail. She was the disappearing accountant. I never saw her put work in my inbox, it would just magically appear.

During the week I worked there they were interviewing for an additional junior account. There was a parade of people in an out throughout the day. One day after one young woman had interviewed, the junior account from upstairs came to my desk and actually talked to me. She said, "Did you notice that girl I just interviewed?" I said I had, and that she seemed very nice. "Oh," she replied, "you did not notice that **RED** nail polish?" "No, I didn't notice, why?" I asked sheepishly. "Who would have such bad taste as to wear **RED** nail polish to an interview?" Ms. Junior Account replied, her nose inching higher and higher into the air. I thought I saw an icicle fall off! "I don't know," I replied. "Hurrump," Ms. Junior Account said, "she won't be hired here."

As I was stuffing envelopes, I was thinking how shallow and superficial these people were, and I was thankful the next day was Friday. Mr. Noslack happily signed my time card, telling me how pleased they were with my help, and said if they needed assistance again they would request me. "Just what I need, another assignment with these bozos," I was thinking as he signed my time card. I was out of there in a flash. If in fact they never did call me back, I would just dress up like the harlot of Babylon to finish it off once and for all.

My next landing was at Anytown Bank. This turned out to be a very interesting assignment, but it was temporary for a month. The position I was sent on was for a Bank Courier. Someone was being promoted into this position from another branch of the bank. For reasons unknown to me, this person could not start for a month, so they got a temp in to cover until then. At the time, this location was the main office for Anytown Bank. All the US mail for the bank and all of its branches, plus the interoffice mail was sorted at this location. I would be sorting mail in the morning. At ten A.M., I would use a company van to pick up interoffice banking from the four branches. When I returned from the morning run, I would again work in the mail room. At two P.M., I would make another swoop though the county picking up the afternoon interoffice banking receipts. This sounds simple doesn't it, it always does at first. The mail sorting was a cinch, but the courier part was an animal of a different color. I was being trained by an older man who was retiring. He had worked as a police officer for Anytown City and had retired from that job fifteen years ago. His name was Bob and he was a dream to know. He reminded me of Mr. Bailey from Venezuela Products. He was a sweet dear man; everyone at the bank loved him. Bob knew every short cut through the city as well as how to bypass the worst traffic in the county. I thought I knew my way around Anytown until I met Bob.

The vans that Anytown bank owned were worn out pieces of crap. They were old, and Anytown Bank was squeaking out every last mile they could get out of them. The one I drove had a sloppy transmission and made a horrifying screeching noise when I gave it the gas. Bob went with me the first few days of the week. By Thursday I knew my route, and Bob would only occasionally accompany me. During my training, Bob drove and I observed where we were going and what we did once we got to the banks. I also observed Bob popping nitroglycerin tablets at an alarming rate while he was operating the van. This made me very uneasy. I did not relate this to anyone; I figured it was none of my business. One afternoon the man running the show in the mailroom asked if Bob was taking medication while driving. I told him I had seen him taking nitroglycerin. He said, "I thought so, other people have come to me about this." I didn't want to get Bob in trouble, and I told the boss, "Please don't say I told you this." He told me not to worry, it was common knowledge, but now since I had actually seen Bob taking this drug while operating their vehicle, they could get him off the road. I felt like a traitor, Bob was so helpful and pleasant. For the rest of the week, Bob rode in the passenger seat and I drove. Bob never said a word to me about what had transpired between him and the management of the bank. I pretended I did not know anything about what was going on. He continued to be as sweet as ever. On the following Monday I was on my own, Bob had retired.

When I would go to the branches, I would take a large heavy blue bag with me. Once at a branch, I took this bag into the teller area. The tellers would place their morning paperwork in small brown bags which they would zipper up and lock. At each bank I would have four or five of these small bags placed in the large blue bag. By the time I got to the last branch, the blue bag was heavy. I would then drive back to the bank and take the bag to the second floor where accounting personnel would *grab* them from me and rapidly begin the reconciliation process.

The only drawback with this job was the weather. It rained for a week. I was soaked by the end of the runs. Once in the bank, customers in line would watch the tellers putting the brown bags in my blue tote. I knew they probably thought I was transporting cash. It made me feel uneasy. I could just imagine being robbed or murdered for deposit and withdraw slips. I had made it to the conclusion of another assignment. The Anytown Bank employees were a pleasure to work with. They made sure I had excellent training, even if it was a little scary in the beginning.

Mrs. Walnut called me to ask if I would like to try an assignment at a Delivery Company. The position would be dispatching drivers and processing the account receivables. This job was temp to permanent. "Yes I would!" I replied with great enthusiasm. "Great, you start Monday." That is how I ended up at Rapid Delivery Company in June of 1989.

CHAPTER 8

I used to be concerned but now I take a pill for it.

Mrs. Walnut told me on the Q.T. that Rapid Delivery was a Christian business. I did not think this would be a problem. I had never worked in a business that revolved around being saved. I figured at least they would not swear and throw office manuals at each other. After all, I was an Episcopalian, and wherever you find four Episcopal priests you find a fifth. There were three owners Sean, Cindy, and Mitchell. They had worked for a major manufacturing company in the accounting department. When the company they worked for was purchased by a competitor, their positions were phased out. They put their heads together and opened Rapid Delivery. Sean was always in the office and was the brains of the daily activities. Sean was a very abstract thinker; he helped me figure out whom to send out on the deliveries. He also processed the accounts payables. Besides the delivery service, there was a division that did industrial cleaning. Sean also ran that division.

Cindy would be my trainer and she was a super teacher. My capacity with computers came from her patience and training. She would teach me everything about computer spreadsheet accounting. They used Lotus 123 for their accounting process and Word for billing and correspondence. It was a very simple set up, only two computers on the network. This was the first time I used a personal PC. I had only worked on large networks. Cindy took all the time I needed while teaching me. The only problem was that Cindy was not in the office full time. Even though she was a full time partner, she only came in two or three days' a week. Cindy was *always* available to me by phone if I needed help.

Mitchell was seldom in the office. He was a C.P.A and had a home business. Mitchell was very pleasant and always made it a point to chat with the employees when he dropped in to visit us.

The owners were about the same age, I would say they were in their early forties. They were serious about making their business a success. Rapid Delivery is the only company I have worked for before or since where the owners did not live out of the receipts. Sean, Cindy, and Mitchell were salaried employees and that was it. They did not lease luxury cars, use an expense account, or submit personal credit card expenses to the company. They lived within their means. It was very refreshing to work for honest people for a change.

The delivery company employed six drivers. I had the privilege of getting to know them all. There were four local drivers and two of those drivers covered the deliveries around Anytown City and County. The other drivers handled long distance deliveries that encompassed the Harrisburg to Baltimore areas. There were two drivers who drove large trucks. They made product deliveries to major manufacturing companies. I did not have much interaction with them, but like the other employees they were very nice to me. As for the local drivers, Mark and Tracy I got to know them very well. Tracy was Sean's wife and had a primo route. She would pick-up and deliver all around the city of Anytown. Tracy was a lovely lady, happy and friendly. Mark was very pleasant, alas a born again Christian, who wore his religion like a big shiny badge on this sleeve. The long distance driver, Shana, was very serious and it was difficult to get a laugh out of her. She wanted people to think she was a tough girl, but she was a softy underneath, all the gruffness a false persona. Shanna was a very down to earth gal and not a born again Christian. Shana prided herself on making rapid *on time* deliveries. She was known to have made the Anytown to BWI airport run in forty five minutes. This run was normally scheduled for an hour and a half.

One afternoon the drivers were returning at the end of the day. Everyone was congregated in the office foyer joking and relating the day's narrow escapes on the highways. I heard Mark say to Shana, "Hey Shana, I saw that the Anytown Police had you pulled over again." Shana was always getting speeding tickets. "Yeah I got pulled over but I didn't get a ticket this time." she stated. Mark replied in a surprised tone, "How did you manage that, I was behind you and I **know** you were over the limit?" "Well," Shana explained (I couldn't wait to hear this story; Shana could get *out* of tickets too.) "As the cop got to my window, I blew off a horrible stinky fart when I rolled down the window." Everyone was now listening with rapt attention. Shana continued, "He tells me, "Madam, do you realize you were driving twenty miles over the limit!" Shana replied, "I have diarrhea, I am sick and I'm trying to get to a bathroom!" "So," Mark asked, "What happened?" "Well," Shana continued, "he just looked at me with his nose wiggling and said, 'I hope you make it.' He returned to his cruiser and took off." Everyone rolled with laughter, Shana had done it again.

During my time at Rapid Delivery, there would be some personnel changes, but for the most part, the employees whom I met on my first day were there when I left. The company paid well, and they rewarded hard work and loyalty.

Sean taught me how to use the two-way radio system. I took all the incoming calls, wrote up delivery slips, and then would figure out whom to assign it to. I also did all the invoicing for the delivery service and the cleaning company. Sean taught me how to process the payroll. Sean and Cindy never *dumped* a new task on me. They made sure I was comfortable with the work, and then they progressed to the next step. The position I was hired for had been newly created. Rapid Delivery had only been in business for three years. By the time my ninety days was concluded, I had an excellent grip on what was expected of me. Once I had most of the job under my belt, Sean would be free to leave the office and pursue new clients.

The company was situated at the crossing point of two major highways. They had an excellent location for a delivery company. The building they were in was a business co-op with three other companies in it. One office in the co-op was occupied by a private investigator, I thought that as cool. I had never known a real life *P.I.* The private investigators' secretary was a nice woman, and we would become friends as she was a smoker too. Things progressed well for the first year and then I began to have problems with the drivers. When the drivers were not out making deliveries, they would sit directly across from me. The office was too small to have a drivers lounge. While I was on the phone, they would ease drop and make comments. These comments were not intended to be offensive but they were annoying. One day the two drivers, Mark and Steve, who were born again Christians, began reading from the Bible aloud. I would sit there answering the phone or doing invoicing while this drone of God's spoken word went on and on and on. Sean was usually in his office but he kept his door shut. I tried to tune it out and was somewhat successful. After all I had worked at McCoy's. Sean, Cindy, Mark, and Steve went to the same church. I did not want to appear unchristian like so I did not complain about the reading aloud. There is a time and a place for everything; I did not feel religion had a place in the office.

We had a bulletin board on the wall like most offices and there were notes and fliers pinned to it. Only on this one there was a flier announcing a church service. Everyone was invited on Monday mornings to worship, the service would be held in Sean's office. Sean held church service from eight am until nine A.M. in his office. I usually arrived at nine, so I didn't particularly care what was going on when I wasn't there. One morning the church service was still going on when I arrived. I got started on the tasks of the day and the phone started ringing. I could hear them speaking very loud in Sean's office; suddenly I realized they were speaking in tongues. The hair stood up on the back of my neck.

I was trying to talk on the phone and the person I was speaking to asked, "What is going on in your office?" I told the customer, "They are having a meeting." I left it at that. About that time, the private investigator's secretary,

Karen, opened the door and asked, "What is going on in here, you can hear them down the hall." I simply told her about the service and she knew they were all born again Christians. I felt I needed to explain, so I said, "they are speaking in tongues." She stared blankly at me and said, "Better you than me." She quickly shut the door. I did not say anything to Sean regarding how I felt about them bringing religion into the office, but I did mention it to Cindy when she came into the office later in the day. Cindy listened to me very carefully, all the while nodding, taking it all in stride. I told her about all the reading out loud and the church service. She was very understanding and did not seem in anyway offended. She said she understood. After we spoke, she went to her desk and I returned to my work just like any other day. Cindy's desk was in Sean's office and at one point they closed the door. *Wham!* The door flew open, Sean stomped out of his office and went to the bulletin board and ripped the church fliers off of the board. As he turned to go back into his office, he glared at me. "Oh," I said to myself, "that went over well." Sean never said anything to me about the incident, but coolness developed between us. He was never as friendly to me as he had been. Sean always professed what a good Christian he was, how liquor had never passed his lips. Well he didn't have any reservations when it came to gouging a customer for an emergency pickup or delivery. He would just make up an outrageous cost. He knew they would pay it no matter what the cost, they had no choice otherwise.

One afternoon there was yelling in the office. Mark and Sean had a difference of opinion regarding the speed limit. Apparently Mark was late delivering a package to BWI Airport. The package missed the flight. Sean was very upset about the late delivery. He had *promised* the customer delivery on time. Sean told Mark that if he had driven faster he would not have missed the flight. Mark was just as adamant that he tried not to break any laws . . . *Gods or man's*. Mark said he was not going over the speed limit just to get a delivery made on time. Shortly after this, Mark quit. I couldn't help but think that this would never have happened if Cindy had been in the office that day. Cindy could always calm a situation and bring people back together.

I had been working at Rapid Delivery for about a year and a half and traveling from southern Anytown County. I lived in Jakeyville, and there was no direct route to Anytown. It took me forever to get to work everyday. My relationship with Smithy had finally hit a brick wall. Smithy and I decided to call it quits for good.

I began apartment hunting. One day I was in Joann's Fabrics Store and ran into my old buddy Dee from Rock Solid Insurance. We talked and got up to date on what we had been doing for the past few years. I mentioned I was looking for an apartment in Anytown City. Dee was living on Linden Avenue and the house she owned had a first floor apartment that was vacant. She said if I was interested to come over and take a look at it. The apartment was perfect. The house was an old Victorian structure that had been divided into two apartments. The rooms had big windows and sunlight filled every corner of the apartment. Dee, her husband and daughter lived upstairs. I signed the lease and within a week I moved back to the city. I continued to work at Rapid Delivery. Now there were no church services, no speaking in tongues, and no reading aloud. Business was good and we were busy, but Sean was no longer friendly. Nothing had changed between Cindy and me. She was always a dream to work with.

A few months after I moved to Linden Avenue, I went on a camping trip with my girlfriends. It was July 4th, 1990. We drove to Woolrich, Pennsylvania to attend a weekend Biker Party. We had a blast! I met the man of my dreams that weekend. Jeff was to become the most important person in my life. After returning from the camping trip, he called me and we began dating. Within six months our relationship had become very serious. Jeff was in the middle of a divorce and we decided he should move in. When his divorce was final, we planned on getting married.

For some reason, Sean began to speak to me again. He would lecture me that I was going to hell because I was living in sin. When I would get to my desk each morning, I would find religious pamphlets called tracks in my "In" Basket. These tracks declare what terrible sinners we were and that we must repent! Well, at least he was talking to me again. It was very irritating but I didn't say anything about it at that time. On sunny afternoons, Jeff would come to Rapid Delivery on his Harley and pick me up. As I left and jumped on the back of Jeff's motorcycle, Sean would pull a long face. He did not approve of my lifestyle. I could not understand why it would even matter to him.

About this time, Cindy's husband became very ill and died suddenly. Cindy was devastated. She put on a brave face and for a time came to the office, but after a few months she sold her share of the company to a man in Lancaster. Cindy had become the buffer between Sean and me. I could not imagine working there without her. I only continued working for them another six months. Work was different without her, it lacked satisfaction. Jeff had gotten divorced and bought out his ex-wife's share of his home. On Memorial Day weekend, 1991 Jeff packed me up. Sean offered us the use of one of the Delivery Trucks to move. I took him up on it and one of the drivers, Buddy, helped us out. Buddy was a driver that had been hired after Mark quit.

As I suspected, it wasn't long before Sean returned to being unfriendly. Sean and his wife Tracy were always badgering me about my personal life and it was getting old. They loved to harp upon me about how we were living in sin. Baugh, Baugh, Baugh. I was ready to move on. Jeff was very supportive and told me that if I felt I should leave Rapid Delivery's employment. "just do it." That was all I needed to hear. I gave Sean two weeks notice shortly thereafter. Guess what I left on the back of my chair in my rush to get out of there?

I planned on taking my time to find a position that would utilize all the computer knowledge I had learned at Rapid Delivery. I took a Microsoft course at a local vocational school. I was able to improve my skills during this time of unemployment.

Jeff had a friend who was an accountant for a construction company. Jeff had run into Allan at the Slow Pony Bar watering hole in the area. Allan had related to Jeff that Edgar Construction would have an opening for an assistant accounting clerk in two weeks. Allan wanted to hire someone as soon as he could. Alan wanted the girl who was leaving to train the new person. When Jeff came home he told me about this job opening and encouraged me to call Allan for an interview. I also knew Allan and his girl friend. They were Harley owners and I had met them at various Harley outings. I went to Edgar Construction and interviewed with a very old man who was the owner. Mr. Edger did not believe in computers. Even though he disapproved of doing business with a computer, he allowed his accountant Allan to purchase one for the company. I would not be using this computer and would be back to doing the bookkeeping journals by hand. Mr. Edgar also told me they did *not* dress up (I had worn my best black suit to the interview). Since I already knew Allan, I figured he would be comfortable to work with. When Allan called and offered me the position, I accepted. Edgar Construction's office was located in a garage next to the owner's home. I did not realize it at the time of the interview but there were no bathrooms in the office. They had a "*jiffy john*" outside next to the building. In addition, there was only a wood burning stove to heat the office in the winter. I had not anticipated I would be roughing it at work.

The girl who was leaving trained me as best as she could. I could tell there was friction between her and Allan. She was very helpful and I thought I had a good grasp on what I would be doing. On Friday, as she was leaving, she stopped to talk with me. I told her, "thanks for all the help and good luck on your new job." She looked at me and said, "You're the one who is going to need the luck." With that, she left. I was on my own. I worked though the first week and was getting the hang of their billing and office procedures. Using a jiffy john with no running water was not pleasant. It was autumn and the mornings were very chilly. The office was cold and it was only September. I could not even guess what it would be like by December. I would definitely need to buy a new white office sweater! I had to have something to leave on the way out anyway!

I made it though the first week but I was very sorry I had gotten myself into this situation. On Monday I would learn more about working with Allan. Allan had lost a leg in the Viet Nam War. I had known this before. He usually got around with one crutch. I did not know the pain he was in or how a severed limb affected a person's life. He lived on aspirin and was very hyper. Instead of the crutch, Allan used his wheeled office chair to maneuver around the office.

Towards the end of the second week, tempers were getting short. Allan was always correcting what I did and told me, "I don't care what she taught you. Do it this way!" I was so nervous; I was making all kinds of stupid mistakes. I was sitting there trying my best to accomplish a ledger task, and apparently muttering to myself. All of a sudden he came *screaming* over to my desk in his chair. I looked up and we were eye to eye. "If you are talking to me you need to speak up, I have hearing damage." he barked. Then he started jabbing his finger in my face and continued raging. "If you are talking to yourself, shut the f . . . . up!" Wow. I just stared at him. I was at a loss for words. Allan went skittering back to his desk and resumed working. I did not utter a sound for the rest of the morning. At lunch I drove to a Rutter's Store because I wanted to call Jeff. We did not have cell phones in those days. I was fuming, and I was going to quit on the spot. When I got to the pay phone, I called Jeff at work. After I told him what had happened he agreed with me that Allan's behavior was inexcusable. I went back to the office after lunch and retrieved my mug just like I did at the Edward S Young Company. I told Allan "I won't be back." I walked out the door. Unfortunately this situation did affect our personal relationship with Allan and his wife Lenore. Gratefully, after some time had passed, Allan apologized to me and all was forgiven. He was no longer working at Edgar Construction either. Mr. Edgar had retired and the company was no longer in business.

I think that employment position was worthy of a record. I made it exactly two weeks. I decided to call Mrs. Walnut, once again.

Chapter 9

Too many freaks, not enough Carnivals.

Mrs. Walnut was delighted to hear from me after so long a time. She was interested to know what had happened at Rapid Delivery, as they had placed me in the position. I was forthright and she said she would have done the same thing. I did not mention the fiasco at Edgar Construction. She told me they had a position from AWI come in, and if I was interested she would forward my resume to them. She told me it was long term temp. I would be filling in for a woman who was on disability leave and it would run six months. I could not be picky so I told her "please do." A few days later Mrs. Walnut called me and said, "It's a go at AWI." I was on my way the next Monday.

AWI is a wholesale grocery warehouse. Every item that was sold in grocery stores was trucked in from the manufacturers. These products were then received in the warehouse. As orders from the grocery stores were placed with AWI, the items would be "picked" by the warehouse personnel and shipped to the stores.

I arrived at AWI and was greeted by a delightful receptionist, an older woman with a big smile and a twinkle in her eye. I would discover later that Carol and her husband were professional clowns. Carol had a vanity plate on her car that read 2CLOWNS, and a clown she was. She was well suited for her position as receptionist at AWI. She told me to have a seat and buzzed the Human Resources Department. Another smiling young woman came to the reception area and leisurely escorted me to the department I would be working in. This department, Wholesale Accounting, consisted of one other person, Beverly.

Beverly was in her early sixty's and very attractive. She was a bundle of energy topped off with a pleasant smile. Beverly was a sincerely caring person. Even though she was very busy, she took the time to train me properly. She knew this was going to be a long term assignment and that we had to work together to keep abreast of the work. There was a lot of work and a lot to learn. I would be receiving the products into the computer that the personnel in the warehouse processed throughout the day. After we processed the receivers, we would match up the invoices from the vendors and input the invoices. I slowly picked up the procedures, and with Beverly's help did not get into too much trouble. She told me she knew the system inside and out. "If you make a mistake, I can fix anything you do. Don't worry about it, mistakes happen," she continued, "tell me right away." I followed her advice. Beverly could fix any mistake I made. At times I believe I made her really scratch her head. We progressed though the learning curve and things fell into place after a few weeks.

When we would input invoices to be paid into the computer system, we would print an edit report prior to posting the data to the general ledger. The reports were printed on old fashion green bar paper. One morning as I was checking the invoice against the report, I could have sworn a decimal walked off the page. I stared as the dot moved across the page and disappeared. I called to Beverly across the room, "Beverly, I think I need to take a break, the decimals are walking off the page." To my surprise Beverly told me, "oh yes that happens. We have paper mites." She added, "There are a lot of old records stored here. They don't bite." I had no idea such creatures existed. You learn something new everyday.

We received our work from the warehouse via a tube air system, similar to the tubes used at some drive up banks. The warehouse was on the basement level and it was huge. The receiving people would place the completed receivers in the tube and send it to our level. When I heard the soft whoosh, I would get up and go into the hall and retrieve our work. From there, it was just a matter of matching up items to the matching vendor invoice. It was as simple as it sounds. The hard part was wading though the pages and pages of the invoices. The items went on forever; there were packs, grosses, boxes, all types of odd quantity break downs. With Beverly's unrelenting patience, I learned what to do.

At this time Jeff and I had set a wedding date for November. I was busy doing all that is needed for a small wedding budgeted on a temp salary. I certainly wasn't going to be wearing a Vera Wang on my wedding day. A November wedding would mean I could have a wintery outfit. I had found a white faux fur muff, a hat, and my wedding dress at the Salvation Army in Anytown City. All I needed was the coat. I could not find a white faux fur coat anywhere.

One day I was lamenting to Beverly that I could not find a white coat. Beverly told me she had one from the 1970s. She had kept it in a storage bag for all these years, would I like to see it? Well you don't have to ask me twice! Beverly brought the coat in the next day and it was a perfect fit. I was so touched by her generosity. She would not let me pay her for the coat, she told me to consider it a wedding gift. That is the way it was at AWI. Everyone was nice, I don't recall ever hearing anyone complain or bicker. The only strange thing was that the woman I was replacing was named Jane Crouse. Her name plate was on the outside of our office door along with Beverly's. I thought that it was odd, maybe it was an omen? The spelling of our last names would be identical when I married Jeff. This spelling of Crouse is unusual here in Pennsyltucky. Crouse is usually spelled *Krause*.

I had been working at AWI for five months and three weeks when the cheerful human resources lady called me and requested that I stop in her office. At this meeting she told me that they did not expect Jane Crouse to return, as they had not heard from her or her doctor. She asked if I was interested, they were offering the position to me. I told her, "I would like nothing better!" "Terrific," she responded, "we will do your paper work next Friday." I floated out of her office. Beverly was pleased too.

Well guess who walked in that following Thursday morning: Jane Crouse. I was sitting at her desk dumbfounded. She greeted Beverly and I. "Hi everybody, I'm back." "Hi there, nice to finally meet you." I said to her, I was dying inside. Just then the phone rang; it was the human resources gal. "Judy, she says, "please come to my office right now." I could hear the panic in her voice. "Sure, I'm on my way". I forced myself to sound cheerful.

When I got to the Human Resources office she was waiting for me. She told me, "We had no idea she was coming back. Tomorrow is the last day of her disability. Since we had not heard from her or her physician, I automatically thought she was not returning. I am so sorry." I was really sorry too. I told her not to worry about it, things happen. To save me from any more awkwardness, the Human Resources lady went back to our office and retrieved my handbag, mug, and my old white office sweater. It took a caring HR rep, but I finally left with my sweater. And that is how my wonderful assignment at AWI ended.

I called Mrs. Walnut and told her my assignment had ended but she already knew. The gal at AWI had called her and explained what had transpired. Everyone was so apologetic, I told Mrs. Walnut, "no harm, no foul, no problem." We left it at that.

I thought about Beverly on my wedding day. It was cold and cloudy that morning, but I was snug and cozy in Beverly's wonderful white coat.

My next assignment would not be so amiable. At the end of November, I began a long term assignment at Boswell Sales. This company sold gas logs, fire places, grills, and lamps to Gas Dealers. There were some customers that were homeowners, but very few. They had a showroom and I sat at the front desk. It was not a receptionist position in the strictest sense of the word. I would be doing a lot of correspondence for the Office Manager, Amy, and the owner, The Big Kahuna, as he was known. There were three customer service ladies who worked upstairs, Big Judy, Little Judy, and Jane. When I was being introduced I thought, how rude, if you're Big Judy. It was determined I would be just Judy. I had very little contact with the customer service ladies, but when I did they were accommodating and pleasant.

The office manager, Amy, was a glamour queen and trotted around immersed in her own self importance. I thought she acted rather ridiculous for a woman in her thirties. After meeting the boss, The Big Kahuna, I suspected they were having an affair. They were a bit too cozy and familiar with each other. They made a lot of eye contact punctuated with secret smiles and glances. There was also a warehouse man; Jim. Amy and Jim had gone to high school together. They were always talking and joking and made a big deal about what wonderful friends they were. Amy needed a lot of reassurance and both Jim and the Big Kahuna gave it to her.

In addition to everyone's daily duties at Boswell Sales, each person was assigned a week of trash duty (except for the Big Kahuna of course). Every afternoon the employee would collect all the trash from the office trash cans. When it was my turn I would stop my normal actives one half hour before quitting time and get a huge trash bag. I would then drag the bag around the office to empty the cans. It gave me a break and I got to socialize with everyone.

As the weeks progressed I had no problems with the work, or helping out with the walk in customers. Amy had given me all the materials and information I needed. Basically it was a rather boring job, but a very quiet environment. The company was very busy as it was the winter months. I helped out in the Customer Service department as needed. I made friends with Jane as she was also a smoker. We started going to breaks and lunches together. We had a lot in common and to this day we are still are friends. During the cool winter days, we ate in the office's little break room. As the weather became warmer, Jane and I would walk to the park across the street and feed the ducks. For some unknown reason, Amy had a problem with Jane and I being friends. One day she changed the lunch schedule. And that was the end of Jane and me going to the park together. I never could figure out why Amy had such a problem with us being friends.

One evening after leaving work I discovered I had left my book at the office. I was half way home and decided to go back and retrieve it. I pulled in and noticed that Amy's car was still in the parking lot. I opened the door, which leads into the warehouse, and there she was going though the trash. She did not see me at first, so I just stood there watching her pull papers out and reading them. About five minutes passed and then she noticed me. "Oh, hi there, I'm looking for something I threw out," she said very quickly as her face turned red. "I left my book, sorry to interrupt you." I replied. I went to my desk and retrieved my book. When I left the building her car was already gone.

I mentioned to Jane the next day that I caught Amy going though the trash when I had stopped back in the office. It was obvious to me that she was not looking for something. She had been reading what the other employees had thrown out. Jane told me, "oh yeah, I didn't tell you that. Be careful what you put in the trash." Jane said "She is looking for anything to use against us." "What could she possibly find?" I asked Jane. "Well", Jane continued, "If you use too much stationary and she finds it in the trash, you will hear about it." I was stupefied. Jane continued, "I just fold my trash really small and put it in my purse, and then when I get home I put it in *my* trash." All I could think was that Amy really needed to get a life. The assignment ended shortly thereafter, it was now April, and their busy season had come to an end. Boswell Sales went out of business a short time later. Jane moved on to a better job and I moved on temping. Pickings were pretty slim at Walnut Agency. I had to go around town registering with every temp Agency in Anytown.

I was placed at Mobile Phone Company as a telemarketer by a company called JFC. This was a typical agency with all the pimps and whistles. I really did not want to take this job but Mrs. Walnut did not have anything for me. When I got to the job I was given an Anytown phone book and a Mobil phone script. That was the extent of the training. I hated the job. I sat in a miniature cubical jammed up against a wall. There were eight or ten other people cold calling and trying to set appointments for the salesmen. I had trouble staying upbeat and keeping a "smile" in my voice. I hate telemarketers calling me at home. There was no way I could do the job with any sincerity. I could not push a call, if the person I was speaking with said they were not interested I hung up. Needless to say I did not get many leads for the salesmen.

I am not sure how this job ended. I think Mobile Phone may have called JFC and asked to have me replaced. Maybe I asked to be taken off. I remember the Mobil office was very *gray*. Everything was gray, the walls, carpet, cubicles, and the phones. Even the people had a gray hue. It was like working in a black and white movie. The young women at Mobil Phone were unfriendly and the other telemarkcters did not bother with the temps. I have never worked for JFC again. Now, I have a great respect for anyone who makes their living as a telemarketer.

I had also registered with an agency called Capitol Area Temps. They sent me on two assignments to a company that manufactured tanks for the Army. The company, M.A.E or Military Armament Equipment, was a big employer in Anytown. Everyone I talked with wanted to work there. Anytown residents would tell me, "Get into M.A.E, they are the best employer in town." Well I was finally at M.A.E.

The first assignment at M.A.E was for one week working in the kitchen as a Catering Assistant. I aced this job in two hours. The title Catering Assistant was a stretch, the job was nothing more than putting dirty lunch trays on a rolling cart and helping the cooks. The duties were the same as what I had done at the Highway House. Everyone was really nice there, and when they discovered they did not have to train me, they were even nicer.

The following week I reported to the Accounts Payable Department at M.A.E for three weeks to cover vacations. This department was no fun. The manager was a skinny old lady with a mean streak. The five accounting clerks slunk around her like cowering dogs. It was disgusting but I picked up the work and got the job done. When I would glance up from my work, she would be staring at me with a scowl on her face. On my last day, which was a Friday, M.A.E was having a huge company party. They had big contracts with the Army and on this day they were rolling out their latest model, The Paladin. All the employees from all three shifts were there, it was employee appreciation day. The speaker that day was Arlen Specter, a Pennsylvania Senator. They had tons of food and a large tent with a couple hundred chairs placed in it. On the stage was a tank with a cover over it. At lunch that day, everyone from the day shift stopped work and went to the party. It was a beautiful summer day, sunny and breezy. I drifted around the grassy area taking it all in. I enjoyed a free lunch and hanging out. As it was getting close to the time when the Senator was going to speak, I wandered down front to get a good seat. I noticed the seats were all taken so I stood on the side lines.

When Senator Specter entered, everyone cheered and cheered. They acted like he was some kind of movie star. They were very excited that he had come to the plant. The Senator walked to the podium and made a speech, which I could not hear; there was a problem with the audio system. He was obviously thanking everyone for their hard work and dedication.

As I was standing there I could not help but notice that all the office people who sit all day were sitting on all the chairs. All the men who stand all day to make the tanks were standing. It seemed wrong. When they unveiled the Paladin, the cover got hung up on the gun torrent. One of the guys from the shop had to climb up and pull the cover off. He got a bigger round of applause than Senator Specter. Now it seemed right. As I drove away from M.A.E on the last day of my assignment, I could not for the life of me understand why everyone wished to work there.

Mrs. Walnut called, thank God, with an assignment at another big corporation in Anytown. I would be assisting the manager of the Marketing department at Anytown International with a special project.

The following Monday I reported for duty. I was taken to the Marketing department and met the gentleman I would be working with along with his assistant. Mr. Gay was a dream to work for, he got me started with some simple tasks, and I had no problem picking up the work. I was assisting him in creating a manual for the dealers who brought products from Anytown International. I learned to use Harvard Graphics and other graphic software. The other women in the department were friendly also. They were always insisting I help myself to the tons of snacks they brought into the office. They always asked me to join them for lunch. It was a dream assignment.

I worked with Mr. Gay for two months until the conclusion of the project. He was very pleased with my performance and positive attitude. He gave Mrs. Walnut a glowing report on my performance. I was such a good little temp, but sadly this assignment was also over.

Mrs. Walnut was out of assignments at this time. I had to shop around doing my best as a temp groveling for jobs. I did not want to go to Peanut Temp service and deal with their snotty little pimps. I thought I would try a larger service and went to a company called ADIA. This was just as typical as Peanut Temps and they had many of the same type of industrial positions. I registered with them with minimal enthusiasm. To my surprise a pimp from ADIA called me with a temp position at a graphics company. I would be logging artwork for a company that created the illustrations for medical and biology text books. This sounded interesting to me and I accepted. The position was only temp for about three months, "but," my sweet little pimp lied, "you never know, it might go full time."

College Art Works was a small start up company. The owners of a larger printing company had taken some of their best people and formed a graphics media business. This explanation was told to me on my first day by the administrative assistant to the manager, Suzan. I can't say this is absolutely true but it sounded good. The manager and the administrative assistant were both in their early twenties. They were very capable and hardworking young women.

I worked with Suzan, the administration assistant. She was a great trainer. Suzan was full of energy but a very serious person. There was very little time for joking around at College Art Works. They employed four artists who worked in computer generated graphics. They had all the latest software and office equipment.

The office was very modern; the entire top of their desks had glass panels with the computer monitor recessed under the desk. The desk I was assigned to work at was modern and beautiful as well.

My job would be to log artwork on Lotus 123 work sheets for each book they were completing. They were busy so there was a lot of new art to log daily. In addition to the new art, there was art being returned by the authors either approving or requesting revisions. Each drawing was referred to by a *figure* with a number, i.e. fig. 10 and so on. The artwork went back and forth, back and forth.

The artists were very cliquey and kept to themselves; you know how artists can be. Suzan and the manager were tight so I never got to know either of them very well. They usually went to lunch later than everyone else. This was another company where the employees were only friendly enough to keep the temp from leaving the job.

Some of the comments the authors had scribbled on the revisions were amusing (to me, not the artist). One in particular stands out in my mind. The art work was of molecular structures, and the artist had rendered the figures in purple. There were about fifty figures in the book and the artist had spent a great deal of time drawing them in different hues of lavender and purple. The author had scribbled in red pen over each and every drawing, "NO PURPLE, PURPLE IS FOR LOSERS!" The artist wasn't amused.

Needless to say the position did not become full time. When this assignment came to an end three months later, ADIA was so happy with my performance at the Graphics Company that they sent me to another start up business called Foremost Capitol Plastics. Happy happy joy joy.

Foremost, Capitol Plastics was a company that was built within and attached to a very large dairy facility. They manufactured plastic milk jugs in gallon and half gallon sizes. There were around ten blow mold machines and a gigantic palletizer. I would be working for the plant manager, helping her with order entry. That is what I was told but I was not surprised to learn there was more to it.

The plant manager and the foreman for both shifts were from the home base in Maine which owned many dairies. My manager Molly was a large boyish woman who could handle any machine or task in the plant. She had worked at the home dairy for years and had worked her way up the ladder from dock worker. Molly would eventually butt heads once to many times with the local management of the dairy faculty and would be transferred to another Maine owned facility down south.

My data entry job would eventually encompass quality control, safety, and cleaning the ladies bathroom. I had discovered by now that it was not unusual that the position I would be sent on was not always what I would be doing. I could usually handle extra tasks as the learning curve shortened. I liked to learn new things but cleaning bathrooms was really a stretch. Everyone who worked there was required to do it except, of course, the management. By having the employees clean it themselves they did not have to hire a cleaning service.

Molly's *girlfriend* also worked at the plant but on the second shift. Anytown is a very conservative area and openly gay relationships are something they do not deal with well. I never had a problem with Molly or how she lived her life but the owners of the dairy did not like it. Molly kept her relationship with her girlfriend strictly professional at work. Molly and the other employees from the home office were in their late twenties and very hard workers. I worked in the office with Molly. The office was very small and the two desks were just about all that fit in it. I would input the orders from dairies throughout the area.

When the truck drivers would come into the office to pick up the paperwork, I usually assisted them.

Foremost Capitol used the drop and hook system for shipments. The drivers would come in with an empty trailer and pull out with a trailer from the lot which was already filled with new milk jugs. It was a very simple system and nothing should screw up, but in reality, it did. A load of empty gallon milk jugs does not weigh much more than an empty trailer. More than once a driver pulled out with no load, something that was not discovered until the trailer was opened five hundred miles away. This did not go over well with management, so we would periodically spot check the trailers in the yard.

There was a great deal of jealously among the managers of the home office's plant. When it was discovered that Molly had an assistant, i.e., me, the other managers complained. They were of the opinion that if Molly had an assistant they should have one too. To quell all this discontent, Molly changed my duties. I would only work in the office assisting her half the day. In addition, I would no longer report to her. My new boss was the general manager for the company in Maine, Nelson.

After lunch I worked in the manufacturing area. I would check for employees not using safety glasses or ear plugs and write them up. I took readings from the blow mold machines, and pulled sample bottles to perform quality control. If the bottles failed the quality control testing, I would have to return to the line and show the blow mold operator. Of course this created friction between the operators and me. The quality control problems I pointed out where *never* their fault, those problems were always caused by something else. Now I was making enemies on the floor because of my new position. Before I had been given these tasks, everyone working in the plant had always been affable, but now I was part of what they deemed the management and was a snitch.

I could have dealt with that if I had the support of Molly and the other foremen but they had their own agendas to pursue. Molly could be rather foul mouthed and aggressive. When I had problems with the quality of the bottles being made, she would tell me to call my boss. My boss was at the plant in the Maine facility. What good would that do me? Once, when I did call him, I had to leave a message with his secretary and he never called me back. I did not know what to do. I should have confronted Molly and told her how unfair she was being. I have never been a person that likes or wanted conflict. I now had wasted nine months at this job. The little pimps at ADIA were of no help either.

When I contacted them regarding the problems I was having at Foremost Capitol Plastics, I requested they find me something else but they could not help me. My ADIA pimp said "I am sorry but that is what is available. If you leave this job, we will not be able to place you anywhere else." The next day I went to work and Molly told me one two many times to, "call Nelson, your boss, if you need help." I knew nothing was going to change. I went to my locker, retrieved my handbag and lunch. Once again I walked out the door. Darned if I hadn't left my old white office sweater over the back of my chair, again.

There is an emotional high that comes from leaving an insufferable work place, but it is short lived. Reality usually sets in for me the next day.

I called Mrs. Walnut but did not disclose to her that I had walked off an assignment with ADIA. She had no problem with me working for other agencies. She knew temps work for who calls first. Unfortunately Walnut Temp Service was still light on work assignments. I had no choice but to call Peanut Pimps, oops I mean Peanut Temps. Peanut Temp Service sent me to That-A-Way Transportation in March of 1994. Being that I had worked in the trucking industry, the Peanut pimp thought I would be a good candidate for a DOT log auditor. She told me they would do the training and not to worry. I could not find anything in the newspaper classifieds and this assignment was better than nothing at all. I worked in the safety department of the trucking company. The manager was a very good looking woman who That-Away Trucking had sought out from another trucking firm. She drove a flashy red BMW and had a vanity plate that read CHERWITAC. I had to ask one of the other clerks what that meant. Cher had worked in the trucking industry for many years. When Cher accepted the job, she brought a fellow worker Phil from her old company to be the senior auditor in the department. Phil was an older man who just wanted to get five more years employment so he could retire. He was very knowledgeable and was a great help to everyone in the department. He was not into standing up for anyone. Phil kept his head down and did not make waves.

There were three other young girls in the department. June was Cher's assistant and there were also two log auditors, Teresa and Jennie. Teresa did my training; she was a good trainer and always had time for my questions. Jennie was a slacker and never had her work current. Jennie was young and enjoyed being twenty-one, she loved the night life. I eventually caught on and became a DOT Auditor.

In the course of log auditing, I would find errors in the drivers' logs. They would be penalized for these errors and this would go against their safety records. The drivers seemed to think that being in one state on Thursday and having a toll receipt that showed they were actually there on Wednesday was not a problem. The drivers got extremely upset when the auditors discovered their travel log schemes and mistakes.

That-A-Way Trucking installed computers in their trucks that summer. This caused a great deal of friction with the drivers. They did not like anyone knowing where they were located. In addition, there were drivers who could not read. These men were older drivers who had grown up on farms in the South.

Since they could not use the computers, That-A-Way fired them. I had never known anyone who could not read, it was so sad.

The drivers would come into Cher's office screaming and threatening her. They would be angry about the log violations in their personal files. Cher was a very hard nosed woman and could shout down any man. By the way, she also carried a gun! These drivers would be so upset with the audit department, I really thought one of them would come in the office one day and take us all out, just like you see on television.

As time progressed at the trucking company, we began to hear rumors of mismanagement by the owners. That-A-Way was owned by four brothers. We had heard, though the rumor mill, that there was a lot of infighting among the family members. There were also rumors of drug use and misappropriations of company funds. I learned from Phil to keep my head down too. So imagine my surprise one morning when I pulled into the parking lot and saw that the fence was locked. There was a sign hung on the fence that simply stated, CLOSED. I had been hired after thirty days but seven months later they had shut the doors for good. We found out later that the company had been sold to another trucking company. We were all out of jobs this time. This time I wasn't allowed to get my white office sweater from the back of my chair.

After I went to the unemployment office to open a claim, I went to the Highway House Bar for a beer. I discovered that Susie was no longer working there. She had gone to work for a real estate appraisal company. Susie and her husband were having dinner and asked me to join them. As we are dining, Susie told me there was an opening at the company she worked for. The position was for a data input cleric and receptionist. Susie had gotten her real estate license and was out of the bar business. She told me the job provided staff support for five other appraisers and that she was sure I would have no problem learning the job if I was hired. I went to the company the following Monday and met with the owner, Mr. McMaster. He was a small man with a very loud voice. I thought he was suffering from the Napoleonic Complex. I found out later I was right about that.

Mr. McMaster was an absolute tyrant. He strode about the office pushing out his chest and yelling at everyone. I tried my best to learn what was required. The software I was using was designed for the real estate business and I had never used it before. However, the software was Windows based and I was picking it up rather quickly. I was only there two weeks when Mr. McMaster started screaming at me for making errors on an appraisal. After I entered the information on a template, I would "save as" and then go to the next appraisal. Apparently I must have saved one under the wrong name. Working at this company was working amidst structured chaos. Susie forgot to tell me one rather important fact. The woman who was there before me had walked out two weeks earlier. No one had done any of the appraisal reports. The first day I sat down at the desk, the in bin was overflowing. It was still overflowing when I walked out two weeks later.

On the Friday of my second week, Mr. McMaster came to my desk. He began his screaming rant and rave routine. His face was red and he was blown up like a puffer fish. I got up, put on my coat and I walked out the door. I was not going to put up with him anymore. By the time I got to my car, he realized I had quit. As I got into my car, he was running across the parking lot, yelling, "I am sorry Judy, don't leave." I just kept going. I drove straight to the Unemployment Office. I told them of the hostile work environment. I was able to re-open my unemployment claim. The UEC agent told me they had another person collecting benefits from Mr. McMaster's company. The claims person at the UE office I spoke with told me they understood that the working conditions at his company were appalling and very unprofessional.

When I returned home that evening, the light was flashing on my phone. There was a message from one of the little Walnut pimps. She had a part time position at a company called Development Topographers. It was only expected to last two weeks. Was I interested? I called her back and said, "Sure, why not." This would be a proof reading position. This company manufactured books. I would be proof reading art work for medical books. I could not believe it. After having worked at College Art Works, I knew what to expect. The manuscripts were not bound and I would be making sure the figure numbers and the captions were correct.

I worked with another temp and she was a very nice gal. We had no problem doing a great job immediately. The only distasteful thing about this position was the subject matter of the manuscripts. They were medical text books about abnormal psychology. The pictures were very depressing; we tried not to read and just proofed the work.

The end of this assignment ushered in the year 1996 as luck would have it. I would work at eight more companies before the next New Year.

Cling Brothers Insurance Company

St. Lemon

Boon Tune Hallway

The VNA

You can pull it off.Community Transit

Nuts and Bolts Industrial

Medical Records Dept. Anytown Hospital

My Cardboard Desk Cedar Grove Commons

Anytowns Finest P LICE

Easter Seals

PCI

Author Incognito

CHAPTER 10

You can pull it off

I decided the New Year would *not* find me working for a temp agency. I had been working for temp services for the past five years and it had gotten me nowhere. I answered ads I found in the newspaper. I went on one interview after another. I revised my resume to include all the skills I had developed over the years. I would sit in the lobby of companies and pray someone would hire me. As I was leaving from the interviews, I usually saw the next candidate for the job waiting her turn. The candidate was always younger and more attractive than me. I became more and more discouraged. I was forty eight years old and I was competing with the cream of the crop. I had never been to college or vocational school. More and more of the clerical positions were requiring a business degree. I had gotten caught up in a cycle of bad decisions on my part, compounded by long futile temp assignments. As the months passed, I had not been able to get a *real* job. I had no choice but to contact a temp agency. This was a depressing and desperate decision I had to make, like it or not.

I contacted a new agency called the Brazil Group. I heard though the temp grape vine that this was a very posh agency. They were no different that any of the other places I had been. The only distinction I could see was that this outfit had spent more money to decorate their lobby. The woman running the show was a Super Pimp boss. She had the same typical sidekick pimps working for her. They were very impressed with my skills and sent me to the Boon Tune Corporate offices in East Anytown. I would be working in the corporate accounting department. I readily accepted the position at the Boon Tune. I had worked there before and looked forward to returning. The Boon Tune had recently bought out another chain of department stores and they needed extra help converting the new accounts into their system.

I spent eight hours daily, imputing information from twelve inch stacks of green bar paper. I loved it. I would put on my headset, turn on the music, and go into a data zone. The accountants I worked for were very supportive and professional. They always had time for questions. The other ladies invited me to join them for lunch and smoke breaks. They truly had the munchies at this office! However, this assignment was only booked for three months. On the last day of the assignment, I went to the Human Resources Department and filled out an application. I hoped to be hired for any job they might have. I knew I would get a good recommendation from the Boon Tune Credit office and the accounting department. The HR woman I interviewed with, Yolanda Tall told me they had nothing at that time but to call and keep in touch with her. I would call every week just to check in with her.

One afternoon I was aimlessly driving around East Anytown wondering what to do next. I saw a sign which said "Kelly Employment Service, Positions Available!!" I was dressed suitably and I always carried copies of my resume in the glove compartment of my car. I decided to drop in and check out this agency. Maybe I could be a *Kelly Girl!*

Kelly Services was no different than any other agency I had been to. They cheerfully stuffed my information into their data base. The pimp I spoke to was typically juvenile, pretty, and animated. She assured me that if anything came in that matched my skills they would give me a call. She told me they where busy and I could expect to be working very soon. I had stupidly confided to her I was collecting unemployment and needed to find a job.

A day or two later, Ms. Kelly Jr. called me with an assignment which she wanted to *feel* me out about. The job was at a Wally-Mart in East Anytown. The job was a make-up demonstrator for Max Factor and would only be for three Saturdays afternoons. I told her I was not interested in such a job. I did not feel it was beneath me, but I did not possess the people skills the job required. In no uncertain terms, she informed me, "You have no choice." I asked her what she meant by that? "You're collecting unemployment and if you don't do this I will call the state unemployment office and have your claim denied. I *can* do this because you turned down available work." I could not believe I was going to be bullied into doing this B.S. job. All of a sudden Ms. Kelly Jr. was no longer cheery or bubbly. I ended up going to Wally-Mart for three Saturdays to show uninterested shoppers Max Factor's latest spring make-up shades.

After a week or so went by, I received a call from the pushy pimp at Kelly Services. Ms. Kelly Jr. forced me to take a position at a company called Swiss Habitual in Anytown City. This company made tiny components for circuit boards. Swiss Habitual was a sub contractor for The Amp Company. This was a temp to perm placement and I knew this was going to be a tragedy. I told her I did not think I could do this job. She let me know what to expect if I turned it down. In no uncertain terms Ms. Kelly Jr. reiterated, "You know I can *yank* your unemployment." Yeah, I knew that was coming. Off I went to this challenging position. On Monday morning I showed up at Swiss Habitual dressed in jeans, ready to do my best. I had to park on the street in a ghastly neighborhood. The work areas were filthy and old. They only employed about ten full time people who went out of their way to either ignore me or refer to me as "that temp" or "the temp".

I was put at an inspection station and would be inspecting teeny tiny cooper parts. The parts were so small I used a large lighted magnifying glass to see them. I wear bifocals glasses and I just could not spot the cracks in the parts. After three days, the supervisor took me off the job. Next they put me on a grimy die stamp machine. This was really a disaster. I had oil all over the place and the parts backed up on my line. By Friday the supervisor called Kelly and told them, "Judy is a great gal, we love her determination, but she is not suited for this job." I gratefully thanked the supervisor and skipped out the door. Kelly had one more *required* job I would have to go on before I could get away from them. Next, Ms. Kelly *requested* I go to United Connectors in Glen Stone, PA. Glen Stone is a long way from where I live and the drive is cross country. There is no direct highway to get there from Thomas Town. I knew I could not turn the job down so I bit the bullet and grudgingly showed up on Monday morning at United Connectors.

I was one of five temps from Kelly Services who had been sent to this job. We would be entering the data collected from the company's most recent inventory. Steward connectors requested five temps so that the job would be completed in five days. We were taken to a conference room with five computers and were given huge stacks of hand written inventory sheets. We could use a headset and listen to music while we worked.

All the temps went to lunch at the same time so we never met any other employees. The woman supervising us was all business but very helpful if we needed assistance. About the only thing any of us needed help with was trying to decipher hieroglyphic handwriting. By Friday we had finished the inventory job. The supervisor we reported to told us what a great job we had done. Since we had completed the project, we were told to take the afternoon off, but they would pay us for the entire day. All things considered this had not been a bad assignment. That was the last time I ever had any contact with Kelly Services. Luckily when they did call me, I was on another adventure in employment for a more trustworthy employment service. I never had to deal with that contemptible little pimp again.

I received a phone call from Yolanda Tall at the Boon Tune. They had a clerical position as a floater and offered me the job. My title was *Part-Time Seasonal on Call Floater*. This was not what I was hoping for, but it was a start. I did not realize it at the time but I would work a week or two, and then it would be months before The Boon Tune would call again.

I called Mrs. Walnut to see if she had any work. She told that she did not have anything temp to perm. I explained to her the arrangement I had with the Boon Tune. Mrs. Walnut thought we could work around my commitment. As it came to pass, I would work for Walnut and if The Boon Tune called I could always give them a start day. This worked out well for sometime. I kept hoping that I would get lucky and the Boon Tune would hire me full time. Yolanda from the Boon Tune called and had a short one week job for me. I would be working in the inventory department. They were receiving the inventory for the Christmas season. I was quick to say "yes, and I can't wait to see you again."

I enjoyed my week at the Boon Tune, entering receiver after receiver. The job was very straightforward. I would be inputting the items the distribution center had received. I would be using the AS400 computer system. I never had a problem with signing into the system. The IT department at the Boon Tune always had me set up and ready to go the minute I sat down. There were three other people in the department and they were thankful for my help. The biggest selling point here was that I only required minimum training. The days flew by and soon the job was over.

Mrs. Walnut called and told me she had as assignment at the Out of Date Plates Human Resource Office in Thomas town. This was a great location for me as it was only three miles from my home. As I was not needed at the Boon Tune, I was grateful for the work.

Out of Date Plates always a good place to work. The employees were very helpful. This time I was working with the Workman's Compensation Claims Handler, Sara. The buyers for the company were also located in the building and they were a fun, energetic group. I was updating the compensation claims into an Access Data Base. During the six weeks I was there, the buyers were also rearranging the display cases.

I had a set of Out of Date Plates called Secret Rose which had been discontinued. During the course of my assignment, I had noticed that there was a complete set of the pattern in one of the display cases. One afternoon a buyer was emptying the displays near my desk. I offered to help her and she gladly accepted my assistance. As we were packing the dishes up, I inquired as to what they were going to do with them. "They are going to the crusher plant." she said. "They were sample runs and are of no use since the pattern is discontinued." I told her I loved the pattern and had a set I was not able to complete. The buyer told me, "If you want them, you can have them." I was flabbergasted, "Can I pay for them?" I asked. "No," she told me. "Just pack them up and put them in your car." I continued to help her get the displays of dishes packed and out the door for the shop to pick up. I put my set in my car. Cool! I completed my assignment at Out of Date Plates. Sadly, they, like so many other companies in Anytown, have scaled back their operations. I will never forget how generous and friendly their employees were to me.

After that, Mrs. Walnut sent me to The Veranda Shoppe for one week in March. Mrs. Walnut would often call me in the morning and ask if I could go to a job immediately. Sometimes she would only give me an hour or two notice. I could usually get out of the house in about an hour and a half. After all, I did not make a habit of sitting around the house in a suit. I always got the job completed in a timely fashion. The Veranda Shoppe was a business that designed kitchens and bathrooms for residential builders and homeowners. This job was for a receptionist and an order entry person. I was not replacing anyone on the job. The woman who did this job had carpal tunnel surgery and could not use the computer keyboard for a week. She sat next to me most of the time and guided me through the order forms. The architects were very snotty, and did not mingle with the woman I was working with or myself. She told me they were full of themselves and to just ignore them like she did.

One of the design orders I entered into the computer that week was for a plaintiff's attorney (i.e. ambulance chaser's) mansion. Mr. Attorney's kitchen was to be forty feet long by twenty feet wide! The counter tops would be made of tangerine (*NOT ORANGE*! I was told by the designing architect) marble from Italy. The appliances that he had ordered were all to be stainless steel. The extras for this kitchen went on and on. The cost for this monstrosity of a kitchen would be over thirty-five thousand dollars! I just could not wrap my mind around such a vulgar display of excess. But that is the way they lived. I enjoyed my week at the assignment. The woman I worked with was down to earth and very amusing.

Without skipping a beat, I was working at the Fritz Company. Fritz had originally been owned by the Ribners family of Anytown. They still had offices on the lower floor of the building, which were staffed by crabby old ladies. I was never informed as to what they did, besides being crabby. This assignment would last six months and it was a temporary to permanent assignment. Fritz was a wholesale grocery store warehouse. I would be working in the warehouse accounting department. This was a good job for me as I had preformed basically the same tasks at AWI.

There were two accountants, Shawn and David. There was also the manager, Mr. Cook and one data entry clerk, Cindy. Cindy was fun to work with and an excellent trainer. She was making a lateral move into the customer service area. I thought this was strange, especially once I got to know the people in the department. They were a dream to work with. I could not understand why she would want to leave the department? Cindy told me she had been working for six years in the accounting department and needed a change.

About five months into this job, I heard rumors that the accounting department would be moving to Mechanicsburg, PA. I also noticed that the two accountants were faxing their resumes and they seemed to have a lot of hushed phone conversations. Mr. Cook eventually called me into his office to offer me the position and confirm the rumored move was true. I had to decline the offer since Mechanicsburg was too far for me to travel. He told me that he too was being replaced by an exact duplicate named Simon. Our new manager would be taking his place the following Monday. That explained a lot of the rumors. I walked over to Cindy's area and asked her if she knew about this move. "Yes, I have known for five months, that is why I took this lateral move." She told me she lived in Wrightsville and there was no way she could travel to Mechanicsburg. I totally understood but wished she had been up front with me. If I had known about the move, I would not have wasted five months at this job.

The new manager, Simon Bennington arrived on Monday and we were introduced to him at a meeting. He was not nearly as nice as Mr. Cook. He approached me about going to work at the new location. I told him I could not drive that far for what I was making an hour. He did not offer me more money and the conversation drifted off into la la land. When Mr. Cook left, he was missed by all of us. Since I had turned down the position, I would have to train the new person. I had no problem with that and Mr. Bennington had indeed hired a very capable gal.

I was at Fritz during football season and I put my dollar in the company football pool just like everyone else. Amazingly I won the final score pool. The payout was two hundred and fifty dollars! Shawn had also won for the half time score. Shawn told me to go to the Ribners department downstairs and collect my winnings. When I approached the lady at the desk, she informed me I could not have the winnings since I was a *temp*. I was not going to argue with her and went back upstairs. When Shawn asked me if I got my money, I told him what had happened. Well, believe me; Shawn took the situation in hand. He grabbed me and said, "We're going back downstairs." When the Ribners ladies saw me coming with Shawn their tune changed. They had to have the last word, "We **never** allow temps to participate in *our* football pools." Shawn said, "Well we do NOW, give her the money she won." The crabby lady forked over my dough with a scowl and we left. During my last week at Fritz I was involved in a dreadful car accident on my way home from work. My totally restored 1973 Ford Maverick was broadsided by a SUV. It had been snowing and the driver of the SUV slid though the stop sign. I suffered a fractured neck and a broken foot. I would spend the remainder of October and November in a halo and a cast. I never got back to Fritz to say goodbye to the first rate people I met there. And of course I left my white office sweater draped over the back of my chair.

I was ready to get back to work when Yolanda Tall from the Boon Tune called me. She informed me that they needed help in the Marketing Department. For two days I updated store employee records for one of the marketing associates. They did not have anywhere for me to sit so I worked in an office with him. I sat facing him and used a laptop. I had to sit sideways as the desk had a solid front on it. It was pretty agonizing after being off with a fractured neck. The

Boon Tune had another area which also needed help. I was sent to the Human Resources department to assist in the process of sending the yearly retirement statements to the retired employees. In addition to the Boon Tune retirees, we were incorporating the retirees from the stores they had bought out. I would be working with a temp, Gloria. We had two weeks to get this project completed but they had not figured out where to put us.

Soon they found one. We would work in a hallway outside of the Human Resources Department. The only lighting was the over head lamps and they were not very bright. They brought in four eight foot by three foot tables and set up our task. All of the labels were pre-printed, and it was just a matter of walking up and down the length of the tables, picking up the information, and stuffing the envelopes. The hallway was cold and drafty. If I had not worked with such a nice lady, it would have been unbearable to me. We were working during the first two weeks of December and The Boon Tune was having a Christmas party for the office employees. Gloria and I could overhear the people in the HR Department calling the catering company and making arrangements for a three piece string ensemble. Boy, this was going to be quite the bash. As we were stuffing our envelopes, we overheard this conversation between Yolanda Tall and another HR employee. HR employee: "Do we have to invite the temps to the Christmas party?" Yolanda Tall: "Of course, why?" HR Employee, disgusted: "Because they eat all our food, they are always hungry!" Yolanda, her tone stern and appalled: "Well, they are to be invited!" Gloria and I looked at each puzzled and shrugged our shoulders. We eat all their food? What was that supposed to mean? Did we look like Ms. Pac-man's?

Gloria and I did go to the Christmas Party. The decorations were beautiful and the food was great. The soft music of the chamber orchestra floated through the dining room as Christmas Carolers drifted from office to office. When it was time for our department to go to the celebration, Gloria and I strolled in and ate our little Pac-man heads off! Wonka-wonka.

We returned to our work station after the lunch party and smiled at each other. We stuffed the last of the envelopes and placed them in the mail bin. Gloria and I said our good-byes and walked to our cars. It was the Christmas Season and I was out of work once more. Happy holidays to all.

I ushered in 1997 yet again out of work and calling around town to the temp agencies again. Mrs. Walnut called me back with an assignment at St. Lemon in Anytown City. The company was a commercial architectural firm. It would start on a Friday and continue for one additional week. The person I was replacing, Jennifer, would only have one day to train me. She was going out of town for her company's yearly trade show. This young woman was the secretary to the President of the company. "Hold up, Hold up," I told Mrs. Walnut, "you know I have never worked in an executive office." "Judy, you can do it. They don't expect a wonder woman," Mr. Lemon is a nice guy." Sure I thought, I just I bet he is. Mrs. Walnut had a way of talking me into situations. I could not say no to her. On Friday I dressed in my best black suit and reported for duty. Upon my arrival at St. Lemon, I walked into a beautifully decorated lobby. I was greeted by a lovely young woman named Jennifer. She took me around and introduced me to *everyone*. I would not see any of these people ever again. I stayed upstairs for the entire week. They had their own lunch room and bathrooms so I never had to go downstairs and mix with the common folk. In the evening I would leave from the executive's rear *private* exit. Bond . . . James Bond.

I met Mr. Lemon and the vice president, Wilson Pratt. Mr. Lemon reminded me of Santa. He was not a fat man and did not have a beard but he seemed very fatherly and had a sparkle in his eye. Jennifer introduced me to Mr. Pratt. He was a different story. He was very tall with angular features. There was a sinister air about him. I was glad I would not have to deal with him during my assignment. Jennifer told me to type and save whatever Mr. Lemon gave me to do. I would sort his mail and answer his phone. She also told me that Mr. Lemon's previous secretary was just down the hall and would help me if I had any problems. I was feeling more relaxed now and knew if in fact this was all that they expected of me, I would do just fine here.

Monday when I got to my desk I had letters to type. I sorted the mail and answered the phone. I had to announce Mr. Lemon's calls, which is something I hate to do. It makes me feel self-conscious. I was typing a spread sheet when Mr. Lemon came to my desk and asked if I had heard from Jennifer. I told him no. I had checked the voice mail and there were no messages. He seemed worried. Around mid morning, Mr. Lemon asked me to call the airport and the hotel to see if she had arrived in Las Vegas. I called the airport and the flight had landed late, there had been a delay in Chicago. I called the hotel but Jennifer had not checked in. When I told Mr. Lemon what I had discovered, he became very worried and visibly upset. Mr. Lemon was very worried that something had happened to Jennifer. He had told me that she had lived her life in Anytown and had gone to Anytown College. He seemed to think she was not capable of taking care of herself. My impression of Jennifer was that she was a very bright self-assured young woman. I did not think he was giving her enough credit.

During all the conversations Mr. Lemon and I were having, the Vice President's door was always open. At one point, Mr. Pratt actually walked out and stood behind my desk. I knew he was listening to Mr. Lemon's frantic conversations with the Convention Center's office. Finally, at two thirty, I heard Mr. Lemon on the speakerphone with Jennifer. He was very upset that she had not called sooner. Actually, she had spoken to Mr. Pratt *before* she left the airport. Whoa . . . . .. silence in Mr. Lemon's office, he got up and shut the door.

When Mr. Lemon came out of his office, he came to my desk and told me that the reason the hotel did not have a record of Jennifer checking in was because she didn't. Since her flight was late getting into Las Vegas, she went directly to the trade show. As there were no phones at the trade show booths, she had no way of calling. This was before *everyone* had cell phones.

Mr. Lemon then strode into Mr. Pratt's office and shut the door. It did not matter that the door was closed, I could hear them shouting. I never found out why Mr. Pratt would be so hateful and purposely upset Mr. Lemon. The week progressed very uneventfully after that. The people were very accommodating and it was a pleasure to assist such a kind man. As I was leaving the parking lot on my last day I thought, 'I guess not all CEO's are ogres and not all vice presidents are knights in shining armor.'

Mrs. Walnut called with another assignment. I was off to Cling Brothers Commercial Insurance Company for the next three months. This was another good assignment from the Walnut Temp Service. This job was part-time about five hours a day. I was helping out the insurance agents. I would type insurance binders and send renewal policies to clients. I was replacing a woman on maternity leave. Thankfully, she never came to visit with her bundle of joy. Or if she did I wasn't there. Baby visits always cause such confusion at the office. This was an easy going pleasant group of people. The gentleman I worked for was a doll. This was another great assignment that sadly came to an end.

Mrs. Walnut was famous for sending me on one day assignments. These were usually tough for me, especially receptionist positions. I would be going to Crackers Packaging to cover for someone who had called in sick. This was a receptionist for a department, not a front desk receptionist. I thought I could handle that. I got to their office at eight A.M. and would be answering the phones for the sales department. The only problem was that none of them would be there. The young woman in charge gave me a phone list, told me they would be back at four and to have a great day. As they all ran out the door, I felt like they had given me a grenade with the pin pulled! I spent the entire day reading a book I had brought. I took messages for the sales staff when the phone occasionally rang. That was about it.

Yolanda Tall called from the Boon Tune with a three day filing job in the visual department. No problem. The visual department was interesting. I was filing advertisement and ad copies. It was pretty straight forward. I did my very best impression of a happy employee. They told Yolanda I did a great job.

Whenever I would work at the Boon Tune, I would always check the bulletin boards for job postings. One day I spied a job posting for a buyer's assistant. The requirements for the position were the standard clerical duties. An associated degree in business administration was not required for the position but would be considered a plus for employment. I did not have an associates degree but I thought, what the heck, why not apply, I had nothing to lose.

To my surprise, Yolanda called me and set up an interview the following week. I was excited about the prospects of getting in the door at the Boon Tune permanently. I had received a call from Mrs. Walnut for an assignment but I could sneak an interview in. When I arrived at the Boon Tune, I was ushered into a small interview room where I anxiously waited. The woman I was interviewing with was the Better Dresses Buyer. The buyer came in to the interview room and introduced herself. She seemed very rushed and rapidly went over the duties. I did not get a warm and fuzzy feeling about our meeting. Her demeanor was very abrupt and stern. She thanked me for my time and *dismissed* me from the room. I walked out the door knowing I had no chance of being hired for the position. I had tried my best.

As soon as I finished the job at the Boon Tune, Mrs. Walnut called me with a four day filing assignment at PRN Company, a.k.a PMS Company. This was a medical office and all I did was file patients charts. I replaced a woman who was on vacation. As quickly as I filed the charts, the harried nurses would pull more, and I would file more. I never got ahead of the piles and piles of charts. But at least it was open shelf filing, which was always a plus. The employees at PRN were not at all friendly. I truly felt like wall paper at this assignment. I spent my lunch hours reading in my car. It was a lonely experience. I had to start keeping a day book at this stage. I was getting confused as to where I was going and where I had been. One morning I drove half way to the Boon Tune before I realized I was going to the wrong company.

It got a little crazy that spring.

Next I went to Berry Advertising for Walnut Temp Service. This was a three day assignment and I replaced the receptionist. To this day I have absolutely no recollection of this job. But since I have it on my list of jobs, I must have been there. I found a reference to this company on the Internet. Bill R submitted a review which said, "Run by the pushiest, most obnoxious tool I have ever met. Shoulda' been a lawyer." I am glad I don't remember that place!

During the summer of 1997 I was back at the Boon Tune. I worked for a Junior Clothing Buyer. Melissa was in her mid twenties and had worked for the Hess department stores. When the Boon Tune bought out the Hess stores, Melissa transferred to the Anytown corporate offices.

Melissa had hired an assistant but she would not be able to start until August. Her assistant had graduated from college in June but was traveling in Europe for the summer. I found it interesting that I was good enough to fill in on a job that required a college degree but I was not good enough to be hired for the job permanently. I only had a B.S. Degree.

Melissa taught me what I needed to know and supplied me with my *temp disk*. This would be my temp Swiss army knife. I would have all the Microsoft Word and Excel document templates on it that the Boon Tune required for data entry. Since I would often not sit at the same desk everyday, I would need to carry it around with me.

I learned to do Melisa's travel planning for her monthly trips to New York City. I processed the mark downs and entered the new styles she would order. Melissa was a pleasure to work for; she was even tempered and friendly. I was at the Boon Tune during a busy season and they were buying for the fall retail season. There were about thirty buyers in the department and it became hectic at times.

Not all the buyers were as nice as Melissa. I became friendly with a young girl, Shannon, who worked for the Better Dress Buyer. I knew of this buyer because I had interviewed with her once. I thought she was pushy and snippy. Needless to say she did not choose me when I had interviewed for the position. The person she had hired no longer worked for her. Her assistant had requested a transfer. The girl I was friendly with, Shannon, was very young and easily pushed around. I would meet up with Shannon at the copier or fax machine throughout the day. Shannon was very unhappy working for this buyer, sometimes she would be in tears. Shannon told me her buyer was hateful towards her and would yell at her for the most minor of errors. I told her to go to the Human Resources Department and see if they could help her out of her dilemma.

The months passed and Melissa's assistant returned from her vacation. I was now sent to assist the China and Silver Buyer. This buyer's assistant was on maternity leave. I really enjoyed this department. All the items were beautiful. The buyer was laid back and the atmosphere more relaxed. I would still see Shannon around the department and sometimes we would go to Annie Ann's Pretzels for a snack. Shannon was still stressed out working for the Better Dresses Buyer. She had gone to human resources and requested a transfer. One afternoon Shannon stopped by my cubicle and excitedly told me that she had been transferred to the Foundations Buyers. I knew these ladies and they were so sweet. I was really glad for Shannon.

I was on the last leg of my assignment with the China Buyer and things were winding down. On my last day as I was walking out the door, (with my white office sweater over my arm) Yolanda Tall came running up to me. "Hi Judy, I need your help for another buyer." she told me. "O.K.! Who and when?" I asked with a smile. Yolanda then told me."The Better Dress' Buyers assistant was transferred and we need someone to fill in until we can hire someone." I was thinking to myself, no way in hell, and she added, "no one has entered Purchase Orders for two weeks!" My smile had faded.

I told Yolanda "I'm sorry but I can't work for her." She asked "why not?" I said, "Yolanda you know why." "No I don't, you tell me why?" I replied, "look, Yolanda, you know what the problem with that buyer is, and if you don't I am not going to tell you. I simply cannot work for her." With that Yolanda said," then we will not have any more need of your assistance." She turned on her heels and walked away. On my way out the door, I tossed my temp disk in the first trashcan I passed. That was the last time I ever worked for the Boon Tune. In retrospect, I should have gone to Yolanda's boss and pleaded my case. I doubt it would have made much difference. I have always believed the Boon Tune was a good place to work. Unfortunately Yolanda was a poor representative of their company.

I called Mrs. Walnut and let her know I was available again. I did not mention the Boon Tune situation. She sent me back to Anytown International this time to work in the Engineering Department. The assignment would be for three weeks.

I would be assisting the Engineering Department's secretary with a special project. I would learn to read compressor drawings and file them. The boss of the department was a super guy. There were about eight other engineers and I helped them out with whatever they needed done. I would learn the importance for keeping a daily log. Everyone at Anytown International kept a daily work log. They would note phone conversations, issues they had with other departments, customer calls and so on. The secretary I helped out impressed upon me the need to C.Y.A. I completed the assignment and wished I could have continued working there.

The following Monday morning Mrs. Walnut called me at seven and asked if I could get to the ARC of Anytown by eight thirty I said, "of course I can, no problem." She said it would only be for the week. I would be replacing the receptionist who had been in a car accident over the weekend. I got dressed and flew out the door. The ARC is a non—profit organization. They advocate for people with intellectual and other disabilities. Non-Profit organizations are always great places to work. They use a lot of volunteers and are well prepared for people who are not familiar with the jobs they are asked to do. The woman who met me at the door was happy and grateful that I could make it on such short notice. She took me to the receptionist's area and gave me a quick rundown on the company and what to expect. When I told her I had worked at Shadowfax, she breathed a sign of relief. She knew I would not feel uncomfortable with the people who would be coming in and out during the day. She also gave me a complete up to date phone list in alphabetical order by *last* name, how refreshing!

The ARC had a small staff of personnel in the building. I did not have a lot of calls, and the woman supervising me gave me some quick and easy tasks throughout the week to keep me busy. One day I updated an Excel spread sheet for her. She had told me to deliver it to the C.F.O down the hall when I completed it. I strolled down the corridors and found the gentleman's office, the plaque on the door said. "Simon Bennington, C.F.O."

I could not believe it. The exact duplicate accountant from Fritz was now a big wig. I peeked around the door and said, "Hi there, remember me?" Mr. Bennington looked up and said, "You look familiar, do I know you?" I refreshed his memory and he appeared to remember, but I think I embarrassed him. He sheepishly told me, 'oh yes, how you are doing?" That was about the extent of my dealings with Mr. Bennington. He made himself scarce for the remainder of the week. After that, when I had work to return to him, I just placed it in his mail box down the hall.

Mrs. Walnut next sent me to Stepping Stone Counseling. I would be replacing someone who was on vacation. This assignment was another one week position. This company offers substance abuse treatment. I would be helping out in the filing room and processing drug testing forms.

The people I worked with there were upbeat and caring. The environment was laid back and congenial. The employees at Stepping Stone were a pleasure to work with. I personally would not have chosen to work in this field. I found checking urine samples repulsive. But it was a tolerable for a temp assignment.

After a week with no work, Mrs. Walnut called me with an assignment at Anytown International's Granite Road facility for three weeks. I would be replacing a person on surgery leave. Since I had done so well at St. Lemon, she felt I could work for the Vice President of Human Resources. The Human Recourses Departments were split at Anytown International. The Human Resources department at the Granite Road plant was the location for the manufacturing division's union employees.

I arrived all bright eyed and bushy tailed as I liked working at Anytown International. They had large parking lots for easy parking and a lunch truck that came twice a day (this truck was referred to as the *Slop Truck*). I arrived at the assigned plant door and was escorted to the department by a guard. I would have to get a badge to work at the Granite facility. After I had my picture taken, I was met by one of the human resources representatives I would work with. Barbara was a lady of color who had worked her way up a very steep ladder of success. She was the second in command at the Human Resources office. Barbara was very nice and would be conducting my training.

I would be updating and calling employees who had been laid off. Anytown International had gotten some large contracts and they were recalling welders and machine operators. I would also be assisting the Vice President, Chester Muffard, with his correspondence, answering his phone and sorting his mail.

Barbara took me to my desk and got me settled in. There was a glassed in office directly across from my desk which was Mr. Muffard's office. Barbara told me he was often in meetings with union representatives, and that he was not in the office much. She also said that when he would have people in his office, it might get heated and *loud*. After lunch, Mr. Muffard came into the office and introduced himself to me and he seemed very polite. He was a tall man and had a rough demeanor. I got started on the work Barbara gave to me. Shortly thereafter, Mr. Muffard buzzed my phone and asked me to come to his office. I got up and rapidly went to his office. He asked my why I did not have a steno pad with me. I told him I did not know I would need one as I did not take shorthand. Mr. Muffard then told me, "When I buzz you always bring something to write on. I am going to be giving you five or six directives at a time. Do you think you can remember all I will be telling you?" "No, I am sure I would not be able to remember." I replied, I felt like a jerk. Mr. Muffard continued, "no problem, lets start over." I trotted back to my desk, got a steno pad, and never ever went into his office unprepared again.

I met some other temps who were working there at lunch time. Everyone was trying to make a great impression in the hopes of getting hired full time. One of the male temps, Jay, told me at lunch one day that temps could only work for thirty days at a clip. He went on to explain that the clerical employees were also unionized. The clerical union had made rules that would protect them from the company hiring temps at lower pay rates. Jay also told me to keep an eye out for "Creepy Charlie" from the clerical union. Jay told me that Creepy Charlie was always slinking around spying on the temps and checking assignment start dates. He reported temps that had stayed on past their thirty days. I asked Jay, "what if your assignment is not complete?" Jay said, "You only have to be gone one day and then you can come back." All this sounded pretty stupid to me. Jay pointed out Creepy Charlie to me one morning at break when we were outside at the Slop Truck. Yes, he was creepy and slimy looking. I would discover that the women working in the office with me did not care for Mr. Muffard. They said he was a foul mouth sexist. When Mr. Muffard was in the office, everyone made themselves scarce.

Mr. Muffard would have people from the shop for meetings in his office and it would get loud and foul. This was a part of dealing with some of the people from the shop. I was outside of his office I just ignored it, after all I had worked at McCoy's.

During my second week on this assignment, Mr. Muffard buzzed me and I picked up my steno book and went into his office. He was giving me instructions and I was feverishly writing them down. As I glanced up and made eye contact with him, I noticed he was rubbing his crotch with a pencil while he was talking. He was looking me dead in the eye, stroking himself and smiling.

This, I also totally ignored. As I went back to my desk, I thought how disgusting this was. Every time I went into his office, he would get out his pencil. I would cringe when he would buzz me on the intercom. I mentioned this pencil habit to Barbara. "Oh yeah, he does that, he is a pig." she continued. "He won't be around here for long, so don't get upset." she added with a little secret laugh, "I will protect you."

On the third week of my assignment I did not see Mr. Muffard at all. His office had been cleared out over the weekend. Everyone in the department was smiling and seemed much happier. Barbara was *really* happy. I never learned what had become of Mr. Muffard. I was just glad I did not have to deal with him for the rest of my assignment. To his credit to this day I always have a pad and a pen handy just in case I need to write something down.

Mrs. Walnut called me and told me Anytown International had requested me for a one week assignment. This would also finish out my allowed thirty days according to the union's contract. I went back to the corporate building and assisted the UPG Division entering purchase orders. They were also busy in their department due to the new contracts. I finished up the week working in a very pleasant department. I kept my eyes peeled for Creepy Charlie.

When Mrs. Walnut called me she had two assignments for me. First I would be going to the Anytown Newspaper Company for two weeks to cover for another vacationing person. After that, I would be going back to Anytown International. She also told me to drop the Mrs. and just call her Janet. The HR department at Anytown International had requested me. Janet sounded thrilled and told me they were extremely pleased with my performance. For now, I would be going to the Anytown Newspaper Company. The position at the Newspaper Company was assisting an advertising marketing person. I had never been inside a newspaper company. I wondered if it would be like it was in those old 1950 movies, with cub reporters and crabby Head Editors yelling, "Stop the presses, Stop the presses!" but it wasn't at all like that. It was a normal, boring, large office.

I met the woman I would be helping. She was very bouncy and full of smiles. She handled the advertisements for the Home Realty Section of the paper. I would assist her with getting her ads ready for the press room. She told me her name was Casey and she would be in and out of the office. She liked the manner in which I took charge of the job and the fact that I was so well organized. She told me I was anal retentive, "but I love it," she added. I proof read her advertisements and opened the mail. I would get her ads and photos for the CD ROMs assembled for publishing. I would take them to the drop off area for the typesetters. The job was fast paced but not difficult. When the assignment ended, Casey told me she would miss me. She told me her regular cleric was not nearly as efficient or pleasant.

The other employees at the newspaper were very pleasant also. They always had a smile and a good morning for me everyday. Before anyone came up to my desk to give me work, they always greeted me first. They did not start by giving me orders. They were an excellent group of people to work for. This was another assignment I would have liked to have gone full time. The only down side was that I did not get to meet Mike Argento.

When the assignment ended at the Anytown Newspaper, I went back to Anytown International for a four week gig in the Treasury Department. This was in the corporate headquarters again but this time on the top floor. I would be working on the executive story. I was apprehensive about working in the Ivory Tower, as it was called, but I should have known better. The people in the Department were very straightforward and down to earth. When I arrived the first day, I met the woman who would be my immediate boss, Winifred, the lady who was training me, Carolyn, and the Boss, Mr. Blackstone. The first thing Mr. Blackstone told me was to call him Eric. This was an excellent sign. This was another case where I was replacing someone who had been hired but could not start right away. Carolyn got me settled in and began my training. She was leaving in two days to start her new job with the School District. Carolyn had been a teacher and had left the field for a few years. She was now returning for the next semester. We had to cover a lot of ground in the next two days.

My main duties were reconciling expense reports for the executives and the personnel in the Treasury Department. I helped Winifred with inventory reports and assembled weekly cost accounting reports for Eric. This was not very different from other jobs I had done. The biggest difference was that the figures on the spread sheets had more commas than I was used to seeing. I was not accustomed to seeing such high dollar expenditures on the expense reports I audited either.

When I questioned Eric about the validity of certain line items he told me, "I understand where you are coming from. Just highlight anything you think is unusual." He added, "I will authorize them and return them to you." This system worked out great and I never felt ill at ease approving the items for payment. I remember one expense report in particular that I highlighted. The item in question was a lunch receipt from a restaurant in Hong Kong for $1,000.00 for four people. I thought that it was a lot of money for lunch. Eric reminded me, "That is the *wooing* cost of doing business. Everyone here at Anytown International is equal, but some people are more equal than others." I got the picture.

I would occasionally have to go to the other side of the floor where the President and Vice President of the company had their offices. Usually I would be hand delivering expense or payroll checks so everyone was glad to see me.

The secretaries were very nice and always accommodating. I never got a peek at the President because his door was always shut.

However, I did see the Vice President, Mr. Wipple, every day in the designated smoking area. He was very arrogant and would act as if he was on his cell phone when he would see us coming out the door on break. He would move away from us like we had a disease or something. Well, we did, it is called middle class. Sometimes the ladies and I would walk around the patio area just to keep him on the move. We would move, he would move, we moved, he moved. It was very silly of us, but we could not help ourselves, it was so amusing.

The girl I was filling in for, Ginny finally showed up and we began her training. The job required an Associates Degree in accounting, which I did not have. I was only doing about 40 percent of the job; Winifred had been picking up the rest of the slack. Ginny was young and newly graduated from college. She was an entertaining girl to be around. I wish I had not lost contact with her. We enjoyed amusing lunches and herding Mr. Wipple around the patio courtyard on smoke breaks.

Winifred, Eric and all the employees of the Treasury Department were a fine group of professionals to have known. I will always remember how patient Winifred was during my training. She was a war bride from England and I loved to hear her speak the King's English. Anytown International is another casualty in the war of corporate buy outs. They are now owned by Johnstown Controls, and I suspect all the people there I knew are now scattered to the winds. Now it was time to move on once again.

Mrs. Walnut had another short assignment for me. This time I would be going to BH Labs. This was a water testing lab that provided services for commercial and residential customers. BH Labs was a very small company. There were only five people employed there, but they were very busy. I was filling in for the receptionist. The young women I worked with were helpful and pleasant. Actually this was a very boring job. I was instructed to bring in a book to read between phone calls. They did test the water from my home for free and it passed their regulated standards.

The next adventure Mrs. Walnut sent me on was to the VNA for three weeks. This position had some odd hours. There would be three temps, also from Walnut, and we would work from five to ten P.M. Mrs. Walnut told me that The VNA provided in home care to people in need of medical and in-home assistance.

We arrived at the VNA ready to burn up the keyboards, only to be told we would be training as a group. The woman training us was from India and she spoke perfect English. She told us that VNA nurses filled out eighteen page reports during their home visits. The reports were then to be fed into the company's data base. The VNA was in the process of giving the nurses laptops so that the reports could be done at the patients homes. The nurses were *not* happy about this change. For reasons unbeknown to me, they were extremely behind in the department which filed these reports. The reason we were working at night was that the VNA did not have enough computers for us to assist them during the day. We would only be able to input three to four home visit reports a night. I had no experience in medical terminology and neither did the other two temps I was working with. Our trainer had been a teacher in India and could not get her teaching certificate in the United States (she did not tell us the reason for this). She was an awesome teacher. We asked hundreds of questions and she was never annoyed or condescending.

The gentleman running the show at the VNA also stayed in the building each night until we left. He made sure we went on breaks in groups of twos. He did not want us outside alone since the building was located downtown. When we left at the end of our shift he walked us to our cars. The other temps and I enjoyed being at a company that valued their employees well being and safety.

We managed to get the VNA totally caught up and they told the agency what a great job we did. The nurses were given their updated laptops and we went on our merry way.

My next assignment from the Walnut Agency would be the last time I would work for them. Janet called me with a position at the Community Transit Authority. This company was the city bus transportation system. I would be inputting payroll and I would have a trainer for two weeks. This would be a three month assignment to cover for an employee on pregnancy leave. She told me the learning curve was long on this assignment, as it was a union payroll. Up until this time, the only experience I had with payroll was strictly adding up time cards and inputting the hours. I did not have experience with payroll taxes or tax forms.

When I got to the Transit Authorities offices, I was greeted by a very pregnant young woman. After the grand tour, we got down to work. By the end of the first day on the job, I was totally overwhelmed with the magnitude of the position. The drivers got on and off buses, one driver could have ten time cards for a pay period. This information was inputted into a huge spreadsheet. I was told that I could not make one mistake. She also told me that I would be totally on my own with no supervisor. No one in the company knew how to do her job. If I did make an error computing a driver's payroll, the union would file a grievance against the company. I wasn't sure what this meant but I was pretty sure it wasn't good.

The more the day went on, the more I knew I did not have the background for this job. By Tuesday morning I was convinced I was in over my head. I told the lady training me I was very confused and did not have any experience with payroll taxes. She seemed very surprised and worried. She told me she only had two weeks to train the person taking over her job. She also was puzzled that since I had a degree in accounting, why would I not know how to do payroll taxes. I told her I did not have an accounting degree, and I had never been to college. She told me, "We have to go see the boss."

I told her I needed to call the agency first and update them regarding the difficulties I had encountered. She replied, "No problem, I am going to go talk to my boss, and then you can join us after you make your call."

When I called the Walnut Agency and spoke to Janet, she said, "You have two weeks to learn the job, don't sell yourself short. You can pull it off." she told me. "Janet, I would need to go to college for four years before I could pull this one off!" I could tell by the tone in Janet's voice that she was not happy. She told me to speak with the boss of the Transit Authority before I made any decisions about leaving the assignment. I hung up the phone and slowly walked down the hall to the boss's office.

When I got to the bosses' office, the woman training me was already there. She introduced me to the director of the Transit Authority, Margie Thompson. The boss lady got up and shook my hand and said to me, "how nice to meet you. Have a seat and tell me about yourself." I proceeded to explain to her what I had told the sweet young lady who was training me. "Well," responded Ms. Thompson, "when I called the Walnut Agency I requested a Junior Accountant." I told her, "I don't know anything about that; all I know is that I am NOT a junior accountant." Ms. Thompson was very nice to me and told me not to concern myself. She was very happy that I had informed her of this and not two weeks later. She also said she would call the Agency and get this situation straightened out. Ms. Thompson signed my time card and said how sorry they were about the confusion.

When I drove out of the parking lot, I was very irritated that the Walnut agency had put me in this position. I decided to go to the agency and drop off my time card rather than mail it in like I usually did. I wanted to talk to Janet and clear up any misunderstanding. When I got to the office, I was told by the little Walnut pimp that Janet was unavailable. All of a sudden there was a noticeable chill in the air. I left my time card and asked the pimp to please have Janet call me. She never called. I would call periodically but I would never be able to speak with her. The pimps would only put me into her voice mail. After a time, I just stopped calling.

I heard through the temp grape vine that Walnut lost the Transit Authority contact and apparently I was the blame. I was livid about this turn of events. All the years I had worked there I had made them tons of money, and now because "I could not pull it off, I was the bad guy? What happened to all the praise and goodwill I had created on jobs for them? What always infuriated me was that the owner would not speak to me and take the responsibility for this failure.

Needless to say I never heard from Mrs. Walnut; just call me Janet, again. The Walnut Agency went out of business not long after my last assignment with them. Possibly, they sent out too many temps on jobs with the instruction "you can pull it off."

Anytown is not a big city but there are lots of temp agencies. There was a new temp agency on the circus roster, The Coconut Personnel Service. I called them and made an appointment for an interview. As another Christmas season began, I found myself out of work once again.

CHAPTER 11

I did not know whether to turn left or right, but it did not much matter.

When I arrived for my interview at Coconut Personnel, I was impressed with the layout. Their offices were in a large building with other businesses. The workplace was newly decorated in a contemporary low key style. There was a lot of gray and silver. The receptionist was very professional. She set me up on a computer to fill out my application and proceeded with the testing. I did amazingly well on all the Microsoft programs. I was surprised since I usually don't test well.

While I was waiting, I scanned the area. There where two pimps in the front of the office, and a rear office which had a sign stating Industrial Division. I thought that rather silly, since the office was so small. The receptionist was very busy directing calls and taking messages. I could overhear her verifying a tee time at a golf course. The two pimps in the front office were more mature people than I usually saw at temp agencies. There was a rather hefty gal whose name I would learn was Carla. The other pimp was a young man named Mark. He was also a marketing executive, which is a fancy term for a salesman. I could see there was an older man and a younger woman working in the Industrial Division office. After a momentary wait in the testing/interview room, the owner came in and introduced herself.

The Owner, Annabel Coco, was all business but very welcoming. She reminded me of Katie Couric from the Today Show. She had that cutesy thing going for her. The reason I had originally called this agency was because they were running advertisements in the Anytown Newspaper. I had seen a position for an administrative assistant. I had applied for it on the application. When Mrs. Coco asked what I was searching for in a job, I told her the one I applied for when I filled out the application. Duh? Mrs. Coco informed me, "oh no, we filled that position but I have other positions available. I am sure you would be a perfect fit for one at M.A.E." "Oh no, please not M.A.E." I could not help remembering the pinched nosed old bitty who was the accounts payable supervisor and how she would stare at me. I kept my misgivings and the fact that I had worked there previously to myself. I had now been a victim of the *old bait and switch* in job advertising. This is a common practice at every temp agency I had ever worked for. I never seemed to be able to get to the agency before that excellent advertised job (which never existed in the first place) had been filled. We shook hands and Mrs. Coco thanked me for my time and told me my *coordinator*, i.e. little pimp, would be in touch as soon as they had verified my references, and completed a background check. She stuffed a handbook about her company and a time card in my hand and hurriedly ushered me out the door. I guess I was cutting into her tee time.

I received a phone call from Carla, my pimp, at Coconut Personal a few days later. Carla told me that she would be my *coordinator* and that they had a position at M.A.E. This was a two month assignment in the Human Resources Department updating employee records in an Access Database. I had never worked in this department before at M.A.E. I accepted the assignment. When I arrived, I was directed to a guard shack. After countless phone calls between the guard and whoever was in charge of this project (was it the wizard behind the curtain?), I was given a *temp* badge. This badge would stigmatize me for my entire assignment. The guard aimed me towards a trailer with a sign that read Human Resources Dept. I was finally at the right place and it only took one hour.

I was greeted by a very polite woman. We did the introduction dance and the blow by blow tour. By ten, I was finally seated at a desk and given a gigantic stack of employee personal files with updates to be inputted in an Access Data Base. This was a very straight forward job. The employees would fill out address changes, marital status changes, add, or remove dependents and department changes. There were also raises that had to be documented along with write ups. I noticed during my stay that there were many more raises given to employees than write ups. I filed the folders after I had finished the necessary updates. All and all this assignment was enjoyable. The people were very nice and always had time for questions. When I had down time, the gal I worked with usually would find little jobs no one else wanted to do.

Every where I went, either in the department or to the cafeteria, everyone always knew I was **the temp**. The temp badge pretty much kept anyone from bothering me. When the job was completed, M.A.E told Coconut Personnel what a terrific job I had done and that if they need a temp again they would request me. Three cheers for me!

After the position at M.A.E was completed, Coconut Personnel placed me at U.S.A. Nonstop. I had heard from friends that U.S.A. Nonstop had a reputation for not being a pleasant or decent place to work. I was told the people who worked there were very cliquish and that the president of the company was a little Napoleon. But since the assignment was not a temp to permanent one, I did not think it much mattered. U.S.A. is a direct mail and commercial printing company. I would be working in the accounting department. Everything I had heard about this company was true with the exception of the woman I worked with directly, Helen. Helen was in charge of the accounts payables and the printing of the checks. She had an enormous amount of work to do, so the company had gotten her a temp. What I did not know, at the time, was that the temp who had done this job before me had walked out. Helen was very nice but always seemed overwhelmed.

I matched purchase orders to invoices which I then posted for payment. I also inputted and tracked the postage accounts for the customers on a spread sheet. The computer system was an ancient MAS 90 DOS system. They were also using Lotus123, when every company I had been to was using Excel. The owner of this company was a short, sullen, surly man who walked through the halls glaring into the offices and scowling at people. If anyone used the microwave to cook fish, he went off the deep end. He would scream and bellow about the odor wafting into his office. I thought it was very amusing. While I was listening to his ranting one day, I had one of my evil little thoughts. I was thinking, "wouldn't it be fun to bring fresh dog poop in a baggy and stick it in the microwave on high for five minutes, and just leave the building." It was only a passing thought.

In addition to Helen, there were two Junior Accountants, a Senior Accountant, and the Accounts Payables Manager in the department. The two Junior Accountants were young and thought they were God's gift to the accounting planet. The Senior Accountant was an elderly man who never left his office. I did not have any interaction with the manager so I had no opinion of him at all. For two months, I struggled along helping Helen as best I could and looking forward with great anticipation for this job to come to a conclusion. No one ever invited me to join them for lunch or to go on break. This was another lonely existence on a temp job. I was always like that white sweater, left draped, alone, over the chair.

The manager asked me to come into his office one afternoon. He coyly let me know the job was available to me if I would be interested. He never came right out and presented the job to me. He did tell me the pay rate would be two dollars an hour *less* than I was making as a temp working there. Mr. Manager told me they were happy with my performance. When I told him I was not interested in working there, he seemed a bit taken back. At that point he told me he had a lot of work to get done and I should leave his office. I presume he must have called Coconut Personnel. When I returned home from work, there was a message for me to call Carla on my answering machine. I returned her call the next morning from my desk at U.S.A. I told her I did not want to work there. It was a cheap, nasty place to work. She said, "That's fine, I understand, we have had trouble keeping temps there. I will find you something else. Just finish out the week until I can find a replacement for you."

When I was taken off the U.S.A. Nonstop job, I was given the temp *punishment*. Coconut Personnel did not have anything for me to fit perfectly into. I was on my own now. I had been put out to sea without a life raft. When I heard that U.S.A Nonstop was acquired by a company called SITERV Communications, I wondered if the little man was still strutting up and down the corridors and peering into the offices.

Jeff came home one night and told me the company where he was employed, Shipley Energy, had a temporary job opening. They needed someone for three months to help out in the Bulk Fuel Department. I called and made an appointment to apply for the position even if it was only temporary. I went to their office the following day, and to my surprise they hired me on the spot. I met everyone in the Bulk fuel Department, John Rotsa who was a salesman, Dave Wilson, the Vice-President, Lori, who I would work with, and Mr. Shipley's secretary, Barbara. I would occasionally see Mr. Shipley. I never had the opportunity to speak with him. There were also two fuel buyers, but I had little to no interaction with them. The only time I ever spoke to either of them was on the dock during a smoke break.

Lori had been out on maternity leave for three months and apparently no one had kept her work up to date. I assisted her as best I could. The job was extremely difficult and confusing. She would give me the billing for the inter company bulk fuel plants. I would also post the fuel that was purchased from the pipeline. This was a very difficult job. I did not do as good a job as I would have wished.

At one point the Vice President, Dave, had Lori show him what her job entailed. He was sure he could develop an easier, less complicated manner in which to process the billing procedures. Dave was always gracious to me and he had a "Good Morning" smile for everyone he met. All the employees in the Bulk Fuel division were a pleasure to have known. Lori was a doll and had infinite patience. Bob was a delight to know, I think he felt sorry that I was having such a tough time with the job. Mr. Shipley's secretary, Barbara, was pleasant and helpful. I was glad I had the opportunity to work at my husband's place of employment. It is not often you can get an inside look at what your spouse does for a living. On my last day, everyone was cheerful and Lori thanked me for trying so hard. As I pulled up in my driveway I realized, "Darn if I hadn't left my office sweater over the back of my chair." It was a Friday night and I had been anxious to get home. Jeff brought my sweater home. He just *knew* I would leave it behind again.

I continued to scope out the newspaper ads for a job. One day I saw a job advertisement that Shadowfax was running. The position was for a computer coach. I went to their office and applied. I had a slight advantage as I had worked for them before. It must have paid off as they rehired me for the job.

One of the jobs in the sheltered work shop concerned scanning time cards for large companies. The time cards were scanned then a back up disk was burned. The disk was sent to the company and the original time cards were shipped to a storage faculty. This was the job I would be teaching. Shadowfax had received grants to re-educate people coming off the welfare rolls. I did not know at the time that the job hinged on grant money. I worked with the selected recipients of the education program. I would teach them the basis of computer operation and software programs. I thoroughly enjoyed working with the women I had in my class.

After four months, the program was discontinued as the funding had dried up. I was sent to the main building to assist in the reception area and to process payroll for the sheltered workshop. I was very distressed by this turn of events. I went to Shadowfax to specifically work with people with intellectual or physical challenges. I did not like working in the reception area, and I did not like working downstairs in the accounting department. I had nothing negative to say about anyone at the main office, I just did not want to work there in that capacity. I had been employed for about six months when I received a call from Coconut Personnel. Mrs. Coco called me with a proposition. There had been a power outage in East Anytown and the entire grid had gone down. Consequently they had lost over two thousand of their applicant's information in their computer system. For some reason, the backup for their system had failed. Mrs. Coco asked if I would be interested in helping her receptionist, Tory, re-enter the missing information. I had never had the opportunity to work inside a temp agency (this was novel). I told her I would *love* to help them. We agreed on a wage and I reported to her office the next week.

I was given a small office in which to work. It had been an office of a coordinator that was no longer with the company. I heard scuttlebutt to the effect that she had sabotaged their computer system. From my vantage point, I could overhear both Carla and Mark calling temps to fill jobs. They would also make appointments with prospective clients and were often out of the office.

The receptionist, Tory, and I would pull handfuls of hard copy applications and re-enter them into the computer system. Coconut used an aged DOS based system and the monitors were a nasty blue color. The applicant's data was input on two screens. The first had the applicant's personal information. The second screen was all the resume information. When the system had failed due to the power outage, only the second screens had been wiped out. We were only fixing the second screens. The only problem was that it was all free form typing. Some of the resumes were professional applicants who went on and on describing their accolades. They were just wonderful.

While I was inputting the information, I could not help but overhear the conversations between Mrs. Coco and the pimps. One day I overheard a conversation between Mrs. Coco and John, the man who operated the industrial division. They were discussing an upcoming contact which they were hoping to secure. If they got this contact, they would need to hire a fairly large number of people. They decided to run a help wanted advertisement in the local paper. Now mind you they did not have this contact as of yet. I discovered the agency was running ads for jobs that did not exist. The pimps did this not only in the industrial division but in the clerical division as well. The point of this was to get people in the office filling out applications so the pimps could justify their own jobs. They were busy all day interviewing, testing and giving people who sincerely wanted to work, false hope. "So," I thought, "that's how it works." What a bunch of crap.

I did not have much contact with John. He was an extremely nice man, very polite. He was always joking around. The young lady working with him was named Maggie. She was pleasant and was *always* on the phone. John had a sign in his office that read, "Companies Lie, Temps Lie, Only Agencies Tell the Truth." Boy, what a crock!

For some stupid reason, I felt very humbled and special due to Mrs. Coco inviting me to work in her company. Looking back I am sure it was only to see what my work ethics were. I was very eager to impress her and my big pimp. I would readily jump to assist them with any little thing. I would ask, "MAY I get that for you? MAY I copy that for you?" or "You stay where you are, I can do it!" I was beyond a doubt a disgusting suck up.

Tory and I labored for two months updating the data base. When it was completed, Mrs. Coco was very pleased with the speed in which we had accomplished so much work. My main focus at this point had been to obtain a full time job at Coconut Personnel. All of my showing off had only gotten me another temp assignment. Mrs. Coco asked me if I would be interested in a short term job at a friend's business. Of course I said yes. My mission for Mrs. Coco would be at a company called Ultimate Systems. Mrs. Coco made it a point to tell me she had gone to high school with Tom Foltz, the man who ran this company. She said he was an important client as she also placed industrial temps at his company. Ultimate Systems was a powder coating facility. There was also another division called Foltz Textures which was run by his father. "Oh happy, happy, joy, joy, "I thought, "Another family run business, I can't wait." There was not a clear-cut end date for this assignment. I would be updating a customer data base in Access. The job would come to a conclusion when I got it completed. As it turned out, I would end up being there for two months.

When I arrived at Ultimate Systems, I was met by Tom Foltz. He took me on the grand tour and introduced me to René, the Customer Service Representative. There was also a salesman who was in and out of the office. I don't recall his name but he was always smiling and laughed a lot.

Rene' got me started with a gigantic green bar paper printout of their customer listing. I would call each customer and verify if they were still in business. Originally the listing had two thousand entries. By the time I had finished calling and updating the Access data base only two hundred-fifty were viable companies. During my stay at Ultimate Systems, I experienced the one week "every one on their best behavior" syndrome. Rene was always pleasant and helpful, but she did a lot of shopping on the Internet. Rene was the only CSR in the department and there were two empty cubicles. I thought they may have been short staffed in the department. Tom was a bird of a different color.

Tom was decidedly feminine in his appearance and mannerisms. He had a mean streak that would surface at the slightest provocation. On more than one occasion he was very short with me. I just tried to stay out of his way. No one ever asked me or included me in lunch runs. I was the invisible temp. Basically no one ever spoke to me except for Tom. When he did talk to me he made snippy remarks if he thought I was not *slaving* away (but it was OK for Rene' to be on the Internet shopping all afternoon). I did not miss going back there once the assignment was concluded. There is an old proverb which says, 'Fish and guests smell after three days.' No argument here.

Mrs. Coco called me and said she had a short five day assignment at St. Lemon Design in East Anytown. I would be working with another temp from Coconut Personal. We would be inputting data for the design engineering department. I was curious about the company since as far as I knew St. Lemon was in downtown Anytown. Mrs. Coco explained the owners of the company had parted ways. Mr. Lemon had started his own company in East Anytown. Apparently Mr. Lemon had parted ways with Mr. Pratt over the direction in which he wished the company to go in the future. The fact that he had kept part of the name of the original company must have caused some confusion within the industry.

I arrived at St. Lemon Design and joined the other temp from Coconut Personnel. As we waited, we surveyed the impressive lobby. The building was contemporary, with large living potted trees throughout the room. The sun poured though the vaulted glass ceilings. It was considerably more attractive than the St. Lemon offices downtown. There was one tree I thought might be a Jade plant. The plant was so large I had to ask the receptionist what is was. She told it was in fact a Jade Plant. I had never seen one that was five feet tall with a stem at least eight inches around. The tree was covered with pale pink blooms which were the size of roses. She told me with a smile, "that Jade has

been in Mr. Lemon's family for over fifty years. Everything grows big in here."
I was sure it did.

The other temp and I were set up on two computers in a conference room. One of the designers brought us the data work to do. We were left to our own devises to find the break room and bathrooms. We would stroll around at lunch checking the place out. To my delight I did run into Mr. Lemon, but only briefly to exchange a pleasant greeting. At least he remembered who I was.

We completed the job in just three days. Everyone was impressed with what we had accomplished in such a short time. The fellow who was in charge signed our time cards and sent us on our merry way. When I called Ms. Coco to tell her we had completed the assignment, she was surprised. They had contacted the job for five days. I could not figure out if she was pleasantly surprised that we had done such a good job, or disappointed that she had lost two billing days.

She told me to "Just call me Annabel. We do not have to be so formal." 'Boy,' I thought, 'it's about time.' Annabel had another assignment starting on the following Monday. It was at Anytown International in the accounts payable department for the Unitary Products Group or UPG Division. This would be an indefinite long term assignment. The woman I would be replacing was having heart surgery. Her name was Penny and I would be there for training for two weeks. I readily accepted this assignment.

I pulled up at Anytown International with a big smile on my face. The guard had been notified that I was expected and had a visitor's badge waiting for me. No delay at this company. I was allowed to park in the visitor's parking lot for the entire time I worked there!

When I went in to the Lobby, the receptionist, Corinne, remembered me from the times I had been there before. We said our hellos and giggled about how we used to herd Mr. Wipple around. I took a seat and shortly thereafter Penny exited off the elevator to greet me. I did not normally use the elevator when I worked at Anytown International. I needed all the exercise I could get and I used the stairs. Penny was not in the best of health, having had congestive heart failure. Penny was a real character. She was in her late fifties, very petite and attractive. I am sure in her youth she was a real beauty. Penny was always smiling and bursting with happiness. It was hard to be solemn when Penny was in the room. When we got to the department where I would be working, Penny introduced me to everyone. She showed me where the coffee niche was and the ladies rooms. She could not do enough for me. Penny got me settled at her desk and pulled up a spare chair and we began my training. The I.T. Department had my user ID set up. She gave me the run down on her job and a stack of invoices. I was now officially a UPG Accounts Payable Clerk.

There was another AP cleric in the department. Myrtle was a bit older than Penny but just as nice. She came over to us as I was training and told me to feel free to ask any questions of her. After Penny was gone, Myrtle would be my savior and mentor.

Once I got the hang of the system and had an understanding of the position, Penny was in the wind. She was the social butterfly of the company. She had been there for twenty-five years and knew everyone. She would flit around and stop back to check on me and then she would be off again. By Wednesday of the first week, I was doing well and figuring out what reports I needed to run and how to input the coded invoices. Like Myrtle, I would be paying invoices for five branches of the Anytown International Company. The invoices were for the expenses which were incurred by the branch offices. Twice a day I would receive interoffice envelopes stuffed with invoices. The invoices were always properly coded and ready for payment. Anytown International maintained a tight ship when it came to company policies. I seldom had a question on an invoice. I rarely had a vendor call me about a payment being late either. Like I said, Anytown International ran a smooth operation.

On Wednesday of my second week, I did not see Penny anywhere in the department. Myrtle came to my desk and said Penny had been taken to the hospital Wednesday night. She had become very ill due to her heart condition. She would be having open heart surgery as soon as it could be scheduled. Myrtle reiterated to me, "don't worry you will be just fine. We will work together."

There were two Cost Accountants in the department, a young woman, Gertrude, and an even younger man named John. I would have very little work contact with them. Gertrude was very nice and had just returned from pregnancy leave. John was in a world of his own. He was totally engrossed with the splendor of the general ledger program. I did not interact with the manager of the department, Mr. Smith. He was usually in his office and the door was always open. My main contact was Myrtle. I had no problems with anyone or anything when I was at Anytown International. I would be there for four months. When Penny returned it was a very sad day for me. Much to my total amazement the employees of the department threw me a going away party. They gave me gifts and a card, and they had even gotten a cake. I was nearly in tears; they had kept it a big secret.

I sadly pulled out of my personal visitor parking space with my gifts on the front seat and never returned. I kept the card with their good wishes in my scrapbook along with the pictures I had taken while I worked there.

While I was at Anytown International, a terrible industrial accident occurred. Unbeknown to me, early in the morning before I left for work, a propane tank exploded in the factory. One of the men in the shop where this happened was killed. The explosion was so violent a roof top air handler was thrown five blocks away and landed on the sidewalk of a company called TEETH R US. The blast was felt ten miles away. People reported knickknacks on shelves had fallen of the walls. That was a terrible day. Many of the employees were in tears and had to leave work. Several of the employees in my department had known this man personally. After a few days, a collection was taken up by the employees of Anytown International for his family. Everyone chipped in, including me. The employees collected close to twenty-five thousand dollars for the family. This was truly a testimony to the kindness of Anytown International workers.

I ran into Penny at the Strand Capitol Theater some years afterward, she had not changed one bit. She told me she had retired and now she was *really* having the time of her life. I was delighted to see her so healthy and still in high spirits.

I stopped in at Coconut Personnel just to check in on the afternoon I left Anytown International. Annabel knew my assignment was in the closing stages. She had lined up a few quick jobs for me. I grabbed a few time cards and proceeded to my next job quest. I went to a company called The Design Center one day in August of 2000. This was a commercial graphics and design company. When I got there I was introduced to no one. The woman I was working for walked me directly to a conference room where I would spend the entire day alone assembling manuals and binding them. The machine which I used to bind the manuals was a desk top spiral binder. I finished up the project and proceed to try and chase down the woman who was in charge of this project to have my time card signed. After I had wasted a half hour tying to find her, I boldly walked in an office occupied by a man who looked like he was in charge. I explained my plight to him. He graciously signed my time card and I drove of into the sunset. I have no idea who he was, but I got paid just the same.

The following Monday, Annabelle had me out at a company called Smith and Company. It would only be a four day assignment. This was another snotty accounting firm where no one acknowledged my presence. I ate and read in my car at lunch. I sat in a grimy attic room with poor lighting assembling tax forms and stuffing them into envelopes. Coconut did not send me on the best assignments. It was better than collecting unemployment. I had to keep hoping something better was just over the horizon.

Next, I ended up at Diebold for one and a half days. I was filling in for a receptionist who had taken a week's vacation. I was sent there on a Thursday afternoon. Apparently the girl covering for the receptionist was so backed up trying to do two jobs; she threw in the towel and called for a temp. This company serviced ATM machines and also installed security systems. I was alone in the office with the girl who was swamped with work. The technicians were in an out all day and they seemed like a fun, friendly bunch. The phones were not very busy and I took messages all day. In a flash, this assignment was over and in that same flash I was out of there.

Annabel called me with another short assignment. I would be going to the Anytown County Literacy Council for two weeks. I was covering for the receptionist who had taken two weeks vacation. This was an interesting place to work. The people who worked there were teachers and social workers. They were a very caring bunch of ladies. The director was a very pleasant woman who seldom came out of her office. They did not have a full staff so everyone was always busy. I answered the phone and like all good non-profit agencies, the job came with a small instruction manual explaining the job accompanied by a phone list in alphabetical order by *last* name. It's the little things that matter. Trust me!

I learned the Literacy Council had many projects going on throughout the city. They sponsored a reading program in the schools. They had volunteers which helped people of all ages with Spanish to English programs. They did much more than just teach adults to read. This was another place I would have liked to have been hired. They did so much good for the community. It was not meant to be and before I knew it I was getting my time card signed for the last time. I headed out the door once again.

It was now November of 2000 and I did not think I would ever have a permanent job again. Carla from the Coconut Agency called me with a position at Screw & Nut Industrial, a local manufacturing supply company. I would be entering invoices for payment in the Accounts Payable Department. Carla told me there was a good chance this could go permanent. They were placing two other temps there along with me. One of the temps, Isabel, would be working in the Customer Service department and the other temp would be working in the warehouse. Carla went on to tell me Screw & Nut Industrial had acquired another company in Scranton, Pennsylvania. She said she felt the company would continue to expand and would be a good long term employer. Again I said, "Sure, I can't wait."

The following Monday, I reported as always, bright eyed and bushy tailed. Screw & Nut Industrial Supply was a nationwide supplier of maintenance, repair, and operation products. They sold anything and everything to manufacturing plants. When I arrived, I met the two temps who were starting along with me. Isabel was a beautiful dark haired beauty form Dallas, Texas. She was of Mexican descent and was very lost in Anytown. While we were waiting, Isabel told me her husband, Mel, had been transferred to Anytown from Dallas. Mel was a plant manager and had been sent to an Anytown division of his company to trouble-shoot some problems at the plant. She had a little boy, age six, and hated living in Anytown. She missed her family and could not practice her profession as a pharmacy technician. She had to reapply for her license in the state of Pennsylvania. Isabel was just waiting for the day she would be licensed in Pennsylvania and she could apply for a job at one of the pharmacies. She was working as a temp for Coconut just to make some quick money. The other temp was a guy named William; he was going to work in the warehouse. He sat there with us but did not offer much conversation. Finally the supervisors came to the reception area and we left in different directions.

My supervisor was a tall imposing woman named Denise Raven. She was in her late fifties and kept a very distinct wall between herself and the employees of her department. She spent most of her time in her office.

The other women in the department in which I would be working were Mildred, the head AP clerk, and Valarie and Deloris. Valarie and Deloris were the AP data entry clerks. I was trained by Valarie and she too could fix anything. The system was an updated AS400 with all of the Microsoft products. I would also use a scanner when inputting the invoices, this was great since the invoices were then boxed up and stored, and saved hours filing them.

I settled in and began my training with Valarie. Valarie was twenty-five years old and had been employed by Screw & Nut since she had graduated from high school. She was a happy pudgy Garth Brooks luv'n Anytown Country gal. She had a casual style in dress and the farthest from home she had ever been was Ocean City, MD a couple hundred miles away. Valarie was a good hearted individual. She was very knowledgeable and conscientious. During the two years I worked at Screw & Nut, Valarie only dressed in leggings, tights, and big tops. She had the wildest collection of leggings I had ever seen. The only time I ever saw her dressed any other way was on blue jean Fridays. Valarie's cubicle was decorated in cutesy bears and with the crafts she made. Valarie was very talented and creative; she had a little sideline business going on in her cube.

Delores had been a registered nurse and (for reasons she never disclosed to me) had left the nursing field. She was a hard working quiet lady. She was in a great deal of pain with a bad hip. She was looking forward to having hip replacement surgery. I never heard her complain, but on a bad day she had a very apparent limp.

When I first met Mildred, I was definitely taken back. She was very gruff and curt when Denise introduced me to her on my first morning. She could hardly be bothered to even look up from her desk to say hello. Mildred was from New Jersey and could have easily been a mafia hit woman. She was short and as big around as she was tall. Mildred had the standard Anytown County short "wash and go" hair cut and never wore makeup. She was married to a man on permanent disability and often bemoaned she *had* to work due to his failings. I thought she was cold and callous. She had pictures of her pretty teenage daughter all over her cubical walls but not one photo of her husband. In Mildred's' defense, I will add she was swamped with work. Her bad manners and razor sharp temper may have been due to the many duties that had been heaped upon her. She processed and printed all the checks and credits for the accounts payable department. When she did a check run, there were usually hundreds of checks to print and stuff in envelops. Valarie and Mildred were very tight and had worked together for years. Mildred was a stone cold bigot, a trait I personally can not tolerate. I found her bad jokes (recanted in a pronounced jersey accent) and remarks about people of color to be very hateful.

The building Screw & Nut was in was relatively new. The accounting and the executive office were all on the second floor. The customer service area, purchasing, and the warehouse were on the ground level floor. They also had a large bright break room surrounded by windows. There was a room for large meetings and training. Usually the folding doors were closed on the far end of the room. There were large parking lots and the grounds were planted with shade trees. They had placed picnic tables under the trees for summer lunches. All and all it appeared to be a pleasant place to work, *if* you're looking in from the outside.

The president of Screw & Nut was a young man named Robert Rip. He was the son of the former owner. Mr. Rip was a good looking tall man and he knew it. During the first weeks I worked at Screw & Nut, Mr. Rips' secretary retired. She was an elderly lady and had worked for his father for many years. She and Mr. Rip had been interviewing for months for her replacement. One day I was in the break room and met a tall lanky blond named Dora. She was very friendly and as we made our introductions she told me she was Mr. Rip's new secretary. She was training with the "old bag". I was surprised that she would say something like this to someone she had just met. Dora was very up front and she did not pull any punches. Dora was a super hero secretary. I think she was hired for more that her administrative abilities. Dora was thirty-two when I first met her. She was on the surface the blond bomb shell, or so she thought. Dora had long blond hair to the middle of her back and long legs to match. Typically men did their dog drool routine when she was in the room. I have always thought Mr. Rip hired her because of her looks. Dora had a dear little boy from her first marriage. She was engaged to the owner of a small time construction company. Surprisingly, Dora and I would become friends.

Over the next six months, I settled into my routine and the job became a data drone position. I got along well with most of the employees at Screw & Nut. Dora, Isabel, and I became the three musketeers. We went out to lunch and shopping at the mall together. On occasion the three of us would go for a drink after work. Dora was a social butterfly and often stopped by my cubicle. When Mr. Rip was not in the office, she became restless. She told me she did not have enough work to keep her occupied for the day. "Well," I thought, "come over here and pound some invoices in the system." Our department always had so much work it was hard to keep current. On an average day, I inputted one hundred and fifty to two hundred invoices. After about a year,

Screw & Nut was acquired by a company called ABC based in Georgia. There were rumors flying around as to the effect that the company would be trimming back personnel at our location. None of this was true, and if anything a few more people were hired. Some of the personnel in the I.T. Department left. The atmosphere had changed at Screw & Nut. Many of the employees were unhappy with the procedural changes ABC instituted. None of this affected the day to day activities of my department, except that another young girl was hired and her name was Julie.

Julie was hired as the Accounts Payable Department supervisor. Up until now, Mrs. Raven had been in charge. Due to the changes in the I.T. department she was handling the I.T. and Accounts Payable departments. I don't think Mildred was very happy about the change or Julie being hired as her boss. Julie was capable and knew what she was doing. She had an Associates Degree in Accounting and Business. I figured better her than me. I could never have filled her shoes. I thought she did a great job. Julie had a very bad lisp that had not been corrected. She would get up in front of all the employees at staff meetings and speak. I could not have spoken at a meeting with a lisp, comfortably. I thought she was brave. Dreadfully, Dora would make fun of her. I should have spoken up when this would happen but I did not. Dora was one of those women that looks first-class on the outside but is like a Cadbury Easter Egg; sweet on the outside . . . you know the rest. She was very immature for someone of her supposed stature. During the time all the changes in management were taking place, there was a big stink about something Isabel had reported to the office in Atlanta. I never found out what she had gotten herself into but it was not good.

Mildred had never liked Isabel and went out of her way to cut her down when ever she came into the department. Isabel was in customer service and sometimes had dealings with the AP clerks about why a payment had not been made to a vendor. After Isabel would leave, Mildred would make nasty remarks about Isabel's Mexican heritage and call her a wetback. Mildred would never say those things when Isabel was in the room. One day there were a lot of phone calls between Mildred and one of her buddies in the CSR department regarding Isabel. Dora had called me on the phone and told me Isabel had been fired. About the same time, some one from downstairs called Mildred and told her the same thing. What transpired next between Mildred and Valarie was absolutely sickening.

Mildred hung up her phone and literally sprang out of her seat. She was jumping up and down and squealing like a pig" Valarie, Valarie, they did it, they did it, they fired that Mexican wetback!" She was beside herself with hateful glee. Valarie just sat there with a stupid smile on her face. I had to get up and leave. I went outside for a smoke and pondered how people could be so hateful.

I disliked Mildred for many reasons. She was a bigot; she was mean and would not help me if I had questions. Every other word out of her month was the F word. But this display of hate was more than I should have had to deal with. It was hard to ignore Mildred's domineering presence. Now Isabel was gone from our circle. Dora and I continued to go to lunch and breaks together but Isabel's absence was very apparent. We tried to stay in touch with her but I think she had such bad memories of Screw & Nut she wanted to forget us as well. Dora told me she had discovered through the Screw & Nut's grapevine; Isabel's husband had been recalled to Dallas. They had moved back to their home, I know that made our friend very happy.

I continued to plug along, inputting invoices and trying to keep out of Mildred's line of fire. In July of 2001 my father was diagnosed with terminal cancer, he was eighty-one. I was spending a lot of time traveling to Baltimore. I would go with my mother to John Hopkins when my father was having chemotherapy. Mrs. Raven had told me to take all the time I needed for these family obligations. My father was sent home in September with a death sentence of two months. It came to be he would only live for two more weeks.

One morning I got a phone call from a friend of mine Cindy, at CCC. She asked me, "Did they have the TV on at work?" I told her, "I don't know, what was going on?" Cindy told me a plane had just flown into one of the Twin Towers. Just about then, I could hear the other people in the office getting the word about what was happening. As I hung up with Cindy, Dora showed up at my desk and we went to the break room with everyone else. Someone had turned on the TV. We walked in as the second plane hit the towers. Dora and I stood there in total disbelief.

Over the course of the next two weeks, I was traveling to Maryland every other evening. Every weekend I went to visit with my brother, Oscar. We spent as much time with my father as we could. On a Sunday night at eight-thirty, my Dad passed away. I called Mrs. Raven and informed her of what had happened and that I needed to take off. She told me no problem and that I had one week of bereavement leave. Unfortunately after the first week had passed, I was not ready to return to work. There had been delays in having my father buried and we could not get everything done in one week. I called Mrs. Raven that Friday and told her I would need another week off, and that I did not expect to be paid for it. Mrs. Raven was horribly snippy and said to me, "we need you here, the work is backing up, and it is the month's end. If you don't come in on Monday, don't come in at all." That was the way I left Screw & Nut Industrials Employment. Darn if I hadn't left my white office sweater over the back of my chair, yet again. Thanks for the memories.

CHAPTER 12

Don't stray from the beaten path

Having left Screw & Nut under the circumstances I did, I could not use them for a reference. I contacted Coconut Personnel to feel out Mrs. Coco. She was very glad to hear from me after two years. I informed her of what had transpired at Screw & Nut. Annabel was shocked that a company would be so unsympathetic to an employee after a death in their family. Annabel's company had prospered during the past two years and she had moved to a newer building. She had also modified the type of personnel she recruited, focusing the main core of her business to the medical professions. Consequently she no longer had as many clerical or accounting positions in the mix. She told me I was welcome to stop in and update my paperwork. Annabel's new location was close to a hospital. She was in a partnership with the other owners of the structure. Within the building there were many doctors, dentists, and ophthalmologists offices. The building was a one story structure with well manicured lawns and newly planted trees. The building even had a small cozy coffee bar with snacks. There was a steady stream of patients entering and departing the building.

Annabel was looking good and driving a red Audi these days. Her office was rather opulent, with white antique furniture and pastel paintings on the walls. She also had all new personnel. Not one person from the old office worked for her any longer. She had eliminated the receptionist position. The two new pimps, Beth and Shannon covered the phones. They were both in their early twenties and were clones of Mrs. Coco. They were preppy, bubbly and pretty, but not prettier than Annabel. She did not like anyone competing with her for attention. People had to have a certain *look* before Annabel would even consider them good enough to work for her.

My new pimp, Beth, processed my paper work and testing results. I was immediately turned off by her haughty better than thou attitude. I hoped I would have as little contact with her as possible. She gave me the impression she was a very spoiled little girl. We shook hands and smiled a lot. Beth assured me she would be in touch if they found a job which would be (please don't say it but she did) "a perfect fit".

I also contacted ADECCO temp service and did the dog and pony dance at their offices. I had no loyalty to any temp service and would work for whoever called me first. The little pimps at ADECCO were not haughty but they were young. I got the same old speech, "we will call if we have anything, but feel free to call every week and check in with us." Which I would do, but I had a harder time begging this time around. I was also answering employment ads in the newspaper and contacting friends for job leads. Out of the blue a friend, Tim, who was also my I.T. specialist for my home computer, called me with a job lead. He had a friend who had opened a business and needed a receptionist with an accounting background. He told me the only draw back was that it would not pay as much as I had been making. Since I was collecting unemployment again, I told him I was not looking to make what I had been making. I just wanted to get back to work. Tim gave me the information and I called Professionals Certified LLD. They set up an interview time and I was on my way.

Professionals Certified LLD was located in Anytown City two blocks off the city square. I interviewed with Guy, who was an I.T. specialist. Guy was about twenty-five and typically dressed in khaki casuals. He was a good looking man with longish blond hair and an encouraging smile. He explained that they were Certified Microsoft Engineers, what their company did, and what my duties would encompass. We agreed that I was overqualified for the position. He told me I would have a lot of down time. If I accepted the position, I was welcome to use one of the empty rooms for any purpose I wanted. He was thinking along the lines of a small craft business. I told him no, but since I was an avid reader I would just bring a book along. Guy told me I would be free to use the Internet to my heart's desire. All I needed to do was answer the phone, process the Accounts Receivables, and handle the payroll. There were only two employees at PCL and I would make three. I knew I could handle this position. Guy told me that he and Jason had worked together at another company for some years. Jason had left the company and opened PCL. He asked Guy to come to work for him.

After I interviewed with Guy he introduced me to the owner, Jason Kipple Jr. The instant I met Jason Kipple I felt at home with him. He was open and affable. Jason had a rather wild appearance. He had a slight build and was of average height. Jason had very pallid skin, insipid blue eyes topped with bushy black eyebrows. His thick black hair went in all directions. He reminded me of Edward Scissorshand. Jason told me he would do my training. I had not worked in the accounting system they were using, called Quick Books. He assured me I would ace it as it was Windows based software. Jason told me I would have a parking space in the public garage across the street (this is a real plus when working in the city). He showed me around the small offices, which previously had been a tanning salon. Jason thanked me for my time and said he would call me one way or another. I felt good about how the interview had gone and hoped for the best.

I was feeling better then I had felt in quite a while. All the horrible events of the past two months drifted out of my mind that day. The sun was shining and it was warm for a November morning. I strolled around downtown checking out the boutiques, and treated myself to lunch at the Anytown Hotel. When I returned home my answering machine light was flashing. I hoped it was good news. Jason had left a message which said to call him if I wanted to start the following Monday. I called and accepted the position. I had high hopes this would be a long term relationship. The only thing that kept nagging at me was the fact that PCL was a small company and had only been in business for three years. As I had no other prospects for employment, I put these negative thoughts away and looked forward to a fresh start.

I was excited to be working with friendly computer geeks. I just loved to pick their brains. Many people in this profession are not so friendly and seem to think they are above the rest of us. Jason and Guy were never like that. PCL provided secure and reliable networks systems consulting for companies large and small. My duties were answering the phone, inputting and reconciling the billing, payroll input and printing checks. I would make the daily bank deposits on my pleasant walks downtown at lunchtime. I also maintained quality control of the Microsoft updates. Jason handled the Account Payables.

Everything fell into place, and for the next year all went well. At one point Jason hired another part-time Microsoft engineer named Ronald. I never got good vibes from Ronald. I thought he was sneaky, but I could never put my finger on anything. I was usually in the office alone as Jason and Guy were always on site at a company working. One time I did not see Jason for nine days. We kept in touch by phone or instant messaging. As long as he signed my paycheck and it was on my desk every Thursday morning, I was not concerned.

I loved working downtown and walking about the square at lunch. I would go shopping at the Lutheran Secondhand store where I had purchased another gently worn white office sweater. I smiled as I wondered if I had left it over an office chair at a previous job. I became friendly with a young African American woman named Violet from the attorney's office next door. We met while smoking outside of the office one morning. She and I were ready for some fresh air around ten-thirty each morning. We would stand outside watching the pedestrians and traffic go by. On more than one occasion we witnessed drug deals *going down*. As we were only two blocks from the police station, Violet and I thought the dealers were very smart or the police were very stupid. We spied a police van one day and it was missing the O, spelling P LICE, no wonder the drug dealers did business out in the open.

After about a year and a half, Jason began having family problems. He separated from his wife and became embroiled in a tangled divorce. There were all kinds of problems with the home, vehicles, and the children. Shortly thereafter the money stream started to dry up. Jason's father, Mr. Kipple Sr., came to the office one day and took over one of the vacant rooms. Jason told me his father was some sort of a consultant and would be paying the rent. I knew this was killing Jason relying on his father to help him out with his finances. Jason confided in me his father had been ousted from a high position he had held in the state government during a power play. I never knew the details. I *never* know the details!

Mr. Kipple Sr. was so very quiet; I scarcely knew he was in the office. I offered to do any administrative duties he might need, but he declined my help. He was a very well mannered older gentleman. He spent a great deal of time on the phone with someone from his old office. I knew he was manipulating a situation from afar but I could never figure out what it was about. I did notice Mr. Kipple Sr. had an attitude towards Guy. He never told me what the problem had been. I could tell he did not like Guy working in Jason's company. In July, Mr. Kipple Sr. went sailing for two weeks, it was a welcome break. For that short time, things were back to normal with just Jason, Guy, and myself.

PCL was another of the few companies I worked for that the owner did not live out of the receipts. Jason took a salary and had a leased car through the business. He didn't pay himself bonuses or put extravagant spending on the company credit card. He was very candid and forthcoming in all his business dealings. His customers knew he was trustworthy and honest. Jason was a smart, funny man. He would get excited at the prospect of teaching someone who wanted to learn. He always was encouraging and understanding. He once told me that the average person needs to work at a task seven times before it sinks in. The best advice he gave to me was, "if you didn't create it, don't delete it." The company continued to have severe money problems. Things got so bad; Jason and Guy did not cash their pay checks for six weeks. Since I did the banking, I knew the magnitude of the predicament. Finally, Guy had to find a different job, and sadly, he resigned. Now it was just Jason, Mr. Kipple Sr. and I.

Jason cut my hours to half days and that was okay with me. He told me when business picked up I would be back to full time hours. I knew this was true and I could afford to hang in there with him. Unfortunately, business did not pick up. Finally, one afternoon, Jason sat down at my desk and told me the inevitable. Not only was I being laid off, he was closing his business. He had decided to work from his apartment for the time being. On Friday I got my belongings together and for once I did not forget to grab my gently used white office sweater. I said farewell to Jason. I never saw him again. For a time, we would I.M. when we would catch each other on the Internet. Now much time has passed and I have lost track of Jason. The day I was laid off was my fifty-fourth birthday. Happy Birthday to me, it was also my two year anniversary working at PCL. It was time to call around to the temp agencies once again.

I re-contacted both ADECCO and Coconut Personnel. I had to go back to each agency and test in all the Microsoft programs and update my information. I typed an updated resume and was on my way. At ADECCO I dealt with pleasant but uninterested pimps who spent their time talking to each other about what fun time they had on Saturday night. At Coconut Personnel, I was subjected to my pimp Beth's condescending tone of voice and conceited airs. I did not have much hope in getting an assignment from Coconut. They were doing mostly medical placements. A few days passed and I received a call from ADECCO. They had an assignment at Easter Seals of Anytown county that would go for six weeks, was I interested? Of course I was.

When I arrived at Easter Seals I was met by the director, Mrs. Easter. She was a good looking woman in her mid thirty's. She introduced me to the other employees. There were three other people in the office. I would work with Sara, the administrative assistant for the department. I was replacing a receptionist who had left their employment. When I went to Easter Seals, I didn't realize that it was a school for children with many different types of disabilities. I loved the atmosphere, there were little children running and laughing everywhere. They were well behaved children, but they were still *kids*. The teachers were friendly, kind people. I really enjoyed the time I worked there.

My chief job at Easter Seals was being the receptionist. I also assisted Sara with a major fund raising project. I would type letters of thanks to people who had made donations, made phone calls, helped design booklets, and advertising pamphlets. Sara was a charming young woman who was horse crazy. She boarded a horse in the country nearby and would dash off after work to visit with her horse. I was offered the receptionist position while I was working there. They offered me the position at two dollars less an hour then I was making working temp. I have processed payroll in non-profit profit businesses and I know the kind of money the administrators of these organizations earn. There is no excuse for the meager wages they offer first line employees who work hard and are as committed to the organizations as they are. In addition, it is preposterous to offer a temp a job at a lower wage then what the temp agencies are paying. The people who run these non-profit companies think that because you are working as a temp, you are desperate for an actual job. They believe you will take whatever paltry amount of money they offer. Needless to say when I turned down this offer, Mrs. Easter was none too friendly to me for the duration of my assignment. My pimp at ADECCO understood where I was coming from. She told me no problem, no harm, no foul. I was back to cube one.

I rang in the new year of 2003 with some good news. Annabel called me from Coconut Personnel and offered me a long term floater temp position at Anytown Hospital. I was very excited at the prospect of obtaining full time employment at the hospital. I would be able to check the job boards and possibly apply for a position once I was working there. I eagerly accepted this position. I wish I had known beforehand how much of my time I would waste.

I would first go to the Healthspan office on Duke Street in Anytown City. This was an administrative office that processes the billing for the hospital. I was to work in the Accounts Receivable Department. Originally I was sent to enter expense invoices from the companies supplying the hospital with equipment and products. This was a bait and big time switch. After two days training with another uninterested temp, I was pulled off of the job. I was unceremoniously taken to the collections department and instructed to make collection calls for past due medical accounts. This department had become suddenly short of people. Apparently two people had quit rather unexpectedly. If the manager, Raymond, had not been so adept at manipulation, I would have called Coconut Personnel. Normally I am not very good at getting results making collection calls. Raymond assured me I would be *great* at this position, so of course I had to give it a go. I was given stack after stack of returned mail which needed to be pursued for payment. This way the hospital could hand them off to a collection agency. It became a detective game for me. I would call the person listed in the computer who had signed off on the medical procedure, that is, if I could find a valid phone number. Usually this person was never at home, had moved, or was no longer among the living, or so I was told. Often I could not communicate with whoever answered the phone, as I did not speak Spanish or Jive.

I usually become frustrated trying to collect money. It is not one of my favorite things to do. I was told by the lady who trained me, "just call and call, then make notes on the person's file in the system. We only need to document our attempts." Cool, I could do this. I continued to do this for months until the mail was caught up. I also helped out updating patients accounts in regards to the new HIPAA regulations that had been instituted by the federal government.

I met Lynn, a fun gal from another temp service in Camp Hill. Lynn had an accounting degree and was very unhappy about processing collection accounts. She was looking for employment closer to her home but took this hoping to obtain a full time job at the hospital. We went on breaks and lunches together. After three months Lynn got a full time job, but not at the Anytown hospital. She had been looking on her own and had found a job in Harrisburg. Lynn left and I went to another area to work. Lynn is another of the many great gals I have lost track of in temp land.

I next went to the *heart beat of the hospital*, the Healthspan ROBI building a few miles from the hospital. This building housed the systems that ran the hospitals computers (so I was told) plus the help desk personnel. The ROBI was a relatively new addition to the Healthspan family. The building was new and very modern. The executives on the hospital board were also at this location. I would be sitting in for the receptionist who was on vacation. I was trained by a darling young woman named Tracy. She was extremely efficient and very helpful. Everyone at the ROBI went out of their way to make me feel welcome. This was the first place I worked with a new Dell computer and it had a plasma screen monitor. The equipment the hospital provided for their employees was the most up to date and modern I have ever seen at any company. This was particularly true at the ROBI. Soon the week came to an end and I was off to the medical records division at the hospital.

The medical records division, at the time, was a massive mess of patient's records. I was stunned when I first saw the condition of the file rooms (I have pictures to prove it). File folders were stacked three feet high *everywhere*. The patient's files were towering on the file shelves, on the floor, on the tables, it was unbelievable. There was hardly any room to walk between the shelves. Even so, that would not be my main concern. I would be working on a computer in the hottest, smallest room of the department. I was jammed up with three other employees, auditing duplicated patient records. A duplicated patient record happens often. It happens enough that there is an entire department dedicated to keeping the records straight. Like they say, junk in junk out. The systems are only as good as the people imputing the data. I discovered that errors happened most frequently during the weekends in the ER department. The department was located right next to the boiler-room of the hospital. During the day it would get up to eighty-five degrees in the room. I left my white office sweater at home during this assignment.

I was blessed to be working with the smartest man in the department, John. He had worked in the medical records department for over twenty years. John could find and fix the most screwed up records imaginable. John always had tons of work as he also supervised the micro-film department. I would be helping him get the records caught up. John was a gentleman in his fifties and lived with his aged mother. He was her steadfast loving caretaker. John gave me the impression of being shy and backward. But as I got to know him, he was anything but. John was very funny and sarcastic.

While I was working in this department, I would meet a terrific lady, Kathy. She had been at the hospital for years and was a great help to me. There were two other temps from Coconut there as well, Kim and Sandy. Kim was a groovy gal. She was in her early twenties and very good looking. She had a soft, luminous appearance with long blond hair and subtle blue eyes. When we would go out for a smoke, the hospital guards would flirt with her. Kim was so at home with people and never acted like a diva.

She was a mother to a little girl just as pretty as herself. Unlike some mothers, she did not go on and on about having the smartest, prettiest, most clever child in the universe. Kim actually had other interests and I could have conversations with her on many subjects, not just motherhood. Our supervisor John was enchanted by her. Sandy had been working in the Medical Records department for Coconut Personnel for over a year when I first met her. She had been implanted into Anytown County from New Jersey. Sandy was not as critical as I was about the attitudes of the people in this area. Sandy was upbeat, happy and liked everyone. She was very conscientious and would work as a temp for five years at Anytown hospital before she was finally hired.

During the time Kim and I worked in the medical records department, a new manager was hired. The position had apparently been vacant for some time. We would meet Caria at the department meeting. She was from Baltimore and had worked in the medical records department at John Hopkins University Hospital for seven years. Kim and I thought she would straighten out the department. We never could figure out what Caria actually did except avoid us on Fridays. We needed to get our time cards signed by her. We would have to chase all over the hospital trying to track her down. On one particular vexing exploration, I asked her if she could sign our time cards *before* she went into the bowels of the hospital. Caria told us, "No, how do I know you will finish today? You might leave early!" Kim and I were shocked that she would think that of us. Kim and I would continue to hunt for Caria every Friday. We decided we would leave our work area a half-hour early in our pursuit of her. We got sick of losing a half hour of our time trying to unearth her (when we did find her, she was usually in the neo-natal department cooing with the babies).

As Kim and I became accepted by the full time employees, they shared their thoughts about Caria. They all thought she was in over her head and ineffectual. They had no respect for her and spoke dreadfully about her behind her back, referring to her as *the nutcase*. To me she seemed disconnected from the other employees and scatterbrained.

Kim and I worked a very early day shift. We would start at four and be finished at two-thirty. The hospital had a flex hour program and we could set our own hours, as long as we were constant. I loved the early morning hours at the hospital. It was quiet and we had the place to ourselves until around eight. I discovered a wonderful time of day, twilight. Kim and I would go out for a smoke (you could still smoke outside at that time) and watch the sun rise. I delighted in the peacefulness and beauty of the coming day. We would go to lunch at nine and enjoy breakfast in the hospital cafeteria with the nurses and other hospital staff. The food at the hospital was wonderful and the coffee excellent. Everyone was so amiable during the morning hours. During the three years I worked at

Anytown hospital, not one person who was an employee of the hospital that I had contact with was ever anything except helpful, polite, and caring.

After three months, I had helped John to get the records current and was going on to another department. This time I would be going back to the ROBI center, Tracy had requested I return to help her out.

I was acting as receptionist and helping Tracy with all types of projects. I assisted her on one occasion setting up for an executive luncheon. This was fun and I had a great left over sandwich from Isaac's Restaurant. Remember, temps are always hungry! I couldn't help but wonder what happened to the receptionist. I got my nerve up one day and asked Tracy what was up with the vacant position? Tracy was very frank and told me the person had been let go due to excessive absenteeism. I pursued the conversation asking her when they were going to fill the position. Tracy told me, her voice becoming angry, "probably never!" I did not mention it again. Everyone at the ROBI was a delight to work with as always. After two weeks I was out of there and on to another *real* adventure back at the hospital.

This time I was sent to the Trauma Surgery Administration department. I was a little leery of this job. Sylvia was the woman I would be replacing for a week's vacation. She was the Administrative Assistant to the three day trauma surgeons. She tried to put me at ease, saying, "They (referring to the surgeons) will be very nice to you. They don't want you to walk out." That did not make me feel any better. The week Sylvia was on vacation went very well for me. The doctors were frosty but not disagreeable. I answered the phones and did whatever copying or typing they requested. Sylvia had told me they were the closest thing to God that I was going to meet on this earth. In a way, I suppose this was true.

Next, Coconut Personnel sent me to the Medical Administration Department to assist the head cleric. The woman I would be assisting was new to the department. This department handled all the paper work and arrangements for the new medical students entering the hospital's education programs. The beginning of a new school year overlapped the graduation year. While we were working with the new students, we were also making graduation arrangements. I would obtain medical licenses and update the doctor's files. There were new students coming into the office for all sorts of request. Housing was provided. It was often I would be showing the small living quarters to the arriving students. I assembled and mailed graduation invitations and picked up awards at the engravers. Any task that required running around was given to me. I loved running errands. Everyone was easygoing and helpful in this department. When graduation day was only a week away and the job came to an end, I had worked at the hospital for one year. Now I knew why Sandy was still working there too.

Next I went to the Citterman Building and worked in the employee health department. I would be assisting the receptionist. This department was within the Human Resources Department. While I was there, I asked about obtaining employment since it was obvious the department was understaffed. The human resources person I spoke to venomously replied, "We don't hire temps ever." **Temp** had become a four letter word. Well that pretty much summed up any questions I had about employment. I plugged along for three additional months. One of my duties involved reading PPD test results. I had no medical training whatsoever. I was told that all the employees of a hospital must have this test every two years. I was given reading material on the test. I had been required to have one when I first went to work at the hospital. A PPD test is a TB test, or Tuberculin Skin Test. The purified protein derivative is an antigen, which is injected under the skin in the forearm. After 48 to 72 hours, the injection site is evaluated by a *physician*. I was NOT a physician. This skin test helps determine if a person has ever been infected by the microorganism that causes tuberculosis. I was given a picture of what an abnormal reaction would look like. When employees came back to have the injection site evaluated, I would pull their file and note the negative reaction. I can only hope I did not misread one. Outside of reading PPD test results and filing, I don't recall anything more about working in this department. The assignment came to an end and I would have some downtime until Coconut Personnel placed me on another assignment at the hospital. For now it was the Christmas season and I was out of work once again. Happy Holidays to all.

Kim and I had kept in touch and did girly activities with her dear little girl. One day Kim called and asked if I had gotten an invitation to Coconut's Christmas party. I told her, "yes, but I am not keen on going." Kim said, "Come on it will be fun, we can meet and go in together." I told her "sure, it would be fun to see the girls we had worked with at the hospital." Not long after I spoke to Kim, Beth from Coconut Personnel called me. She wanted to know if they could expect me at the party. I thought this was odd, but I told her yes. I did not think any more of our conversation. I did ask if they had any work and she told me they did but it would not start until after the New Year (of course). The night of the Christmas party I got all dolled up. I met Kim in the parking lot of the Expo Center at the Anytown Fair Grounds. The party was held in one of the banquet rooms. It was a very posh affair. The room was beautifully decorated for the Christmas season. There was a large crowd of about one hundred employees. I had no idea this affair was going to be so large. Annabel and the other women of Coconut Agency were very lovely dressed in their Christmas finery but seemed nervous. We had a wonderful meal and then it was award time. I did not know they would be giving out awards.

Kim, Debra, Sandy, and I were chatting softly when all of a sudden I heard my name being called to go up and accept an award. Kim pushed me out of my seat. I walked up not realizing I was going to be the Employee of the Year! Annabel was standing at the podium going on and on, "'Drop of the hat Judy' **never** says no to anything requested of her, she is always accommodating, always punctual and always has a smile." That's ME! I just stood there smiling like an idiot. Next Kim was called and received an awarded for The Most Persevering Employee of the year. (What did that mean?). We thanked everyone and scooted back to our seats. At the time I was proud of the acknowledgment. Kim thought it was hysterical.

As Kim and I walked out of the party and back to our cars, she told me, "You know, I can get anything I want out of Annabel." I was surprised with her comment and asked, "What do you mean?" Kim continued," She thinks I am so sweet, and so pretty and the world has been soooo mean to me. She perceives me as a struggling single mother. I can play her like a fiddle. Did you know I did not finish high school?" "No, I did not." Kim continued with a little smile. "I buffaloed her and she placed me at the hospital, on the promise I would get my GED, I haven't done it." Then she hit me with a bomb shell, "I was an exotic dancer for five years. She thinks of me as her personal project. She is going to make me into a better person." Kim laughed and added, "You and I have the awards and the big checks, don't we?" With a sweet smile Kim gave me a big hug. I got in my car and drove home wondering what more did I not know about Kim? I wished I had her secret to unlocking the world. Then it came to me that she was pretty, street-smart and conniving. For once I knew the details.

I still have my award. It is in the bottom of a drawer somewhere. AND, I still do not have a full time job. At the time I was pleased to have gotten such an honor. Now I look at it as a testimony to the absurdness of working as a temp.

My next assignment for Coconut sent me back to the ROBI, the heartbeat of the hospital. This time I would be working in the I.T. Department. I was to report to the manager, Mrs. Tuttle. The Anytown Hospital and Gettysburger Hospital had joined forces under the Healthspan umbrella. I would be working with the supervisor of the department, Mrs. Tuttle. When the hospitals joined, the I.T. department ran a duplicate patient record report. This report had every patient that had ever been seen at either hospital. By running certain filters, the reports showed how many possible duplicate records might exist. My job was to audit these reports and incorporate the ones that were duplicates. There were thousand of people on these reports and it was a monstrous job. It was an I.T. function. The people working in the department did not have time to process the information or pretended to be so busy with other tasks that they could not get to it.

Mrs. Tuttle was a small boned woman who appeared to be stuck in the sixties. She had long brown hair to her waist with white streaks running through it. She was dressed in a throwback peasant dress with hemp sandals. She was not at all what I would have expected an I.T. manager to look like. Mrs. Tuttle impressed upon me that I could not make even one mistake. If I had any questions, I would need to find her and she would happy to assist me. One day I ventured over into her cubicle to ask her a question. She wasn't there but the turtles were. Mrs. Tuttle collected turtles and they were everywhere on her desk and on the shelves of her cubicle. There were big turtles, blown glass turtles, ceramic turtles, little tiny turtles, stuffed turtles, metal turtles, cute turtles, sad turtles, turtles that looked like real turtles; she even had a turtle lamp. I wondered how many turtles a Tuttle could collect if a Tuttle could collect turtles. She was nowhere to be found. (Maybe she was hunting turtles) I had to make a decision about what I was doing. It was the end of the day and the system was going to be brought down for the day to process the backup. Needless to say, I made the wrong choice. I joined two patient records that were NOT duplicates.

The next day Mrs. Tuttle found me. She shrieked at me in front of the entire department, "this I.T department DOES NOT MAKE MISTAKES! You made a mistake yesterday and **I** had to handle it." I told her I had been doing this task for three months, it was nearly completed, and I was very sorry. But it was the only error I knew of I had made. She told me, "sorry is *not* good enough; YOU bear in mind WE DO NOT MAKE MISTAKES." I put on my best pitiful puppy temp face on and told her I would be more careful. After her verbal explosion, she went back to turtle world. I would have liked to have told her to have her lazy I.T. people do the report if she wanted I.T. perfection. (I had to listen to them talking all day about their exceptionally bright children and what they were buying on EBay.) After all, I only worked for an I.T. Specialist, I wasn't one. Thank goodness I only had one more month to deal with Attila the Turtle, I mean Tuttle.

While I was at the ROBI, I ran into Tracy and the *nice* folks who I had worked with before. We would have pleasant lunches on the rear patio. There was a gas grill on the patio and the guys would make hamburgers and hot dogs for everyone. At lunch one afternoon I confided to Tracy how Mrs. Tuttle had spoken to me in front of the entire department. Tracy told me, "she is a rude I.T. person, you know how they are." I told her about my experiences working at PCI with Jason and Guy. "You were lucky, you **know** that is not the norm." Tracy replied. The subject was put to rest as we dug into delicious grilled hot dogs.

The project at the ROBI came to a conclusion on a Wednesday and Annabel sent me back to the hospital the next day. This would be a very short assignment in the Surgical Services Department. On Thursday I made my way to the department and was met by a very busy woman. She shoved me into a desk, slammed a disk in the hard drive, and told me I would be updating the hospital's policy and procedures manual. It had to be completed by Monday. She was in a bind and was in deep "do-do". She needed to present the completed manual at a meeting on Tuesday. She dumped the stack of manual pages with the edits that I was to complete on my desk and took off. I did not see her again until Monday. I typed and typed and typed for two days. On Friday the department head signed my time card and I left for the day. On Monday I went back to Surgical Services and began working on the manual. This woman, I never even knew her name, came to me and told me, "you haven't gotten enough completed, I needed a faster typist. *You* need to go. I have someone else coming to help me."

"That's right I don't have feelings. I am the temp; you are allowed to speak to me in any manner you choose. I must say please and thank you. I have to watch my P's and Q's." The things I wished I could have said but didn't. So much for kind considerate and caring hospital employees at least in the Surgical Services Department. I got up and left. On the way out I stopped at a pay phone outside the hospital and called Coconut. I spoke to clone pimp Beth who told me not to worry about it. They would pay me for four hours, go home, and relax. I never expected that.

My final assignment was at the Cedar Grove Microfilm Department located at the Cedar Grove Commons Complex. This was a state-of-the-art building and housed the new Micro film and patient records audit department. The chaos at the hospital's Medical Records Department had been straightened out. I would be auditing, copying, and sending the Emergency Department forms to an outsourced billing company. In the course of a day I would process hundreds of ED forms. I would call Federal Express each afternoon and send two or three large boxes of ED's to a company in New Jersey. I worked in a small room with only a copy machine. I did not have a chair or a table on which to work. My old friend Debra from the medical records department at the hospital was now working at Cedar Grove. John was still the supervisor and came over to the Cedar Grove location three times a week. The only crappy thing about this job was a temp from Coconut named Rachel. I had met Rachel when I worked in the Medical Records Department two years prior. She was a large girl with bleach blond split ends. She had been to college and thought her crap did not stink. She always had an attitude towards me. Kim came over from the hospital for a few weeks and helped us with the billing project. It was great to work with her again. For some reason Rachel *really* disliked Kim.

I was having a difficult time copying all the forms and carrying them from one room to another to collate, staple and pack up. There were other desks but they would not fit into the small copy room. Debra found an empty large screen plasma TV box someone had put in the trash. We dragged it into the copy room along with a chair. Debra got out her handy dandy box cutter and created a desk for me. I have pictures of this also.

One day the director of the hospital's Medical Records Department came to visit with some people from the Gettysburger hospital. I was in my little room jamming to my radio and working away when she opened the door. As I turned to look at her, she had this horrified expression on her face. I learned later she was showing off this newest location. She did not skip a beat as she explained to her visitors, "as you can see, we at Anytown Hospital take recycling very seriously and to a new level." With that she closed the door and they hastily left the building. We never heard anything more about the visit. John did say (with a chuckle) he wished he had been around the day she stopped with her visitors.

After six months this assignment ended. I gave up trying to be hired at the hospital. I packed up my belongings again, my award, my automatic stapler, and my dirty old white office sweater and left the building for the last time. I had been working there for three years. I would not work with Kim again. When her assignment concluded at Cedar Grove, Coconut Personnel placed her at a private medical practice. She worked in their medical records department and was hired full time. Kim and I have stayed in touch and talk on the phone now and again.

I called Coconut Agency and had to deal with snotty clone pimp Beth. She told me they did not have anything for my talents at the moment but to keep in touch. I felt I had been scammed by Coconut. They were never going to assign me to any job which would go permanent. Why should they when I was jumping through their hoops. I would go to any crappy company at the drop of a hat. I had never turned them down on any thing they called me about. It was apparent to me Annabel only placed her favorites in permanent positions. I decided to contact another agency and see if I would have better luck with them.

CHAPTER 13

A rat by any other name is still a rat

I went to all my old agency haunts to update my information and to re-test. I discovered an agency I had overlooked in the phone book called Nuts East Employment Services. I made an appointment and went in and did *their* dog and pony dance. The receptionist was a much older woman that I generally saw at agencies, named Mattie. She was in her mid sixties and had a very genuine air about her. The phones were hectic while I was interviewing with her. She took her time and gave me her full undivided attention. She told me they would get in touch with me if they got a position which suited my abilities.

A few days later the phone rang and when I answered it a woman said, "Hi this is Sara Lee." I replied," "Oh hi there, this is Little Debbie, why don't we get together and bake something?" There was absolute silence on the other end of the line. I hung up. I remembered as this was tumbling out of my big mouth, Mattie had told me the owners name was Sara Lee Swartz. Why did I say stuff like this? I checked the caller I.D. and darn if it didn't say Nuts East Employment. Later in the day I called back to check in with Mattie. She told me the owner wanted to meet with me and see if they could place me in a position. I did not mention my faux pas and neither did Mattie.

Mrs. Swartz was an older woman who spoke in a clipped precise manner. I got the impression she was having a hard time aging gracefully. She was at least sixty-five, very thin, wore heavy make-up, and her hair was dyed jet black. Mrs. Swartz had a hard crispy, edge about her, rather like a chocolate chip cookie with nuts that had been left in the oven too long. She seemed like she was on a life-threatening caffeine high and she was also very nosy. She was curious about my dealings with the Coconut Agency. I told her what had transpired between us. I also told her that I did not feel Annabel was interested in placing me any longer. Mrs. Swartz than told me that Annabel had once worked for her. She went on and on about how Annabel had stolen her book of business when she opened Coconut. I just nodded and I took it all in. She was very bitter about her relationship with Annabel. I thought, "I do *not* need to know these details. She has no business involving me in this distasteful tale of deceit." I let the conversation drop and we went on to other subjects. She told me of a position at a company called Oil and Chemical Services (OCS). It was a temp to permanent assignment. If I was interested I would not have to interview and I could start the following Monday. Of course I was! The position was for a clerical bookkeeping clerk with customer service duties. Mrs. Swartz went on to tell me the company used Peachtree software, and if I knew QuickBooks I would have no problems. She also told me it was an office manager position and I would be the only female working there. The company employed five other employees who were men. The Boys Club! While I was there, Sara Lee called the company, Oil and Chemical Services, and arranged for me to meet the manager Ernie. This way I would be at ease with the surroundings on Monday morning. When I arrived at OCS, the manager, Ernie Nubby, greeted me at the door, and showed me around the office and the warehouse. Ernie was sixty-two years old and told me he was looking forward to retiring in a few years. He was a tall slender man with silvery hair and happy blue eyes. He put me at ease immediately.

Ernie told me OCS was a small company and generated about one hundred thousand dollars a month in revenues. He explained the company supplied business in the Anytown and Adams county area with oil and chemical products. In addition he was in charge of the environmental services company which collected the same products, after they were used for recycling. The recycling company was called Merry-Sol.

While I was there, two of the drivers, Dick and Sam, came back from making their deliveries. Dick was a short stout middle aged man with a boisterous voice, he seemed pushy. Sam was a tall man at least six feet five inches. Sam was in good shape physically and in his early fifties. Sam reminded me of a typical Anytown county good old boy. We said our hellos and Ernie took me back into the office. Ernie told me I would meet the two salesman on Monday, Thomas Snooze and Bert Nubby. Ernie added that Bert was his brother. Bert had been one of the original owners of OCS and was now a salesman (I thought that was strange). In addition to meeting the salesmen, I would also meet Vincent Merry-Sol from the company in New Jersey that owned OCS. Vincent would be here the entire week and do all my training.

There were only two computers in the office. Ernie had a very old computer, but the one in my office was a newer model. Yes, I would have my own office, but unfortunately there was not a door on it. My office was jammed up with four waist high and two tall filing cabinets plus a safe. Ernie told me once I was settled in I could rearrange it to suit myself. Cool. Before I left, Ernie introduced me to the warehouse manager, Harry. What can I say about Harry? He was about fifty years old and seemed friendly enough at our first meeting. I got the impression he was shy. I could not get a good read on Harry.

Everyone I met seemed glad the position was being filled. Apparently they did not like answering the phone. Dick mentioned at the time, "We need a *woman* here to answer the phone when it rings." I let the remark slide, and thought, 'how sexist, Dick must be a jerk.' I would discover in addition to Dick being a jerk, he was lazy, a bully and a racist." Nevertheless, I drove off feeling at ease about my upcoming adventure at OCS.

On Monday morning I arrived at OCS and met Vincent Merry-Sol. Vincent was a large sturdy looking individual and very pleasant. Vincent was a great trainer and I had no problems learning the job or mastering Peachtree. The major problem for me was going to be getting used to the items and products they sold. I had never worked with fifty–five gallon, one hundred ten gallon, carboys and "tote" sized liquid inventory. I became proficient in all aspects of the position. What I would not become proficient in was dealing with Bert Nubby.

I would provide the *woman's* voice on the other end of the phone or the receptionist. I was the primary CSR processing all customer orders. I maintained the accounts receivable, payables, invoicing, the daily banking, and the inventory reconciliation. In addition to all of those duties, I generated the shipping documents, purchase orders, MSDS sheets, and ordered all of the office supplies. Vincent spent the entire week training me. I felt good about having an understanding of the position. Even so, Vincent spent a good amount of time on his cell phone. Vincent was the plant manager at Merry-Sol and the people from the plant were constantly calling him. We took a break so Vincent could get caught up on his voice mails. The salesmen had now arrived and Ernie introduced me to Thomas. Thomas was about thirty-five, married with two small daughters. He had the college boy look but was pudgy and soft. Thomas had worked at OCS for ten years. The only other job he ever worked at was as a shoe salesman. During the next year, Thomas and I would have a good relationship. Sometimes we were even silly. That would all change when he was promoted to Sales Manager.

Ernie's brother, Bert, was sixty-eight and did not look it. I would discover he had his hair cut and colored weekly. He was a vain, selfish man. He acted friendly and at one time I think he sincerely liked me. When I discovered he was stealing from the company his attitude towards me changed. Bert would play nasty little games along with Dick to try and get under my skin. The level of junior high school crap they would pull was ridiculous. The differences between Ernie and Bert were so extraordinary it was difficult to believe they were actually related.

There was only one person I had not met, the accountant Mr. Skinny Pickens. Slim processed the weekly payroll and would assist me with any problems that might arise. The only time Slim was in the office was on Wednesdays. He would arrive with the company paychecks and update the computer accounting software. He was not particularly friendly but he wasn't awful to work with either. He had a bit of a superiority complex but then what accountant doesn't?

I had only been working at OCS for two weeks when Thomas sat down at my desk one afternoon to go over his sales orders. Bert was seated at his desk outside of my office and Ernie was on the phone. Thomas said to me as his voice became stern, "Bert is an Ass." He did not lower his voice and made no attempt to keep from letting Bert hear what he is relating to me. Thomas continued, "Bert is a snake, he screwed Bonnie over," (who was his partner before they sold the business to Merry-Sol). "He got his cut, plus he kept his leased vehicle. By the way, the company still pays his *personal* car insurance, and his job at OCS is only as the head salesman." Thomas further warned me, "don't have anything to do with him." I just took it all in smiling and hoped I would not get caught up in what was going on between them. Thomas told me all the dirty details of how Bert manipulated the buyout and went to New Jersey on the sly to negotiate a juicy package for himself.

Thomas was no saint either. He would pretend he was on the road when he would be home in the afternoon. This way he did not need to hire a babysitter to care for the girls after school. Thomas would call me to see which customers had placed orders throughout the day. I would kid him when I heard his dog Boo—Boo, barking in the background, "Are you selling cleaners at a Kennel?" He would act as if I hadn't said anything. He thought he was *so* slick. Thomas also pretended he didn't know how to use a computer. This was pretty strange, since he had input all the orders when Bert and Bonnie owned the company. Thomas was very sneaky and could not be trusted.

The only woman I had contact with during the course of the week was the gal who did the cleaning, Janet. She was down to earth and we enjoyed many lunches and smoke breaks together. Janet told me one of the reasons Kate (who I replaced) had quit was because of Thomas' romantic advances. Janet said Kate had shown her letters Thomas had written to her. Kate was a single lady and was friendly to Thomas. He apparently read more into it then she meant him to. Janet said the correspondence was vulgar and disgusting. She went on to say Kate should have filed a sexual harassment claim against Thomas. Again I took it all in. I kept my dealings with Thomas friendly but strictly business. I did not want to give him any idea he could do the same to me.

Ernie and I worked together in perfect harmony. He would decide what vendors to pay each week and I would print the checks. I made new forms for the truck drivers and the waste department. When the cell phones, copiers, or printers needed service, I made sure the correct repair companies were called or the items were returned. I ran reports for the sales force so they were aware of their customer's payment status. I called on all the old past due accounts and attempted to collect money owed. I printed inventory reports for the warehouse manager. These reports would inform him of the vendors to use when he ordered products. I maintained the item inventory cards in Peachtree. The items listed in the computer were a mess. There were so many duplications and it was difficult to figure out what was what. I asked the accountant to straighten out the inventory but he could not be bothered. Even the CFO at Merry-Sol would not address the inventory issues. I was in fact the office manager, but only in name. I received no support from the office in New Jersey. I continued to work as best I could. Thomas was an aggressive salesman and brought in many new accounts.

I got along well with Harry, the warehouse manager. With his help I initiated a new and efficient procedure for warehouse receiving. Harry would usually come out and join me for a smoke. I thought we had a good relationship and I felt he was a friend. I was isolated at OCS being the only woman. His attention meant a lot since I did not get along with Dick or Bert. Harry disliked Bert intensely. He felt Bert had screwed Bonnie over during the buyout. He told me Bert was lazy and sneaky. Harry also told me Bert was stealing pails of grease from the warehouse. Bert would "give" the products to vendors or sell them under cost and pocket the money. Harry could never catch him in the act. Bert, like all of us had keys to the building. He could come in during the weekend and who would know. Harry also said Bert was brokering tanker loads of alcohol on the side. Again, he could not prove it. By now I have been working at OCS for one year. I was given a very generous pay increase. Hooray for me! I had not expected to be involved in all the drama going on at OCS. I had hoped this job would be *the* one. Things were not working out as I had planned.

During the summer Bert and his wife went to Finland for two weeks. They went there every year to visit her family and to sell her paintings. Thomas told me Bert's second wife, Helga, was a *trophy wife,* and wore the pants in the family. They went where she said they would go. Helga was an artist and lived a life of luxury. The atmosphere changed dramatically while Bert was gone. Thomas was more upbeat, Harry and Ernie were smiling, and I was ecstatic. The only person who missed Bert was Dick, birds of a feather . . .

I arrived each morning at seven thirty and Bert was always there first. Thomas told me Bert came in at six in the morning because his wife threw him out of the house. She could not stand him being around. The drivers usually got in at seven and would load their trucks and take off for the day's deliveries. Ernie would get in around eight thirty. Everyone would be working, except for Bert and Dick.

Bert would start his morning pacing routine and Dick would sit at the break table in the middle of the office reading the paper. The diesel truck would be running and wasting fuel until nine but Sam was always loaded up and on the road by eight. Since I was the office manger, I decided to cancel the daily paper. I could see no reason to get it as Dick was the only one who read it. I could get him out of the office and on the road where he belonged. Besides I would save the company over a hundred dollars a year by canceling the newspaper.

Dick whined to Bert about the paper being canceled. Bert went to the newspaper company and reopened the account. When the paper was delivered the next morning, there was the typical junior high school snickering between Bert and Dick. I called the company and closed the account again. I called Vincent at Merry-Sol and related the newspaper incident to him. Vincent agreed the newspaper was not needed. He proceeded to call Bert and told him to stay out of the daily running of the office and to turn in his company credit card. Vincent was reissuing *gas* cards for all the personnel with company vehicles. I was responsible for the petty cash. It was kept in one of the unlocked file cabinet drawers. Every once in a while there would be ten or twenty dollars missing. When I mentioned this to Ernie, he seemed surprised. He told me to move it to the safe if I wished. That was the end of the missing money. Harry told me it was Bert who pilfered the petty cash. Bert had always been permitted to take whatever he wanted when he was the original owner. Well he was not the owner anymore! Bert was constantly coming into my office and rifling though the invoices in the short filing bins. He would remove shipping documents and nose in everything. He could not stand knowing he was out of the loop. Finally one afternoon I had enough of his rummaging around my area. With Harry's help, I moved the file bins into the open office area. Now there was no reason for Bert to invade my space. When Bert saw that I had moved the filing bins, he was furious. He had finally lost all control. He should never have been allowed to remain at OCS when the company was sold. Bert could never get used to the idea that he was no longer an owner. At this point Bert began leaving at nine or ten every morning. I was glad he was out of the office. When Vincent would call, he could never talk with Bert as he was never in the office. I did not miss Bert's obnoxious behavior one bit. Bert was the most disruptive person I have ever been around in an office environment. He would pace constantly, pick his teeth, and run his long ugly finger nails across my cubicle wall as he walked up and down the room with his sloppy loafers clicking and clacking. He was a hyper freak who could not sit still. When I would transfer calls to him and the caller would inquire, "How are you?" Bert would answer, "I'm sobering up nicely, thank you." He was so unprofessional. All Bert did was maintain his old accounts. He had all the large primo accounts and had never pursued one new customer while I worked there.

My relationship with Dick would deteriorate over a pair of socks he ruined on the job. Dick was a very distasteful person to be around. If he would return from making deliveries and it was lunch time, he would sit at the break room table outside of my office. While that was not a problem, the fact that he ate with his mouth open was. It was disgusting listening to his chomping. Dick was also overweight so he would be gasping for breath as he ate. I would be in my office with no door on it, six feet from the table. Jeff would usually call me at lunch to see how my day was going. I made no bones about telling Jeff, "I am just sitting here getting sick to my stomach listening to Dick eat like a pig." I knew he heard me. Everyone at OCS except for Ernie always eavesdropped on my phone conversations. When Dick would hear me, he would slam his lunch box shut, stomp out to the warehouse, and rag to Harry about what he had overheard. I used this tactic when ever I wanted Dick out of the office. It worked very time.

Okay, let's now get back to the Tale of Dick's socks. DOT regulations require drivers to wear long pants. It doesn't matter if it's a hot summer day. One would think if your carrying and unloading fifty-five gallon drums of caustic chemicals, one would understand the personal safety issues. Sam and Dick both would wear short pants. There were a couple of manufacturing plants that would not allow them to unload because of this. Ernie was in charge of the drivers and would remind them, "remember you are going to Merry-Sol, no short pants." Ernie was a good guy, and his attitude was to protect them from themselves.

One afternoon Dick came into my office, in short pants, and **demanded** I pay him for the socks he had on. I looked at them and they, along with his boots, were covered in black grease. There was no doubt they were ruined. "I am not going to reimburse you for your shocks, if you had been dressed properly in long pants it would not have happened." Dick screamed, his voice was ear splitting, "they [meaning Bonnie] paid for a pair of pants that Thomas ruined!" I replied to him, keeping my voice even, though I was shaking inside, "Dick, I don't care if they paid for Thomas' pants. That was then, this is now. No one pays for my nylons which I ruin here in the office. I am not paying you for a pair of socks." Dick drew back like he was going to punch me and screamed, "You bitch!" I had made an enemy of Dick. He stormed out of the office and jumped into his good old boy pickup truck, tore out of the parking lot spraying stones everywhere. Ernie had heard everything. He walked back to my desk and gave me his take on what had just transpired.

"If he had spoken to my wife like that she would have slapped his face." he continued, "You need to stand up for yourself." I sighed and said, "Ernie I am not a violent person, I *will not* sink to his level." "Well Judy," Ernie replied, "things will never change then." What a hell of a way to have to work.

In retrospect I should have just given him the lousy two dollars. It was his superior attitude and the way he *demanded* the money that caused me to get my back up. This would go down in the annals of COS history as the *Sox Bow Incident*. Dick created an alliance with Bert to get me out of OCS. Bert told

Dick he would pull strings and Dick would be the next office manager and sales person. They did a lot of whispering and called each other on their cell phones. Like them, I could overhear their conversations as well. This was never going to happen, number one Bert had no influence at Merry-Sol, and number two, Dick was a crude foul mouthed truck driver. He possessed none of the sophistication and charm needed to be a salesman, let alone the computer knowledge to be an office manager. Thomas thought it was all very hilarious.

At this time, Ernie was interviewing potential drivers from Nuts Employment. The recycling department was very busy and Ernie was considering hiring another driver. One afternoon, as Dick was eating like a pig at the break table, a young man of Spanish descent stopped in to fill out an application. Ernie gave him the paperwork to complete and conducted the interview. After the young man left the office, Dick *shot* out of his seat and ran up to Ernie. "Is that Puerto Rican going to take my job, what is going on, are we going to have Ricans working here?" Dick was very agitated. Ernie in his mellow manner told Dick not to be concerned. I just sat at my desk fuming. Another typical Anytown county bigot, no wonder people say, "Anytown is a white man's town." You just can not get away from it.

The summer turned into fall and I continued working at OCS. It had become a distasteful experience but I was determined to do my job. I was not going to permit Bert and Dick to push me out. As the Christmas Season of 2005 began, the show "As the Stomach Turns" premiered at OCS. Like all companies, we began to receive Christmas cards, candy, large cans of snacks and fruit from our vendors. One morning Bert noticed the large can of popcorn we had received from Nickel Chemicals Company on the break room table. He came into my office and had the nerve to tell me, "Any booze that is delivered here is **mine.** I am the only one who can have it." What a total ass, so I said, "sure Bert whatever." Bert was also a drunk. He turned on his sloppy loafer heels and left for the day.

Harry was at his desk when this conversation occurred. He came over to me and said with a smile and a wink, "by the way, you've got to be here to claim it." We did claim three bottles of booze which were delivered. Harry, Thomas, and I were the only ones in the office when it was dropped off. In all fairness, we did leave a fifth of Crown Royal on Bert's desk.

The day before Christmas I went shopping on my lunch hour to pick up some last minute items. While I was in the liquor store, I spied a bottle of Chambord Liquor which also had two beautiful glasses packaged with it. I bought it for Jeff and I to enjoy after Christmas dinner. I wanted it to be a surprise. When I got back to the office I removed the glasses and liquor from the big Christmas box it was in and placed the box in my trash. This way I would be able to sneak it into our house.

Harry stopped in my office to go over the next days' deliveries and saw the box in my trash. Harry suggested to me, "Why don't you put that big box out in the warehouse trash the next time you go out?" I realized what he was planning. Harry continued, "Bert is coming back to the office this afternoon since we are closed tomorrow." I let Harry manipulate me, I could have said no. I took the box with the wrappings and placed it in plain sight in the warehouse trash can. I went back in the office and we picked up where we had left off.

Around three in the afternoon, Bert pulled back into his parking space and entered though the warehouse doors. When he came into the office he made a beeline directly for my office. Harry was still at his desk working. Bert's face was red and I could tell he was fit to be tied. "I told you any booze that comes here is for **ME**! Who took that bottle of Chambord?" I faced him and said, "I bought it for Christmas Eve to have with my husband. Would you like to see the receipt? You are a selfish vile old man." Bert just stood there stammering . . . "I, I, and I". He offered no defense or apology for accusing me of stealing. He walked *very* quickly out of the building and left.

Harry came over to me and said with a big smile, "You really got him. You should have waited a couple days before you told him so he could fume over the holidays." Harry was very pleased with himself, I felt like a fool. Ernie was at his desk and had heard everything. Ernie never offered any words in Bert's defense. He came into my office and said he knew what Bert was up to and what he was like but he could not get involved, "after all, he's my brother." I could appreciate how he felt. Merry Christmas to all! Ho, Ho, Ho!

By the following summer, the situation at OCS was becoming unhinged. I went on a real vacation for the first time in years. Jeff and I went to the Hawaiian Islands. It was wonderful to be away from the ugliness of COS for a time. When I returned on Monday it was a hectic day getting back in the groove and catching up on all the news. I had arranged for a temp while I would be gone. I did not know they had sent a woman of color. On Monday afternoon Dick was at the break table as usual chomping away when the young woman stopped back in to see Thomas. As she was walking up to the door, Dick yelled to Thomas, "Aunt Jemima's here." Thanks goodness she was not in the building yet. Welcome back.

In June, Ernie told us there was a very good possibility Merry-Sol was going to be bought out by a much larger recycling company. The deal was in the early stages of negotiations. During the following months, Dick became very aggressive towards me. When I would be walking out of the building in the evening, he would get in front of me and block me. He also would get within six inches of my face and push his chest out, preventing me from getting past him. I would walk around him and I never said a word. I began keeping a log of what was happening to me and what was going on with Bert.

It finally got so bad I contacted Vincent at Merry-Sol and emailed my daily logs to him. Shortly thereafter Merry-Sol's attorney contacted me. I knew he was feeling me out in case I was going to sue them for harassment. I told him no, that was not my intention. I did want something done about Dick. He needed to be written up or fired. He also questioned me regarding Bert's brokering bulk alcohol with Nickel Chemicals and the missing products from the warehouse. I told him to use my logs in any manner he wished. The following week the Chief Financial Officer from Merry-Sol, Killian, came to the office to do a physical inventory. I thought he was finally going to help me straighten out the database. After the inventory was taken, Killian told me the reason this was done was to obtain a dollar value of the products on hand. He told me he was sorry he could not assist me with the database. He added that he was resigning from Merry-Sol after the merger. Killian and Bert went to lunch after the inventory was completed and Killian returned to New Jersey. I could only surmise that they were in cahoots and things were only going to get worse.

A week later on a Friday morning, Vincent from Merry-Sol came to the office for a meeting. Vincent spoke with each of us separately. Harry and Thomas told me they informed him of the missing products and the alcohol deals with Nickel Chemicals. Ernie and I related the "Sox-Bow Incident" with Dick. I related how I was revolted by Dick's ongoing disparaging ethnic remarks. I also told him something had to be done about how I was being treated. By now it was ten and Bert had just pulled into the parking lot. Vincent and Ernie ended our meeting and went into the warehouse to speak with Bert. I never saw Bert again.

Vincent came back in the office with Bert's keys and the company cell phone and placed them on my desk. Vincent had fired Bert on the spot and Dick was written up. It was too late for any of this to make much difference. Thomas and Harry had gotten what they wanted and I received two supervisors. Harry was now the warehouse supervisor and purchasing agent and I would report to him. Thomas was now the Sales Manager (he would manage himself I guessed) and I would report to him also. Harry informed me that we would no longer be friends as he was my boss now. Thomas was his sheepish spineless self and told me the identical thing. Now I was having fun!

The following Wednesday as I was opening the mail, I came across a bill from the garage OCS used for repairs. The invoice was for six hundred dollars and the items were four brand new Bridgestone tires. Now I knew why Bert was so late arriving at the office the previous Friday. Apparently he *knew* what was coming down and had replaced the tires on his personal Jeep. "That's Bert, what a guy," stealing from the company up to the last possible minute.

In August, Debra from Cedar Grove called me with very sad news about Kim. I had lost touch with her and did not know she had been pregnant. In July

Kim had a baby boy. Her dear baby had died of SIDS and the funeral was the very next day. Debra told me she could not go to the funeral but had already been to the viewing. After we hung up I called Kim and we talked for awhile. She was a mess, and told me the hospital could not give her answers as to why her baby had died. She asked me if I would come to the funeral. I told her, "of course, I will be there." I went. It was the saddest day, I will always remember. There must have been two-hundred people there but not one representative from Coconut Personnel. I could not believe Annabel was not there. Neither were Annabel's little pimps, Beth or Shannon. I was appalled that they did not attend to offer their sympathy and condolences. I was the only one from Coconut who attended.

In September Merry-Sol was sold to Ailoev Environmental Services. Ernie informed me my job would be eliminated as Atioev had an office in Emigstown. All the duties I had performed would be transferred to their accounting departments. I had been employed there one year and 10 months. My husband told me once that I was like Joe Btfsplk from the Little Abner comic. I was starting to believe him. I felt like I was walking around with a dark cloud over my head. It seemed once I'd appear on a job, dreadful luck would befall anyone in my vicinity. I feared an unjustified reputation might be preceding me after this employment calamity. Once again I packed up my belongings. I purposely left my old white office sweater over the back of my chair. I figured I was entitled to a new one after dealing with all the crap. I planned on calling Mattie at Nuts East Employment once again.

Chapter 14

Do you feel Lucky?

My next step after leaving OCS was to call Nuts East Employment. I had successfully sunk into a quagmire at the last place they sent me. What more harm could possibly befall me? Mattie had a position at Zetso Granite requiring an interview process. I really dislike having to interview for a temp job, it is totally redundant. I had already gone to Nuts and had been retested and now I would waste fuel driving to this company. Nuts East was driving *me* nuts! I was ten minutes early for the interview. Being early only added to the time I waited to meet Catherine of the Human Resources Department. When our interview finally convened, Catherine and I waited some more. This time I was waiting for the department head, Loretta. Eventfully Loretta arrived and the interview continued.

Loretta was a well dressed attractive woman in her mid fifties. Loretta and Catherine asked all the same old questions and I gave all the right answers (I must have as I was assigned to the position).We shook hands and I was thanked for my time. The following week Mattie called me and gave me the good news. I would start on Monday and needed to go to the Human Resources Department to have a badge made. I managed to waste two hours on Monday morning sitting around with three other new employees. The only difference between them and me was they were being *hired* for the manufacturing plant. We finally completed the badge routine only to be left in a room to watch the standard safety video.

The room was hot as Hades and it was difficult to stay awake listening to the monotone safety video. It was a good thing we stayed alert since no one came in to shut off the video player. One of the young men showed great leadership and got out of his seat and hit the stop button. Catherine came running in to shut off the video player fifteen minutes later and was surprised to see one of us had already done it. We were finally herded off to our respective departments.

I had to drive to the building I would be working in. Catherine gave me good directions and by ten-thirty I had finally gotten to my destination. The receptionist at this building called to the Account Payable Department and I waited again. I was leafing through their company magazine when a woman named Tabitha came to lead me to the fire below. Tabitha was very friendly and I got excellent vibes from her. She was a slender woman in her early forties with springy brown curls and smiling eyes. Tabitha was a perfect lady with a sense of humor. I never heard a swear word exit her lips. She was always in fine spirits. Tabitha never let someone else's poor mood have an effect on her attitude.

Tabitha explained she would be training me and I would be assisting her. I would have my own work space down the hall from her. Tabitha said she had been a temp at Zetso for three years. I did not like hearing this and it did not make me feel confident about the future. We went down the stairs into the basement area where the department was situated. With the exception of not having windows, the department looked like any other in a large company. All the offices were freshly painted, the walls were hung with the typical motivational posters and the' desks' and equipment were the very latest.

Tabitha and I stopped in at Loretta's office and she formally welcomed me to the department. Loretta was a first-rate person to work for. She generally had time for my questions when Tabitha was not available. Next I met Betty, who processed the expense reports for the company. Betty was around forty years old with blondish gray hair. She had natural clean prettiness and gave me a genuine reception. We made our way to where I would be working. There were three office areas where I was. Verona, the import specialist, was directly behind me, and a very diminutive woman, Becky, was in the adjoining office. Becky was an administrative assistant to a salesman on the first floor. She explained to me that there was not enough room for her upstairs so they had *stuck* her in the basement. She was a little person and the steps were difficult for her to navigate. I would not have many dealings with Becky but when I did she was a delight.

While Tabitha was getting me set up at my desk, I saw one of the accountants I had worked with in the IDG department at Anytown International, Gertrude. She was glad to see me and I was surprised to see her working at another company. Gertrude explained there were changes when Johnstown Controls bought out Anytown International. She went on to say the entire department had been eliminated. Gertrude also had more children than I remembered. She took me to her office and showed me the pictures of her four beautiful children. The last I had known she only had one little baby boy. She had put on a great deal of weight during the years and her demeanor was very serious. Gertrude was not the bubbly energetic person I remembered.

I got back to my desk in time for Tabitha to invite me to join her and Betty for lunch. They usually walked downtown and this was great by me. The building was only four blocks from the Anytown city square. Over the months nothing would change with these great ladies. They would add Verona to the blend and we would enjoy many afternoon strolls. We would go to Central Market and grab a bite to eat as we walked around window shopping. This assignment was a data entry position utilizing Excel Spreadsheets in an AS400 operating system. I would be inputting job costs and journal entries. In addition I would process freight bills for payment and audit invoices for department authorizations.

The manner in which Zetso processed their accounting was ungodly repetitive. It was not unusual to have to enter something four times. Every item had a spreadsheet in addition to being processed in the AS400 system. All payables were cost against a job number, over and over and over again. The spreadsheets themselves were humongous. I processed the journal for the accounts payables monthly totals. This journal often had eight hundred or more entries. If it had not been for Tabitha, I would never have been able master the work.

After the first month, I began to get a sense of the "people" issues around me. Gertrude was horribly over worked. She had changed from the happy go lucky girl I knew at Anytown International. She was short tempered and demanding. The other woman in the department told me she was down right mean on the phone to her children and husband. She was not usually included in our luncheon activities. I did not think this was unusual since she was an accountant. Verona was the only other degreed person in the department besides Loretta. Verona was a sweet young single mother. She was always swamped with work. When she could break away, she would occasionally join Tabitha, Betty and I on lunch walks.

I had been at Zetso for three months when things began to change with Gertrude. Tabitha was having a lot of problems in her dealings with her. Gertrude had made accounting changes which caused friction within the entire company. Gertrude was trying her best to get better control on the invoice flow and authorization process. Many of the employees of the company did not appreciate what she was attempting to accomplish. They would not cooperate and Gertrude found herself up against countless brick walls. Naturally Gertrude took this frustration out on the people in her department.

I was copying hundreds of invoices each day, and I did not have a code to access the copy machine. I had to have someone who did have a code go with me every time I went to the copy room. This went on for weeks. Finally Tabitha gave me her *secret* number and told me, "If you tell anyone I will have to kill you." She was such a cutup. Eventually, three weeks before I left the assignment, the I.T. department finally gave me my own *personal* code.

Tabitha was becoming disgusted with the entire situation at Zetso. She had been there three years and knew she would probably never be hired full time. Tabitha started job hunting and not too long afterwards she left Zetso. I really missed her company. The job I was doing changed from a data entry position into a copy and forward job. All I would do all day is make copies of invoices and forward them to department heads for approvals. I could not enter anything for payment until the copies were returned. The people who needed to approve the invoices did not return them in a timely manner at all. I would often forward invoices two and three times before I finally got an approved copy returned. It was a nightmare and I could not keep up. When I asked Gertrude for help she went into dragon woman mode. She informed me it was *my* problem, and I would just have to work overtime. I could not see any reason to continue beating my head against the Zetso wall. I called Mattie at Nuts East Employment and told her the situation. This was something Mattie did not want to hear, not in the least. She told me they had no other positions and I would have to learn to like it. I told her I was giving my notice but I don't think it sunk in. I continued to call her every other day and to tell her I wanted to be reassigned. Mattie informed they did not have much clerical work.

I put in a call to another agency I had registered with named Accountemps. This company was located in Mechanicsburg, PA. The pimp I was assigned to was named Steve. I really liked Steve when I met him. He was straight forward and pleasant. Steve told me they had an accounts payable position which would start in two weeks at Hauler Transportation Refrigeration in Anytown. He also said it was definitely a temporary to permanent placement. I readily accepted this assignment. It was becoming apparent to me nothing was going to come of staying at Zetso.

During my conversations with Mattie at Nuts, I was also talking with Loretta, the accounts payable manager about the situation. Like Gertrude she could not help me, and let me know she had her own work to do. I was sure this was true. I could see the piles upon piles of work spilling over her in bin. No one was taking me seriously. On Friday two weeks after I had began these discussions, I emailed Mattie and Loretta that I would not be returning on Monday. Apparently this was now a *big* surprise to all. When I called Mattie she was very upset and told me to never call them again. I had put them in a terrible position. I reiterated to her, "I told you I wanted off this job and that I would be leaving within two weeks." Mattie replied, "That is not how it is done, you did not do it right, you can't just walk off." I tried to explain that I had warned her. The telephone went dead. She had hung up on me. I called her back and she told me, "we cannot assist you, don't call back." I can take no for an answer. Nevertheless I was sad that I did not have the opportunity to bake something with Sara Lee.

This is what happens when you do not play their games. Some of the agencies pimps will bully you into remaining on jobs. Once you are placed at a company it can be nearly impossible to be reassigned, unless you like the job. If you are happy and enjoy the job you're doing, you can bet your bottom dollar it will not last. I had confirmed my assignment with Steve from Accountemps and arrived at Hauler Transport Refrigeration the following Monday morning. I was met by Tamari, a young attractive African American woman. She was from the Harrisburg area and had gotten a job closer to her home. Tamari was starting the new position the following Monday. She made no bones about the people I would be reporting to weekly. She said they were very demanding and unfriendly. Tamari also said, "I can't wait to be out of here." This was not a good sign.

The position was not for an accounts payable clerk but was for an Account Payable *Analyst*. I would report to the CFO and the President of the company to explain "Million" dollar account statuses at a weekly board meeting. I would also track this information on very complicated spreadsheets. Tamari told me, "I have an associated degree in business and I still had problems with the complexities of this job." I knew I did not have the experience or training for such a position. We went over the job flow and some of the duties until lunch time. Tamari and I decided I could not handle the work and went to her boss. The manager was happy I did not waste anymore of their training time. I called Accountemps and spoke with Rachel. I informed her of the problems I was encountering. Rachel assured me they understood, to work out the day and they would get a more qualified person for the position.

I helped Tamari with her filing and copying until the end of the day. The other ladies I met at lunch told me not to be upset about leaving. One of the women told me, "it is a very hard, demanding position; we get a new temp in every three months." This did not make me feel real good, but I felt less bad.

This had not been a good move for me to undertake. Now I had no job at all. As the position had not worked out and it was no fault of mine, I was able to open an unemployment claim. I would not work until February of 2007. I could not help but think I should have toughed it out and stayed at Zetso. Steve from Accountemps called me in January for a one day assignment at a company called By-way. The company manufactured metal one gallon and one quart cans with lids. I would report at six on a Saturday morning to assist with their bi-yearly inventory. I joined about fifteen or so other temps from various agencies in the break room. The company had set out boxes of donuts and all the free coffee we could consume. A company representative gave us a comprehensive training session at which time we were each paired up with an employee. I lucked out and worked with a very cool older man. He was delighted I had such nice handwriting. We decided he would count and I would write. As we were working, he inquired as to what my true profession was. (Boy is that a loaded question!) I kept it simple and said "I am in accounting, like 1 2 3 I am a counting, but if I take off my shoes I become a Chief Financial Officer." That broke the ice and we continued *a counting*.

It was very interesting to see how cans were manufactured. I felt as though I was in a real life 'How it's Made' T.V Show. We broke for lunch which the company provided. They had a ton of pizza for everyone. We stuffed our little Pac-man faces and went back to work. The assignment ended around two and all of the temps congregated back in the break room. The man in charge signed our time cards and thanked us for doing such a great job. I jumped in my car and took off for home. I stopped in at the Highway House on my way home for a victory beer. It had been an enlightening and fun day.

I had contacted an agency in Harrisburg called ACSY when I was first out of work. ACSY was a professional accounting placement agency so I did not expect to hear from them. Wanda Marshall called me from ACYS and was interested in setting up a meeting. She was very nice and suggested we meet for lunch at Isaacs' Restaurant in Mechanicsburg, her treat. I could not turn down a free lunch! Wanda asked me to copy my ID and bring it along with me. Wanda would do the entire hiring process at the restaurant. This way I would not have to drive to Harrisburg. This was a great solution to the problem I had driving in Harrisburg, I always got lost.

We met on a cold damp windy January day. I had no idea what she looked like and did not know how I would find her once I was in the restaurant. Wanda had already arrived and had left word at the hostess desk I would be joining her. When I arrived at the table Wanda had a steaming cup of coco awaiting me. I was not used to being treated so nicely. She was in her sixties and was comfortable to be around. Wanda did not have a problem with aging; she had a casual, friendly, natural appearance. We did all the paper work in the restaurant and enjoyed a lovely lunch. Wanda told me she would keep in touch. If she got anything in the Anytown area, she would let me know. Wanda has since retired form ACYS and I am sure she is missed. Wanda called me in February with an assignment at a company called Ground Hog Pools. It would be for about five months. I would be assisting the manager of the customer service department, Chipper Thomas. Wanda said the primary duties would be entering the spreadsheet pricing computations for the upcoming 2007 catalog. I would also be a backup for the customer service department. I would handle customer service calls and enter sales orders.

When I arrived, I immediately had a problem finding a parking spot. This company employed around thirty people and the parking lot was covered with skids loaded with pool accessories. There were piles of skids every where and in every direction. What a mess! What I would find *inside* was even worse. The receptionist buzzed Chipper Thomas who came to get me immediately. Chipper was a large dark haired man. He was young, I would say about thirty. I would discover he knew what he was doing and was an expert in the field of pool construction. The only problem was he would be on pool sites much of the time. I would be working with two customer service women who were *no* fun. Chipper introduced me to Daisy and Ellie May and left me with them.

Ellie May took me to a vacant desk and told me it had belonged to a customer service woman they had fired a week or so before. She told me to get settled in and to go back to see Daisy. Ellie May was about forty years old and was a hard ass old wrinkled up biker chick. I would find out everyone at Ground Hog had a pool in their yards. Ellie May had spent way too much time out in the sun. Her skin was dark and stiff looking. She looked much older than she was. Ellie May's attitude towards me was, I am in charge of **YOU,** and you are my very own personal *slave* temp. Initially she would be somewhat friendly and invite me to join her on breaks, but never to lunch. Ellie May's husband had bought a Harley Davidson motorcycle that spring. She fancied herself to be a biker chick and wore a cheap nylon Harley Davidson jacket to work.

One *casual* Friday, I wore my beautiful American produced leather jacket. I never wore my leather except when I was on Jeff's motorcycle. I could not resist showing it off to her. Of course she did not complement me about the jacket but I saw her look at it as it was hanging on the coat rack. During the time I worked there, Ellie May's husband never took his motorcycle out of their garage. He did not know how to ride and was planning on taking a motorcycle riding course first. Ellie May was just a mean old wannabe.

Daisy was an attractive older woman who was probably very pretty before she fried her skin after years by her pool. She had been employed by Ground Hog Pools for thirty years and told me in no uncertain terms she was an expert in all aspect of the pool business. Daisy added, "I should be the manager and I would be if I wasn't a woman." I was getting a lot of information I really did not want to know on my first day.

The two remaining employees in the department were Ryan, the catalog artist, and Ashley, the pool design engineer. Both of them were terrific. Ryan was about twenty-two and had a punk rock appearance. He had a nefarious sense of humor. Ashley was not your mainstream engineer. She was very engaging and I would assist her when she needed old archived pool plans pulled from storage. Chipper was a super guy, when he was there. His primary function (or so it seemed to me) was to put out fires. Ground Hog Pools was totally unprepared for the coming sales season. Not only was the catalog pricing not done, neither was the artwork. They also had cash flow problems. Vendors would not ship parts needed for spas and pool kits which in turn caused a gap in manufacturing and delivery times. Ground Hog used two major vendors, Amish Plastics and Sunny Liner Company. I would discover all three of these companies were owned by the Sun and Surf Company across the parking lot.

The office area I worked in was on the second floor. There was a powder coating factory on the first floor. The manufacturing area was about the size of an acre. Upstairs overlooking the powder coating facility was the area where the samples and brochures were stored. This was also the area were items were packaged for shipment to Ground Hog Pools' dealers. It was without a doubt the filthiest place I was ever forced to work and it was freezing cold. There was black powder coating dust everywhere. The dust was so thick you could write in it, "Please wash me!" When I had to go out to this area I would ruin my clothing. I kept a Ground Hog Pools sweatshirt over my chair to wear when I would be banished to that area. I certainly was not going to bring in my new black sweater from home just to have it get ruined.

Daisy was in charge of the sample and brochures department. She was another person who was only sociable enough to keep the yearly temp from leaving. Daisy told me she had to instruct a new temp each spring to help her. I think Daisy was genuinely nice but was not interested in being friendly with the yearly temp. They come, they go. At lunch time each day, Daisy would go home to let her dogs out and spend time with them. I wished I had lived closer so I could have done the same thing. One of her beloved pets passed on while I was working there. Daisy was heartbroken. She never missed a beat and gave her clients the excellent service they anticipated.

The entire building that Ground Hog Pool occupied was dilapidated and old. The bathrooms were disgusting. There was no hot water, the tiles on the floors and walls were covered with mold. Half of the overhead lights were burned out the entire time I was there. The only reason I could see where I was going in the bathroom was because there was a window in the room. Not only was there no hot water in the bathrooms, there was no hot water *anywhere* in the facility. When I said something about this to Daisy, she told me," if you have a problem washing your hands with cold water, then you need to bring in a bottle of germicide to use." Apparently the management felt this was an insignificant issue.

I would spend very little time lending a hand to the CSR's. The only time I would assist with customer service was during the lunch hours. Daisy went to lunch at eleven and Ellie May went at one. Every day around eleven forty-five, Ellie May would go for *another* smoke before I went to lunch. I was supposed to go for lunch from noon until one. Needless to say, I never got out on time. She would walk past my desk and say in a very stern voice (I guessed she spoke to her dog like this), "**You sit,** and I am going out for a smoke. **You** just wait until I get back." Baugh, Baugh, Baugh. Every single day for five months, Ellie May ordered me to stay put. She always called me YOU. (She never even called me by my name . . . you know how the song goes) By the end of May the catalog was finally completed. After the catalog was finished, I would spend hours in the filthy second story storage area packaging and mailing marketing aids to the Ground Hog dealers. I packed box after box of brochures with parts samples and placed them on skids for shipment. One of the items included heavy 12 inch by 36 inch pool vinyl samples. Vinyl samples become very heavy and the work was so grimy. This was, in fact, Daisy's job but I would do this most of the time, except when Chipper was in the office.

Ellie May and Daisy had only taught me the basics of the customer service job. I could not effectively help the dealers when they called to place orders. If a call became too technical, I would have to transfer it to one of them. They made sure I was pulling samples or doing their filing. The only time I worked the phones was if Chipper was in the office. They did not pull this crap when he was there. I let Chipper know what they were doing and he made sure I had enough work to keep me busy when he was gone. Chipper told me he would be out of town during most of the month of June. He would be overseeing new pool construction sites and established pools which had warranties issues. Chipper had instructed Carol, the boss of I.T., to utilize me while he was working in the field. Carol was the nicest person I met at Ground Hog, besides Chipper. She was about forty with flaming red hair and dressed in happy island clothing. She was very cool. I helped the I.T. department with the yearly updating of the parts pricing. Again I was inputting from huge stacks of green bar paper reports. Carol was a skillful teacher, and *always* had time for my questions. She kept me busy updating bills of materials in the AS400 program.

Chipper also had given me the daily open back order reports to audit. On any items over two weeks late in shipping, I was to go to the purchasing agent. Chipper instructed me to *demand* an answer as to when the order would be completed. He wanted the backorder report kept up to date. This was not something a temp should be instructed to do. I had to go downstairs to the purchasing agent Milt. He was nice enough and I really hated to *demand* information as Chipper had instructed me. Milt understood and did his best to help me and get answers for Chipper. If Milt could not resolve an issue, he would send me to his boss, Miss. Prissypanties.

Miss Prissy was the beauty queen and the main purchasing agent for Ground Hog Pools. Everyone deferred to her like she was royalty (particularly the men). She had worked for many years at the company. Miss Prissy was a looker and she knew it. She too was a tanning freak. She was conceded and had very little time to be civil. She was another one with long skeletal icicles dangling from her nose. I dreaded going to her when Milt could not assist me. Luckily for me this did not occur often. By the end of June, this assignment was drawing to a conclusion. I will never forget how wonderful it felt driving out of Ground Hogs precarious parking lot on my final day.

Jeff and I enjoyed a superb Fourth of July celebration. We went to the fireworks display in Anytown City on his Harley. I, of course, wore my beautiful black leather jacket. After the fabulous display of pyrotechnics, we stopped to rent a few movies. Jeff got a Bruce Willis flick and I picked out a movie entitled *The Temp* (I am a Timothy Hutton fan). I wholly related to the main character and wished I could have had the lead role. I highly recommend it to anyone considering working as a temp. On Monday following the holiday weekend, I received a phone call from the owner of a collections company. He had discovered my resume on the website Monster. He was searching for a part-time data entry clerk. He wanted to know if I could come to an interview after lunch. Not a problem on my end. I dressed in my black suit (which was holding up well considering how much mileage it was getting) and drove to United Commercial Financial Services.

Their offices were in the same building where Coconut Personnel had been located in East Anytown. United Commercial Financial Services offices were nothing special; it was a predictable gray cubicle world. The work area was a large open space with peewee cubicles. I did notice the employees all had brand new Dell computers. I was greeted at the front desk by an older woman, Cherry who was very congenial. As I sat waiting, I could hear her speaking with clients and the other employees. I got the impression she was extremely knowledgeable in the collections profession. Even though I only waited for about ten minutes, there was a lot going on in the office. There were five employees and they were all on their phones. Their conversations were all low key and they often asked Cherry questions. I was interviewed by the sales manger, Willy Dickers, and the accountant Vanessa. I do not mind being double teamed at an interview. The interviewers think they intimate candidates by doing this. Not me, I figure, "the more the merrier!" Vanessa explained that the position was strictly inputting information supplied from their clients for delinquent accounts. I would be researching debtors using the ACCURNT website. She explained I would be using a windows based collection software program and she would also train me. I would be assisting the full time person doing this job. The position was part-time but it was thirty-two hours a week. They offered me a good starting wage and I felt good about the interview. Vanessa was a generously proportioned woman with long brunette hair and dark brown eyes. She was very down to earth and genuinely sociable. Willy was an archetypical salesman. He went on and on about what a wonderful company United Commercial Financial Services was and what a great opportunity it would be for me. He had a puffed up manner about himself and at one point in the interview, he put his feet up on his desk while we talked.

Mr. Dickers called the owner, Alexander Monday, into the interview and now there were four of us stuffed in his office. Alexander was a small man with a big name and I could tell he was another Napoleon who thought he was dynamite. He was perhaps in his fifties with short balding blond hair and pale blue eyes. His energy level was like two exposed wires making contact and he did not sit down during my interview. I dismissed him in my mind as not being anyone of consequence except to himself. Alexander also told me how wonderful his company was and how busy they were. He dismissed himself as his cell phone rang and left the stifling hot room. We did the "shake hands" all round and I drove back home. To my surprise Mr. Dickers called me that evening and offered me the position. They wanted me to start the following day. He explained the person who had been doing the job had left unexpectedly. By now I know this means one of two things. This person either walked out or had been fired. "Wonderful", I think, "what am I getting into now?" If I had known what a carnival this company was I could have saved myself tons of grief and just said no. I was going to experience something incredible at this company. For now I was thrilled to be starting a *real* job, not a temp job.

On Tuesday morning, I arrived eager to begin my new job. Vanessa would be my tour guide though Area 51. First, I formally met Cherry who was the Office Manager. She told me she had all the answers if Vanessa was not available. Cherry explained she had retired from a bank in Anytown where she had worked for twenty-five years as a loan officer. I would discover by the end of the week that Cherry and Alexander were an item. There would be *lots* of drama between the two of them. Next I met Maurice and Lolita who sat in the same row I was sitting. Maurice was a sturdy, handsome African American gentleman, and Lolita a young Spanish woman who was very good looking. She was built like a brick you know what. Maurice was married with small children. Lolita was married but did not have children as of yet. Lolita would sit next to me and was a big help while I worked there. She and Cherry were very tight. When Alexander and Cherry were having their little tiffs, Cherry would cry to Lolita. Yes, Cherry would actually shed tears in the office.

On the opposite row of cubicle from me was an empty desk, which I surmise belonged to the person who was gone. In the next mini cubicle was a middle aged African American gal, Diamond. She was friendly and invited me to go on break with her, she was a smoker too. Behind Diamond was a pretty young woman named Catlin. She was about twenty-two with long dirty blond hair. Catlin was small gal who was very contentious and friendly. I would find out that she was in charge of the collectors much like a first line supervisor. Catlin was a very smart capable collector. Oh and by the way, I was no longer part-time. I would be working forty hours a week. I had surmised correctly the other person had walked out. Vanessa had me place my tote along with my new black office sweater at my cubicle. I would train in her office. Since the noise level was high out on the collection floor, Vanessa felt I would pick the job up faster in the quiet of her office. By the end of the first day, I was working in the system and catching on to the process.

Wednesday saw me seated at my desk and getting into a routine. I would check on the returned mail in the morning on the ACCURNT website and enter new debtors in the afternoon. I had a phone at my desk but Willy told me it did not work. He said Alexander had a temper tantrum one day and he pulled it out of the wall causing the outlet to split. "Oh, that is just super." I thought. Alexander's office was directly behind me and I wondered what else was in store.

On Thursday Willy introduced me to the two young women who worked for him as part-time telemarketers, Lenora and Angel. They worked in a small room at the front of the office making cold calls from the telephone directory. Lenora was thin with long dark hair and lots of make up. She was a pretty girl, but dressed like a hooker on vacation. Angel was a blond with facial tattoos' and piercings. She wore a tight skirt which only served to accent her baby fat. Both girls wore flip-flops with their short tight skirts and tighter low cut shirts. They had graduated from high school in June and did not show much common sense when it came to office fashion. Willy was constantly getting on them about dressing more conservatively, something they never did. Secretly I think he *loved* the way they dressed.

On Friday afternoon, the crap hit the fan with Diamond. She went into Alexander's office yelling that her paycheck had bounced. The conversation between them escalated into a shouting battle very quickly. Diamond told Alexander she was going to the cops and he could not stop her. Alexander yelled back, "don't you threaten me!" At that point Alexander closed his door. They continued screaming at each other until Cherry ran back and went into Alexander's office. Cherry escorted Diamond out of the building. When Cherry returned she made an announcement to all of us, "Diamond was very upset, and is going to be off until Wednesday." I was sitting there wondering why Cherry found it necessary to broadcast this information and what had I gotten myself into. I looked at Lolita and she smiled at me and said laughingly, "don't worry about the outburst, Diamond has anger issues, just ignore it. She is on probation and is taking anger management class, but they don't seem to be helping." Maurice, Lolita, and Catlin went back to work as if nothing unusual had happened. I put on my headset, found a good radio station, and tried to concentrate on my work. At the end of the day I left with the end of the work week giddies. I pulled out of the parking lot wondering what calamities next week would bring.

On Monday of my second week, I went out to break with Catlin and Maurice. While we were relaxing in the morning sun, Maurice asked me if I had noticed the ankle monitor Alexander wore. I asked, "What ankle monitor? What do you mean?" I noticed Catlin looking at Maurice with one of those looks we all use which conveys 'Don't say anything.' Maurice ignored her and

Catlin when back into the building. After she had left, he informed me that Alexander was on probation for theft by deception and various other charges. He continued, "The office was raided a month ago by the F.B.I. and the local police department. Someone reported him for having *supposed* child porn. That is why we have new computers; the police still have the old ones." Good Grief Charlie Brown! I finished my cigarette and went back inside.

Tuesday and Wednesday were tumultuous days for Alexander and Cherry. They must have had a fight and Cherry was in and out of his office all morning. In between the trips to Alexander's office, she would stop at Lolita's' desk with the play by play. To add to all of the drama, Diamond came in to work late on Wednesday. Alexander called her into his office and fired her. Cherry proceeded to escort her out of the office for good. This place had more drama than Days of Our Lives. During this time I was becoming friendlier with Vanessa. She and I would go out for afternoon breaks and sit at the picnic tables. She told me she had only started working there two weeks before me. Vanessa was a very smart woman and told me she was starting to see the writing on the wall. She said there were money problems and the payroll account was so screwed up she had to close it. I asked her if my check was going to bounce too. "Not this week, I changed the accounts to another bank and I think it is straightened out." Then she added, "for now anyway."

Thursday and Friday of my second week were more normal. When the collectors would get an account settled, they would give the information to Cherry. They would usually get the payment in the form of an automatic check deposit from the debtor. Apparently Cherry would then buzz Alexander on his phone. Alexander would come out of his office and strut around like a cock rooster saying at the top of his lungs, "let's hear it for Lolita or Catlin," or who ever had collected the funds. His loud boisterous behavior was very distracting.

Friday was as normal as any day could be at United Commercial Financial Services. Maurice's paycheck had bounced and he was in Alexander's office when I left. As Vanessa and I walked out to our cars she told me, "call your bank, and tell them your checks might not clear." I just stared at her and replied, "I am telling you Vanessa if my checks do not clear you will never see me again." I had said this to Lolita also. Lolita had checks bounce, but she said, "Alexander always makes them good." Vanessa told me to deposit my paycheck in my savings account and wait to make sure it cleared before I wrote checks on it. This was ludicrous, like everyone else I needed spending money by the end of the week. I knew this was a good idea, and did what she suggested. I had gotten two checks and as far as I knew nothing was amiss. We were standing at our cars getting ready to leave when Vanessa turned to me and said, "For your information, Alexander is under house arrest, which is why he wears an ankle monitor and only works half days." She added," Cherry picks him up and takes him home everyday, he doesn't have a driver's license either." This would be last time I saw Vanessa.

I would talk to her on the phone later after all this played out. During our conversation Vanessa told me she could not expose herself as an accounting professional to the illegal actives she thought Alexander might be involved in. At least she called me.

Week three was a play by play of week two with the exception of a new employee coming on board. Scott was introduced to us by Cherry on Monday, he was replacing Diamond. Scott was an easy going guy and knew Alexander though a casual acquaintance. He had lost his drivers license and was using the bus service. Scott lived near me, so by the middle of the week I would take him home each night. We got to be fast buddies in the short time we worked together. Working at United Commercial was an unbelievably incredible experience. Between Cherry and Alexander's drama, people quitting, people being fired and paychecks bouncing, my head was swimming. Knowing what I did about Alexander, I felt weird when he would come to my desk. I was now into my fourth week at United Financial Commercial Services. I knew this was a limited engagement. I did not realize the final curtain was descending at such a rapid pace.

On Thursday afternoon, Alexander spent most of the morning either on the phone or franticly shredding documents in his office. Cherry was trotting back and forth talking to Alexander behind closed doors. No one was allowed in Alexander's office but Cherry at this point. Lolita tried to keep things light hearted. There was a lot of good natured bantering back and forth between her, Scott and Caitlin. Scott kept glancing in my direction, when we would make eye contact I would just shake my head. I knew Scott was very concerned, he was paying child support. He told me if he had a check bounce he was going to *mess up* Alexander. I knew this was just man talk. As all this was going on, the telemarketers, Lenora and Angel were flipping out to Willy about *their* pay checks bouncing. Just then my cell phone rang, it was my bank. You guessed it ~ my last two checks had boomeranged. This was no longer a carnival; it was now a larger then life three ring circus.

After speaking to my bank representative and getting instructions on how to proceed, I packed up my tote and grabbed my sweater. I said goodbye to Lolita and Scott. He would have to take the bus this night. As I was backing out of my parking space, Alexander and Cherry were running up to my car. Alexander took a hold of my window and told me, "Don't leave. I will make your check good. Judy, don't go!" Oh but I had heard these words before, I think it was Mr. McMaster many years ago. I kept backing out slowly, but Alexander would not let go of my car. I had to stop. I knew I could not run over him, even though

I was tempted to do so. It was all I could do to say," forget it Alexander, you're not getting away with this. I can *not* perform in this freak show any longer." I punched the gas. As the tires squealed I shot out of the parking lot. I drove straight to the Springettsberry Police Department. As I was sitting at a red light, I realized I had left my new black office sweater over the back of my chair. Once I arrived at the police station I sat in my car to compose myself. I was so angry, I knew I was not going to make any sense if went into the station. I sat for a bit and smoked another cigarette. I took a deep breath. I wanted to be calm and credible when I walked up to the desk. The credible part I would not have to worry about. I had never been in a police station in my life. I was so irate that Alexander had caused me to take these steps.

I bravely walked up to the desk and inquired of the officer what I needed to do regarding a bounced paycheck. When I told him the name of the company he smiled and said, "I'll get Detective Tracy for you." The detective took me into a private room where he told me Alexander was well known in the Anytown County court system. He added that the police department along with the Secret Service and the F.B.I. had raided United Financial Commercial Services offices not long ago. They were yet to file charges and the investigation was ongoing. Detective Tracy went on to say that Alexander had been convicted of similar charges in Texas. He was very helpful and told me what steps to take to get my money. I followed through sending Alexander a certified return receipt letter requesting he reimburse me with certified bank checks and have the checks delivered by Federal Express within thirty days. I also sent copies of my correspondence to Detective Tracy. On Monday I received a call from Alexander, he wanted me to meet him at the office at which time he would replace my paychecks. I told him I had been to the police and he would be receiving a letter from me. Amazingly Alexander was very calm and said, "Do what you must, I understand, and good luck to you."

I received my checks on Wednesday delivered by Federal Express. This time they were drawn on a local credit union. I went right to the credit union and cashed them outright. At least I got my money. Sometimes you get lucky.

CHAPTER 15

I will seek the truth.

I had managed to escape from United Financial Commercial Services without much damage. I resented Alexander's irresponsible behavior. I was very happy at the job I had been doing. With the exception of Willy Dickers, everyone else had been a dream. Willy had been such a womanizer. He had his little high school girls to feed his ego so I never had to deal with him. I enjoyed working with Catlin, Lolita, Maurice, and Scott. I could not believe Cherry, who was a smart capable woman, continued working for Alexander. I guess love is genuinely blind.

I was unsuccessful in finding any type of employment temp or full time. I continued searching and called the unemployment office. Just like the police, the unemployment person I spoke with knew all about United Financial Commercial Services and Alexander Monday. The claims agent I spoke with informed me his offices were closed. She enlightened me with an extra tidbit. Alexander was being investigated for not forwarding the deductions he had taken from his employees checks to the proper agencies. She assured me I would have no problem collecting against him and I qualified for benefits! One afternoon I was straightening out a closet and came across a Christmas gift for Annabel. It was a beautiful handmade pillow decorated with reindeer. Annabel collected reindeer and decorated her tree and home with them at Christmas. I often went to yard sales and if I saw a reindeer which was particularly nice, I would get it for her. I must have totally forgotten about this one. I had not seen her in a long time and decided to visit her. The next day I packed up the pillow and drove to her office. It was a very warm October day and nature's fireworks were in full effect. The city was beautiful with the trees decked out in reds, yellows, and coppers. I had not called ahead to see if Annabel would be in the office. I would just leave it for her if she wasn't there.

Beth and Shannon warmly greeted me when I arrived. Annabel was in her lavish office and we had a pleasant visit. She thanked me for the gift and inquired if I was working. I related my latest saga in the employment world, The Alexander Carnival. She was not in the least surprised, she knew *all* about him when her offices were in the same building. At that time she had made me an offer. Annabel needed to create new forms for her volunteer project. I am a wizard in Word Perfect and PowerPoint. She wanted me to streamline the forms, handouts, and testing materials she used in her program. Annabel showed me the old forms and the copies she was using. I figured it would take me about forty hours to get everything reformatted. She told me I could come in each day for about four hours to work on her project. I agreed to help her. Now I was *doing* a project for Annabel. She had always sent me on one project after another when I worked as a temp for her. I spent two weeks typing and laying in new graphics for her program.

I had little to no contact with Beth or Shannon at this time. I would go into a small interview booth and work on a testing computer. I could overhear their conversations and nothing had changed. Beth was now an older spoiled brat who still lived at home with her mother. Shannon worked part-time now as she was a new mother. She was much more mature then Beth, even though she was only in her early twenties. Shannon had a delightful baby girl who she brought into the office with her. Shannon's baby was only about four months old when I started working in Annabel's office. I found it distasteful that Shannon would tell me, "I am going back to the conference room to *pump*." She would then disappear for a time and Annabel would hold her baby. It would become more distasteful when Caroline came to work for Annabel, bringing her infant and pump along too.

When I would go to the kitchen area to use the microwave, I thought it was disgusting having pumping equipment drying in the sink. I thought if someone needed to do this maybe they should stay at home with the baby. Perhaps I was being too old fashioned in my thinking. I kept my opinions to myself.

The accounting clerical was a new employee I had not met before, Rhoda. She was a slim older woman who was painfully conservative. Rhoda was retired and a personal friend of Annabel's. She let it be known in no uncertain terms she was only helping Annabel over the holiday season. (She would be gone by Thanksgiving) Rhoda did not plan on working at Coconut full time.

On Friday I completed the project and stopped in Annabel's office to say goodbye. Annabel asked me to come and have a seat, she wanted to run something past me. She said Rhoda had given her notice. Annabel wanted me to step in and take over the position. Rhoda would be in the office to train me for the next two weeks. I told Annabel I appreciated her vote of confidence but I did not feel I was qualified for the position. The job was defined as bookkeeper and payroll specialist. I told Annabel I had not processed payroll taxes and the job was not something I would be comfortable doing. Annabel insisted I could do the job. I tried to tell her I would be in over my head. Annabel went to great lengths to tell me about the new program she was using called Continuum. She smiled and said, "Continuum processes *everything* for you." This was truly a Hobson's choice for me. I had nothing in the works from any other agency. In my heart I *knew* this would not work out. I wished I had told her NO. She informed me it would only be part-time. She could not afford another forty hour employee on her payroll. I figured it was better than zilch. The first day I trained with Rhoda I was shocked to discover Annabel was still using the old program for payroll called Spectrum. She had been using this back in the eighties when Tory and I worked together. Rhoda explained they were running Continuum on a parallel hard drive. I looked under the desk and there were two hard drives. I could not believe it. The other accounting processes were done in QuickBooks. Rhoda told me they did not have support for Spectrum any longer. She continued, "Annabel had to pay an extra thirty thousand dollars because she did not upgrade within the time frame, but don't tell her I told you." Oh brother, why me?

I never mastered the payroll using Spectrum. Every week Annabel and I would struggle to print checks on an ancient dot-matrix printer and process direct deposits. It was a hateful, drawn out process. I would then input all the payroll information in QuickBooks, another redundant process.

Rhoda left after two weeks and I was not trained in many aspects of the position. Rhoda had been working part-time and she was a very knowledgeable bookkeeper. I would be responsible for maintaining the accounts receivable and payables and the bank reconciliations. In addition, I would be making the federal, state, and local tax deposits. I followed what Rhoda had done previously and for the most part I was successful. When I got involved in Annabel's bank reconciliations and payroll process, I discovered she and her children were living out of the business. Annabel was living the lifestyle of the rich and famous. She was putting nothing back into her business. Her three children were on the payroll and did not work in the office. No wonder she could not afford to pay another *real* employee. They had debit cards and used them as freely as she did. This would not have been a problem if the receipts had been submitted to me. When I was having difficultly reconciling the bank account, she told me to input the entries from the bank statement into QuickBooks and make it match. I did as she said and I made everything *match*, as best I could.

She also paid for her leased sports car, condo payment, groceries, dry cleaning, and gas out of the general account. In addition to those expenses, she ate out at least four times a week; these expenses were listed as client entertainment. And on top of that, she got a weekly paycheck which was not shabby. Oh I almost forgot. She gave herself a monthly bonus.

Each week Annabel would have a lunch staff meeting. Considering only three people worked for her, this was pretty lame. There was always a long drawn out discussion about what restaurant they would order lunch. Once the decision was made, I would be sent to go and pick up the order. Ultimately the meeting would commence. Shannon and Beth would decide what payroll inserts needed to be designed and printed for the check run. I never understood why this was such a big deal. They used the same ones from holiday to holiday and from year to year. Then they would drone on and on about the payroll verses the sales margins and what problems they were having with the temps. It was a boring waste of time. Usually I could get excused after the payroll insert choice was decided. I was just as isolated at this job as I had been at OCS. Annabel and the pimps had little time for me. They made no attempt to get to know me or include me in their lunch plans. There was a snack bar in the building so I usually wandered there for a Latte.

The young woman, Katie, who worked at the snack bar, was a Desert Storm Vet. She was outgoing and friendly. I looked forward to seeing her smiling face each day. One morning we were talking about Coconut Personnel. Everyone from Coconut eventually made a trip to the snack bar in the course of the day. Katie could not understand why I worked with such stuck up people. I told her, "I try to ignore them and keep my head down." Katie said, "It must be lonely for you." It was. Katie thought Beth was very unprofessional in the manner in which she dressed for work (Beth would wear low cut tight tops with her bosom hanging out). I totally agreed. Kate and I laughed about the irony of my situation. I was still a temp working inside a temp agency being treated like a temp. She was the only person I missed when I left Coconut's employment.

Shannon was the master mind for Continuum. She would work with me as we attempted to get payroll running in the new system. December would come and go and Continuum would not be up and running yet. This was going to be a considerable problem when it was time to process W-2's in January. Shannon was working as many hours as she could but there were lots of upgrading problems. One morning Annabel said she had an important project to accomplish. I expected to be told I would be training full-time with Shannon on Continuum. I was not surprised when she explained the project would be to find an upscale restaurant for her holiday party. This celebration would include the four of us and our spouses. It was too late to make reservations anywhere for the month of December. Annabel always did things at the last minute. She was not a planner. I made arrangements at an exceptional restaurant in West Anytown, The Lincoln Tavern, for early in January.

The evening of the holiday party was cold, clear, and blustery. Everyone was dressed in their best celebration outfits. I was shivering in my crimson silk dress. We enjoyed a wonderful dinner, drinks and lots of laughter. We were bantering and telling jokes when I could not resist telling a limerick, "There was an old woman named Judy, who worked temp and busted her booty, a real job it seemed was an impossible dream. So she went to work each day wired, dreaming of the day that she'd be retired." The girls and their husbands were impressed and I received a round of applause. Annabel picked up the tab and it was a hefty one. During the course of the evening Beth and Shannon were actually giddy. I thought they had drunk to much wine. I did not know at the time, Beth and Shannon, had already been hired out from under Annabel's nose. They were going to be working for a client of Annabel's. Talk about your just deserts.

Annabel had promoted Shannon to Senior Coordinator in December. Beth had been working at Coconut Personnel longer then Shannon, and was upset when she was not offered the position. I did not say anything to Beth but I thought Shannon was much better suited for the position. Beth was still a rude little pimp. She spoke to everyone including her mother like they were dogs. Shannon had a lot on the ball; she was very sweet and professional.

One afternoon shortly before Christmas, Annabel had a meeting with the representatives from one of her major medical accounts. Annabel, Shannon, and Beth were in the meeting and I handled the phones for the afternoon. After the meeting everyone was smiling and the visitors left. By mid January I would discover (along with Annabel) things are often *not* as they seem. At this time I was going to the doctors frequently due to an old foot injury. I had been in a car accident years before. I was experiencing horrible pain and I could hardly wear shoes comfortably. It was determined the only thing they could do was to operate on my foot and insert a screw. The doctor said I should have it done as soon as possible. I would not be able to drive or walk for two weeks. When I told Annabel of this she did not *seem* to have a problem with me being off for the surgery.

Annabel went on vacation for two weeks and it was wonderful working along side Shannon. She was always so understanding and helpful. Shannon and I continued running parallel payrolls. Each week Shannon was hopeful we would be fully operational, but it never happened, at least not while I worked there.

Blake from ACYS agency called me with a job offer. There was nothing I could do but turn it down. It would have required me walking out on Annabel, which was something I would not do. Blake explained he needed someone to start the following Monday. I could have screamed.

One morning Beth told me she was still very upset about not being promoted to the Senior Coordinator position. Beth had submitted her resignation and would be leaving in four weeks. She went on to say that she would be working for a large medical office. Beth would not work for the entire time as she planned. Annabel was not happy with Beth's departure and put up a great wall of silence. By now it was the end of January and Continuum was still not up and running live. Shannon was working with the support people and making some progress. Beth was no longer working at Coconut. There had been a heated discussion between her and Annabel due to the fact Annabel had cut off her health benefits the *day* she handed in her resignation. There would be more unsavory talks when Annabel did not pay her for vacation days.

A few days later when I had just gotten settled at my desk, Annabel came in and told me Shannon had left her employment. Shannon had gotten a job where Beth was working. Annabel was very distressed with them for pulling such a *stunt*. Apparently they had already been interviewed and hired for these jobs two months before. To make matters worse, they were working for the clients she had the meeting with in December. She felt it was all very underhanded. All I could think was that whatever goes around comes around. The conversation became even stranger. Annabel began reminiscing about the people who had worked for her over the years. Somehow we got on the subject of Kim and the terrible death of her baby boy. I mentioned to Annabel I was surprised when I had attended the funeral and did not see her or the coordinators there. Annabel told me, "We just couldn't take a chance being there." I was mystified and asked, "what do you mean?" She replied in a whisper," I did not know if criminal charges were pending?" God almighty what is wrong with this woman? How could she think something like this of Kim? I came to the realization about what type of a person Annabel really WAS. Her life revolved around how others perceived her and her company. She was not someone I wished to be associated with any longer. She was shallow and self-serving.

A new face came on the scene to help out after Shannon's abrupt departure, her name was Caroline. She was another one of Annabel's snotty friends who would drag her infant to the office and pump daily. Caroline had an icicle nose and was a very abrupt when she spoke to me. She lived in an expensive neighborhood and expected everyone to defer to her like she was a princess. I was in the office alone with Caroline on an occasion when Annabel was at a business lunch. Caroline walked to my office and demanded I hold her baby while she made a trip to the ladies room. When I told her I felt uncomfortable holding her child, she acted like I had spurned her. Nothing was farther from the truth. I had never had a child and I was always afraid of dropping a baby. I did not think it should be a job requirement either. I did not relate my personal fears to her, perhaps I should have.

Caroline had the baby's jump-chair in her office. I told her, "place her in the jump-chair and I will sit on the floor with her while you are gone." I thought this was a reasonable meeting point. Caroline went to the bathroom for what seemed like a century. I sat on the floor and played *grab my finger* with the baby, who was a dear little one. When Annabel came into the office, Caroline went to her and complained that I had insulted her and her child. It was becoming a distasteful situation. Caroline and I tried working together to finish the W-2 employee listing. I could not work with her. She spoke very curtly to me. I had never given her a reason to be so unfriendly. Or perhaps I had with the Jump-Chair Incident? It was now January 27th and W-2's were still not printed. Annabel kept insisting we could get this accomplished. I knew better. Annabel was like a pit bull with a bone, she would not give it up even when she knew she was defeated. Annabel finally *let go of the bone* and filed for a federal extension on January 30th. Caroline and Annabel completed the list for W-2s' on January 31st. They forwarded it to the accounting firm which would be printing the W-2 forms.

The second week of February the accountant came in with the completed W-2 forms. Caroline dumped them rudely upon my desk and instructed me, "get them in the mail!' Annabel came into my office and asked, "Could you stay and cover the phones while I take Caroline and the accountant to lunch?" I usually left at one and it was now twelve-thirty. Well of course I could! They went to a *valid* client luncheon and I licked stamps. By mid February, Annabel had finally hired another coordinator, Jessie. She was a physical clone of Shannon. Jessie was professional in her demeanor and pleasant to be around. Caroline was still coming in part-time dragging her infant and pump along. I was plugging along and trying my best.

When I went to work at Annabel's, I noticed a great deal of unpaid invoices in the system. I worked at collecting this money for her. Usually it was because a customer had not gotten a bill. I reprinted the invoices and stayed on top of the accounts receivables. I managed to collect over thirty-five thousand dollars in old accounts in three months. I did not get much credit from Annabel for all my efforts. She did not believe in being rude to her customers. I was never rude to her clients, I was persistent. I know how to collect money. Calling customers who are one-hundred and twenty days late in paying their bills is not bad etiquette. Not calling is just bad business.

I made plans to have foot surgery at the end of February. I was not looking forward to the surgery. However, I *was* looking forward to not working at Coconut for a few weeks. I would not have to deal with Caroline's snootiness or Annabel's disapproving look every time I called a client. I was starting to dread going into work each day. I knew I was not living up to Annabel's standards and never would. On a Monday in late February, I cleared out my office and said goodbye. Annabel was her sweet little self and wished me good luck with the surgery and to keep in touch. I had the surgery on Wednesday of the same week. My recovery was going great and I did not have much discomfort. Thursday morning I was checking out the newspaper ads. I saw Coconut had placed an ad, it read, "Clerical AP Assistant PT Clerk needed." I called Coconut and spoke to Jessie. She was very sugary and asked me how I was doing. I was not in the mood for idle chatter and got right to the point, "Jessie is that my job in the paper?" She hedged my questions by playing dumb. I asked her to have Annabel call me. She assured me she would. I continued calling for the rest of the week and on Saturday. Annabel did not return my calls.

I was mystified and my feelings were becoming hurt. The least she could do was to return my calls. Didn't she say, "Keep in touch."

At last Annabel called me the following Tuesday. She was bubbling over as she told me with Caroline's **brilliant** help they had gotten Continuum up and running. She was giving the accountant all of the work I had been doing. There was no reason for me to return. I was dumbfounded. I could not believe anyone would stoop so low as to let an employee go while they were out on surgery leave. I should have known better. I had finally learned after all these years of knowing Annabel, she was an accomplished ecclesiastic.

Once when I was trying so very hard to assist Beth with an employee's hours, Annabel told me not to permit the coordinators to interrupt me. I told her, "I don't mind, I don't want to alienate them." Annabel's reply to me was, "you can't be all things to all people." Truer words were never spoken. I was glad in a way; things had worked out as they had. I was never comfortable working for Annabel. She treated me in such a shabby manner I could only hope I would **never** have to deal with her again. After I was given the green light to return to work, I spent the next few months going to agencies and contacting the pimps each Monday. I was able to reopen an unemployment claim against Annabel. I had no choice as I had no income. I thought I was done with Annabel forever but NO. She called me in April.

Annabel called on a Tuesday afternoon and was frantic. Jessie was on vacation for the week and she needed someone in the office. She had not replaced Beth when she quit. It was only her and Jessie in the office these days. Annabel wanted me to come in for the rest of the week from eleven in the morning until two in the afternoon by so doing; she would be able to meet with some very important new clients. I had no choice in the matter, I had to do it. I knew if I declined she would report me to the Unemployment Office. I could not take a chance losing my benefits. I gritted my teeth and with my best phony smile in my nice sweet voice I told her, "Sure Annabel, no problem, I will be in tomorrow." I wondered how far down her list of *friends* she had to go before she got to me. Annabel gave me a crash course in the data base of Continuum. She left me some work to keep me busy while she was out of the office. I updated the employee address, W-2 withholdings and any other data entry tasks which needed completed. I became bored so I poked around in the accounts receivables' program. Just as I thought, many of the accounts were over sixty days over due.

When Annabel came back from her meeting on Friday, she was in a chatty mood. She told me she was worried about me and my financial situation. Annabel's *act* was so insincere with her fake smile and fawning and verbal nuances, it made me want to puke. I was ecstatic as I drove out of her parking lot. It was a warm spring afternoon and I was going to enjoy the *rest* of my day. As I drove home I thought, "If she was really was so concerned, why she didn't find a full time position for me?" Again, things I wish I would have said. At this point I never wanted to speak to her again for many reasons. The most chilling being her remarks concerning the death of Kim's child. I was not going to be that fortunate. The following Thursday my direct deposit was not in my bank account. This was very unusual for Coconut Personnel. I had never had a problem with my direct deposit before. When the deposit was not in by Friday I called the office. Of course I spoke with Jessie and she said, "Your deposit did not go through, Annabel is not here right now." I told Jessie to have her call me.

I would persist in calling and emailing Annabel for the next five days but to no avail. At this point when I called, I would get the company voice mail directory. I knew Coconut had caller I.D. and they were sitting there not answering the phone. After all I *had* worked there. On April 21st, Annabel returned my calls. She told me my bank botched the deposit. Yeah right. Annabel had told me when I helped her out the week before, "we are scary slow and I don't know what is going to happen." Well I knew what was happening, she could not make her payroll. Maybe if she was on top of her accounts, she would not have to worry about what was going to happen. All is well that ends well, I got my money. This past year I had to call her when I did not receive my W-2 by January 31st. Imagine that! Annabel was very pleasant and inquired as to how I was doing. I was cool in my response and I did not go into any details. She said the reason I had not gotten my W-2 was because I was NOT in the new system. I should have known.

I called around to what agencies I could. There were few jobs during the summer to be had by anyone. The economy was taking a downwards twist and every agency I went to said business was terribly slow. I received a call from Mindy at ADECCO in September. They had an accounts payable position at a dental supply company. I was game for it, and thankful I would be working again. I reported for duty at Teeth R Us on September the 13th, a day that would go down in infamy.

Teeth R Us is a large international company in Anytown which employs hundreds of people. I was telling my husband's biker friend Slick I had gotten a temp job at the Corporate Headquarters. Slick and his wife worked at another Teeth R Us location. He raised his eyebrows and said, "oh lucky you, it's located right in the middle of Needle Park, the building your going to is called the "Snake Pit." Oh great, not only will I have to drive though a bad area, I got to work in it too. Slick shook his head and uttered in a pretend scary tone, "Don't let the boogie man get ya'." I asked him, "but it is the headquarters, all of the companies officers work there, isn't it like Anytown International?" Slick laughed and said, "No, no, they moved the big wigs out of the building, they are in a ritzy safer location downtown. The people you will be working with are office *suits* and snobs." The conversation drifted to other subjects and I tried to think positively about this new assignment.

Wednesday morning would be the end of the world as I knew it. It was still dark and the weather was cold and overcast as I drove into the city. I thought the row-homes I drove past were neglected and gloomy looking. The sidewalks were littered with bottles, cans, and rubbish. There was a lot of pedestrian traffic, children going to school and small groups of young men standing on the corners talking as they glanced furtively up and down the street. I had to drive slowly seeing as there were teenagers dashing across the street in every direction. A repo tow-truck was blocking my lane hooking up to a new Cadillac Escalade. A crowd had gathered and a police car pulled up with its' flashing lights glaring in the morning darkness. There was a lot going on at seven-thirty in the morning. I maneuvered slowly down the street and pulled into the visitors' parking lot. I had made it! As I was walking across the street, I noticed tiny baggies and apparently used hypodermic needles laying in the gutters. Now I get it, *Needle Park.*

I had to buzz the receptionist from outside the building on a call box. I felt a little safer knowing the building had a security system. She let me in and gave me a visitors' badge which I would use to enter the building. I was met by the Accounts Payables Manager, Phyllis Shank, a petite attractive woman in her fifties or so. She walked me briskly back though the department. The offices were a typical cubicle world. As we passed the cubicles, no one glanced up from their work.

I spent the entire morning sitting behind Phyllis observing the computer programs I would be using. She explained there was no place in the department for me to sit. I would be at a vacant desk in another accounting department. It was located down the hall and through a set of double doors. Eventually I would end up back in her department when a woman named Pam retired. Apparently Pam was to have retired months ago. She was having problems selling her home and was waiting for the sale to go though before her big day. Phyllis explained there were ten people in the department but she would spare me all the introductions at this time and just introduced me to Sonia, "Our Calendar Girl". As we walked back through the department, I noticed bags of chips and junk food stacked on every vacant space. Phyllis dropped me off at Sonia's cube and disappeared.

Sonia was a large typical looking woman of German Dutch heritage. She was very pretty and appeared to be in her late thirties. She did not meet my definition of a Calendar Girl. By now it was lunch time, Sonia told me she and her friends, Rhoda and Nancy, were going to walk to the fairgrounds for lunch. She got up abruptly and left me sitting at her desk (thanks for the invite). By now, nearly everyone had disappeared. I was on my own. Sonia's cube neighbor peaked around the corner and introduced himself to me. Darnell was average looking and gave me the impression he was somewhat bashful. He was in his fifties and had pictures of his wife and their cats all over the walls of his cube. I thought he was probably a nice man.

I wandered around the department searching for the ladies room and the coffee alcove. I discovered there was a cafeteria in the building. I did not check it out since I had packed my lunch. I was to realize the cafeteria ladies would be the few people I would consider genuinely friendly at this company. I strolled to my car to eat my lunch and began reading my current Stephen King novel, *The Girl Who Loved Tom Gordon*. It was time to relax for a while; it had been a stressful morning.

After lunch I went back to Sonia's cube and waited for her to return. I was checking out the pictures in her cube of her teenage sons and a dog (another person with no pictures of her husband) and I noticed that she had an amazing amount of calendars on the walls. There were calendars of birds, calendars of dogs, little ones, big ones, I counted twelve different calendars. Oh, I get it, Calendar Girl. I wondered what this collecting behavior implied about an individual. When Sonia returned and plopped into her seat, the first thing she told me was, "I don't have time to train temps, it should be Phyllis' job." Oh yeah big surprise, like I have never heard this before. Sonia picked up a stack of invoices and in a sharp tone of voice said, "Just watch, pick up what you can, and take notes." She added, "I don't have time to walk you though this stuff." Oh great, just great.

Phyllis had only shown me the basics of the Dynamics program. Sonia went on to say in a disgusted tone, the new system was terrible and had lots of bugs. The inter-company invoices she handled were the first ones on the new system. She added that I would be the second person using it. There were test users in every department of the company. I sat there until it was break time watching Sonia race through the screens. At break, everyone began their afternoon *grazing* routine. Expect for one other person, every woman in this department was huge. I retraced my steps and went out to the dock for a smoke. The only other person out for a smoke at the time was a young woman shooting the breeze on her cell phone. When she saw me, she immediately turned her back and walked to the far end of the platform. I smoked my cigarette and pondered my first impressions. So far Phyllis was harried but pleasant, Sonia was not very personable, her office buddies, Rhoda and Jo were downright rude. The other people in the department (with the expectation of Darnell) were uninterested in meeting the temp. The smokers ignored the temp. At that point, my first impressions did not matter. I was thankful my first day was just about at its end.

Thursday and Friday were much of the same. I checked in with Phyllis each morning to see what the status was with my computer sign-ons. Phyllis told me she was fighting with I.T. regarding my sign on and getting Dynamics installed on the computer I would be using in the other accounting department. I continued to watch Miss Personality but could not get any hands on experience. Sonia told me over and over how overworked and unappreciated she was. I could certainly see from the piles of invoices on her desk that she was either overworked or just plain slow. Everyday Sonia and her buddies would make a morning chow sprint to the cafeteria. They were usually gone for 30 minutes or so. I walked down with them on Friday to check it out. They ordered three course breakfasts (no wonder they were gone so long). I picked up a good cup of coffee and returned to Area 51.

There was little socializing among the women in the department. When I was training with Sonia, all I could hear was the clicking of keyboards. I noticed Sonia never answered her phone and let all her calls go to her voice mail. When I asked her about this she told me, "I don't have time for phone calls." She added, "I check them at the end of the day; I can only do so much!" Beside eat . . . Sonia was so unfriendly I could not wait to get away from her. I never figured out what her dilemma was. All I did was observe her work for three days. This had certainly been easy money. I could only hope I would be able to retain the information.

Friday at lunch I was told we were going to a baby shower. This is an office activity for which I have no *taste*. It is another excuse for an extended eating extravaganza. I never knew any of these women and had to sit at the table as they shoved Dutch carbohydrates in their pie-holes at the speed of light. I *had* to go to and appear to be sociable. I knew from experience that once they moved like a herd of cows to the buffet tables and started devouring everything in sight; I could slip away and would never be missed.

I had been given a car I.D. tag to hang on my rear view mirror so I could park in the employee parking lot. The lot was not very secure and I often saw teenage boys walking though and climbing over the fences. No one seemed troubled with their presence as there was a private security force patrolling the lots. The security force was from a company called The Shark Defense Agency. The Sharks are considered to be a joke with most people in Anytown. The company consists of police academy flunk-outs, mustarded-out jug heads and retired cops. They are very polite men and are an excellent source if you need driving directions though. I personally would not have put my safety in their hands unless I absolutely had no choice.

Week two did not begin on an upbeat note! Phyllis was no closer in obtaining a user I.D. for me and continued to fight with I.T. so I spent the morning in her office putting W9 forms in alphabetical order for scanning. Finally she got the go ahead from I.T. and I was able to log onto a computer in another department. I scanned returned customer W9's which I had already put in order for the most of the day. It was wonderful not being around Sonia. The department where I was using the scanning equipment was another corporate accounting department. The woman running this area was Phyllis's boss, Mrs. McFudden. Everyone including Mrs. McFudden's administrative cleric, Karen, was extremely friendly. It was amazing how different one department could be from another.

On Tuesday Phyllis took me to the vacant cube in the Egghead accounting department. She introduced me to the Top Egghead Manager and set me up with her laptop (I.T would never get Dynamics loaded on the desktop computer). I would work on a laptop for the next two months. Phyllis gave me some of Sonia's simple invoices and turned me loose. Now if I had questions for Sonia I had to walk four city blocks to get to her cube. When I did go to her, she was helpful but very cool. The accountants in the area I was stationed in were a chilly cluster of folks. Not one person spoke to me during the entire time I sat in the department. On my last day in their department, I could not resist saying as I got up to leave, "Hey Chuck, It was great working with ya!" He replied, "Who said that?" What a bunch of stuck up eggheads.

On Thursday I checked in with Phyllis concerning my progress. She informed me that I had made no errors and she felt I was doing a good job considering how large the learning curve was. She hooked up a standard keyboard to the laptop to make inputting easier for me. By the end of the week I was getting the hang of the work flow. The accountants sitting around me, Chuck and John talked all day about Penn State Football. I don't know how they got anything done. They would chat, chat and chat some more. I had to go to Sonia about a few questions I had on invoices but she could hardly give me the time of day. On Friday, Sonia did not come into work. She was sick so it turned into a pretty great day for me. I kept plugging away with inter-company invoices.

On the Monday of my third week, Sonia was in during the morning but it was a *non-talk* day. I had nothing to do at this point and I was waiting to get onto the system. Sonia came over to me and showed me five errors I had made. She was very upset and reamed me out in front of the entire department. Considering I had entered over four hundred invoices and it had only been two weeks, I didn't feel this warranted her nasty attitude. She was still sick and left early. Yea!

It tuned out Sonia would be out for the rest of the week. Phyllis was also out of the office for a seminar. I would walk around and beg for work from anyone. I decided to make an executive decision. I went to Sonia's' desk and checked invoices to see if the products had been received so they could be entered for payment. I did pay thirty-five of them. I could only hope they were done correctly. I did not wish to incur the wrath of The Dragon Sonia. When invoices were entered for payment at Teeth R Us, they were stamped with the date. Guess what, I did not have a date stamp. This was another process which was as complicated as getting a computer sign-on at Teeth R Us. Phyllis told me she had ordered one but by week three I still had not received it. Since I was imputing Sonia's invoices, I needed to use her stamp. It was not pleasant having to beg Sonia for the use of her date stamp. Usually I would wait until I was finished my work before going to her desk to request to use it.

One afternoon when I asked to borrow it, Sonia snapped and replied, "No, I need to use it all day!" The wicked witch of Teeth R Us had spoken! It was totally ridiculous. I just smiled my little sweet temp smile and walked away. As I walked back to my area I was thinking, 'why should I bust my butt at this company when all I get is an attitude from her?' I went back to my desk and put on my headphones so I could listen to my favorite website, Beethoven.com. I got lost in my work and the next thing I knew it was three P.M.; Sonia waddled over to my desk, *threw* the stamp on it, and kept on a waddling, never breaking stride. She was so pleasant.

For the next month I would wrestle with the laptop. Phyllis eventually hooked up a desktop monitor to it. Every night I had to disconnect the laptop and return it to Phyllis's office. Each morning I had to retrieve it from her closet. I was told this was because laptops "disappear when left unattended overnight." 'Boy,' I thought, 'what type of people work here?'

The chair I was sitting in was the worst lumpy wobbly chair in the office. I asked the manager of the department if it would be okay with him if I traded my lumpy bumpy chair with a nice soft chair in the adjoining cube. Mr. Manager assured me it was just fine with him. The cube I took it from was only used by the accountants for occasional scanning. One day Chuck went to do his scanning. He wined and complained to the air around him about sitting in such an uncomfortable chair. He kept asking, "where is the red chair, where is the red chair?" I did not say a word. If he could not see where it was, he wasn't very observant for someone with a Masters Degree.

During this time Kim from JFC had called and offered me a full time position. I would have to start the next day. I had to turn it down. The same afternoon Lori from Staffing Associates called me with another "start tomorrow position." Where were these people two months ago?

One morning Phyllis asked me to assist the Accounts Receivable Department in correcting a major accounting error. Some one had made a boo-boo and there were over five hundred entries which needed to be reversed. Of course I said, "Yes, you can count me in." During the course of the next three days, I corrected a total of one thousand four hundred and fifty line items. I did not make one mistake, imagine that. In addition I completed the project in three days. Phyllis was very impressed.

I got a big surprise one day when Phyllis called me in her office and told me that I would be assigned a division of Teeth R Us to handle. It was located in Texas and the company would be going on the Dynamics system. I told Phyllis I had never been properly trained in Dynamics by Sonia. Since I was spilling my guts, I told her how rude everyone (except Darnell) was to me. Phyllis shook her head and said, "I know exactly what you are saying. I am very aware of the people in this department and how they act, but that doesn't change anything." I told her about how nasty Sonia was. Phyllis said," None of us can work with her, but she is invaluable, and I can not afford to lose her. I am already short people. We have all learned to live with her." Phyllis added, "We don't poke the bear."

I became very brave for some reason and told her, "I don't care if she talks to her husband, sons or her dog like she does, but she will not speak to me like that any longer." I added, "I don't speak to her or anyone else the way she has spoken to me." I found it to be unbelievable one person was allowed to affect an entire department as she did. Phyllis changed the subject and dropped a bombshell on me, "When Pam retires you will be sitting at her desk." 'Great, that is just great,' I thought. Pam's cube wall faced Sonia's cube wall. A day or so later Phyllis invited me to join her in a meeting with the comptroller from the Texas Company and her boss, Mrs. McFudden. They would be going over the time line for the start up in Dynamics. I sat and listened but didn't offer much. What could I offer? There was absolutely no reason for me to be in their meeting.

Sonia did cool her attitude with me for a short time. Apparently Phyllis had spoken to her but it was not long before she was again her old nasty self. She came to my desk one afternoon and literally screamed at me again about my errors. I told her to take the invoices in question to Phyllis. I was done dealing with her. Sonia just stared at me as if I had lost my mind. I could see the wheels turning in the gooeyness of her little brain, "how dare her?" Every one in the snooty accounting department could hear her ranting and raving at me.

It was a very strange phenomenon when I entered the invoices for the Texas facility during the last month I worked at Teeth R Us. I had absolutely no errors. Another 'imagine that.' I had the account payables edit reports to prove it. A lot of good this would do me.

I called Mindy at Adecco and told her what I was dealing with in the department. She told me to chill-out and she would call Phyllis. I could not wait for this assignment to end and it is was not even January. Mindy called me back later in the day and told me Phyllis was pleased with my progress. How could that be?

The month of December was not much different either. Whenever Sonia did *not* come to work it was a good day for me. Pam had finally retired and I was now sitting directly facing Sonia's cube wall, joy joy. I got to listen to "A Garth Brooks Christmas" over and over though the walls. It was **not** a Merry Christmas. The I.T. department could not get the computer I was using to accept my sign on. In addition to the computer problem, no one knew what Pam's voice mail password had been. I had to forward all the messages to someone else for handling. It took I.T three days to change the passwords and get the computer up and running. During this enforced downtime, I helped Rhoda with her scanning. She handled the company credit cards. Rhoda told me to slow down and, "you need to make this work last, like we do." I told her Phyllis had told me to help anyone I could. To this Rhonda said, "Phyllis is a nice Christian lady but she is totally ineffectual as a manager and lets people push her around."

One day I had inputted over one hundred invoices and Sonia again crucified me (in front of everyone, of course) for one mistake. I just could not take anymore of Sonia's crap and told Phyllis I needed to speak with her. I told her whenever I would go to Sonia for help on an invoice, instead of giving me instructions on how to handle them, she would snatch it out of my hand and say, "I'll take care of it." In addition, I was tired of the raft of crap I got from her. Phyllis suggested I sit with her and she would help me with some of the problems I was having in the Dynamics software. I was sitting directly behind Phyllis on an occasion when she received an email from Sonia. The email stated that Sonia could not handle the pressure she was under. She did not have the time to correct errors or train a temp and she was crying at her desk. Baugh, Baugh, Baugh, she could not *take it* anymore and if something wasn't done (about me) she was going to the Human Resources Department and request a transfer. Phyllis suddenly realized I had read this email too. She apologized all over herself about what Sonia had written. Phyllis was very understanding and told me "Sonia is a very unhappy person, you must not concern yourself." She reiterated that, "we don't poke the bear."

Darnell would stop by my cube with friendly support and a daily smile. He told me he disliked Sonia and said he has learned, like everyone, "not to poke the bear." I continued to call Mindy at Adecco and she would assure me, "Phyllis was very happy with your performance." Mindy said she understood about the issues with Sonia and I needed to ignore her. Easy for her to say. I had no way out. All of a sudden I started making all types of errors. I was so unhappy that I literally could not think straight. I finally went to Phyllis about my problems working in this position. Phyllis told me she was aware of the errors I was making and wanted me to explain what the problems were. She said to me, "you are making errors now which you had not made during the past three months." I told her, "I am so nervous I am afraid to enter *anything*. I don't know, maybe I am old and burned out. Maybe I hate it here, maybe I am self destructing, take your pick." My voice was quivering and I was fighting back tears. Phyllis told me to calm down and said she wanted to offer me the job full time, I told her, "no, absolutely not!" I added, "You need to call Adecco and tell them I am not suited to work in your department."

Phyllis was a very nice person, but she buried her head in the sand hoping anything distasteful would just go away. I was not going to continue working with Sonia who was impolite and mean. I had enough of those circumstances at OCS. Mindy called me back and told me she had spoken with Phyllis. Phyllis told Mindy she regretted the problems I had faced. She also told Mindy she understood and felt I was not the right choice for the position. Mindy told me what I wanted to hear. Friday would be my last day.

This had been without doubt the epitome of the worst temp position I had ever been assigned. During my entire assignment, I was never invited to join anyone for lunch. I seldom conversed with anyone on the dock. It was a lonely mean existence. Slick had warned me, "it's a Snake Pit", and I wished I would have listened to him way back when.

I do not feel bad about my efforts at Teeth R Us. The people in some of the Teeth R Us departments need to take a long hard look at themselves. With the exception of the cafeteria ladies and the Shark Patrolmen, there were few friendly faces. If it is a matter of being overworked and shorthanded then the management of Teeth R Us needs to look at how they staff and run their company. Teeth R Us was one of the most antagonistic work environments I have ever been subjected to work as a temp. Alas, I haven't been able to come across work since. I continue to apply for positions I find on the Internet and in the newspaper. I've had some time to reflect on my life and how I am perceived. I am by no means perfect but I have always tried to be a conscientious, agreeable person.

In March I saw a position Adecco placed on CareerBuilder. The position was for an accounts payable clerk in a large manufacturing company. I applied for the position on Adecco's site. Mindy emailed me and said, "Guess what, that is the same job you were doing at Teeth R Us." Her email continued, "The person who replaced you left also." Hmmm, what does that say?

Mindy called me the other day to see if I was still looking for work. We talked a bit and Mindy asked, "What have you been up to?" "Oh not much," I replied, "I am thinking of writing about some of my temp adventures." Mindy said, "I can't wait to read it!" I told her with a smile in my voice, "it's just a thought. Keep me in mind and take care Mindy, talk to you soon." As I hung up I was thinking to myself, "I can't wait for you to read it either."

Like Scarlet, I stand in the soft fertile soil of my garden dressed in my tattered black suit clutching my office sweater, the rising wind whipping my hair in all directions. The blazing red and orange sun sets as dark threatening clouds thunder across the horizon. Drawing a deep breath, I raise my fist to the heavens and swear,

"As God is my witness I will never work temp again!"

The End

CHRONOLOGY

Chapter 1   First Day and the Agencies'

Chapter 2   1967-1980   Coopers Glen Arm MD
                                    Chemical Company Cockeysville MD
                                    Dept of Welfare Baltimore MD
                                    Eastinghouse Cockeysville MD
                                    GEICO   Towson MD
                                    Veterinary Office   PA

Chapter 3   1981-1982   Cottage West
                                    Leotards & Lace
                                    D'namra R. Smith
                                    Postmen's
                                    El Jefe's
                                    Biller Skate Company

Chapter 4   1982-1984   Agway
                                    Rock Solid Insurance
                                    Edward S. Old Insurance
                                    Bowen Insurance

Chapter 5   1984-1985   Serpentine Cadillac
                                    Tri-Glory Electric
                                    Venezuela Products   Red Leopard PA
                                    Anytown Snacks Downtown
                                    Anytown Snacks   Emigstown, PA
                                    YMCA
                                    Greenhouses

Chapter 6   1988-1988   Highway House Restaurant
                                    State Ranch Insurance Company
                                    Btines Printing Company
                                    McCoy's'

Maple Squash
Out of Date Plates

Chapter 7	1988-1989	Shadowfax
		Washington Inventory
		Boon Tune Department Store
		Coon and Noslack Accounting Firm
		Anytown Bank Anytown
Chapter 8	1989-1991	Rapid Delivery
		Edgar Construction
Chapter 9	1991-1994	AWI
		Boswell Sales
		M.A.E
		Mobil Phone Company
		Anytown International
		College Artworks
		Foremost Capitol Plastics
		That-A-Way Transportation
		Appraisals
		Development Topographers
Chapter 10	1995-1998	Boon Tune
		Wally-Mart
		Swiss Habitual
		United Connectors Glen Stone PA
		The Boon Tune Anytown PA
		Out of Date Plates
		The Veranda Shoppe
		Fritz Company
		The Boon Tune
		St. Lemon
		Crackers Packaging
		Cling Brothers Insurance
		The Boon Tune
		PRN
		Berry Advertising
		The Boon Tune
		Anytown International
		ARC of Anytown

Anytown International
Anytown International
The Anytown Newspaper Company
Anytown International
BH Labs
V NA
Community Transit

Chapter 11	1998-2001	M.A.E
		USA Nonstop
		Shipley Energy
		Shadowfax
		Coconut Personnel
		Ultimate Systems
		St.Lemon East Anytown
		Anytown International UPG
		Design Centre
		Smith and Company
		Diebold
		Anytown County Literacy Council
		Nuts and Bolts Industrial Supply
Chapter 12	2001-2005	PCI
		Easter Seals
		Anytown Hospital
		Healthspan Facilities'
Chapter 13	2005-2006	OCS
Chapter 14	2006-2007	Zetso Granite
		Hauler Transport Refrigeration
		BY Way
		United Commercial Financial Service
Chapter 15	2007-2008	Coconut Personnel
		Teeth R Us

Get Published, Inc!
Thorofare, NJ 08086
19 February, 2010
BA2010050